THE
CONSPIRACY
OF *US*

THE
CONSPIRACY
OF US

MAGGIE
HALL

G. P. PUTNAM'S SONS

AN IMPRINT OF PENGUIN GROUP (USA)

G. P. Putnam's Sons
Published by the Penguin Group
Penguin Group (USA) LLC
375 Hudson Street
New York, NY 10014

USA | Canada | UK | Ireland | Australia
New Zealand | India | South Africa | China
penguin.com
A Penguin Random House Company

Library of Congress Cataloging-in-Publication Data
Hall, Maggie, 1982–
The conspiracy of us / Maggie Hall.
pages cm
Summary: When sixteen-year-old Avery West learns her family is part of a powerful and dangerous
secret society, and that her own life is in danger, she must follow a trail of clues across Europe.
[1. Secrets—Fiction. 2. Secret societies—Fiction. 3. Identity—Fiction. 4. Family—Fiction.
5. Voyages and travels—Fiction. 6. Mystery and detective stories.] I. Title.
PZ7.H14616Co 2015   [Fic]—dc23   2014015540

Printed in the United States of America.
ISBN 978-0-399-16650-1
1 3 5 7 9 10 8 6 4 2

Design by Marikka Tamura.
Text set in Adobe Caslon Pro.

For Andrew. This book wouldn't exist without you.

CHAPTER 1

The piece of paper could have been anything.

The spotlight behind me flashed acid green, then pink, then went dark. The pink still seared my retinas, lending a rosy glow to the folded page clenched in my fist.

I stared at it for a few seconds, then reopened it.

The six-inch square had just dropped out of Jack Bishop's bag.

Jack Bishop, the new guy, who had transferred to Lakehaven High at the beginning of this week. Who had shown up here at lighting tech rehearsal, even though he was the last person I'd expect to be a theater kid.

He'd glanced at his phone and hurried down from the catwalk, and was now making his way across the stage below, his footsteps echoing through the theater. His white T-shirt went orange with the next floodlight, then blue, a bright spot in the dark.

I made sure no one was watching, then smoothed the paper flat again.

It was a photo. A photo of a girl with long dark hair and matching dark eyes focused just out of the frame.

The girl was me.

CHAPTER 2

I watched Jack until he disappeared.

On the other end of the catwalk, Lara Sanchez, the lighting director for the spring play and the person who forced me to come today, leaned over all the new theater techs to demonstrate how another light operated. It made the whole structure shudder.

I clutched at the wire mesh with white-knuckled fingers and glanced at the photo again. In it, my lips were slightly parted, my head turned, like I was talking to someone. He must have gotten it online. Lara posted a ton of pictures. For Jack Bishop to go to the trouble of searching one out meant . . . Well, there weren't many reasons a guy would be carrying your picture around.

I suddenly realized how stagnant the air up here was. Hot. Stuffy. I was doing better than I thought I would, but I wouldn't say no to an excuse to get down.

I scrambled to my feet. "Sorry," I whispered to Lara as I stepped over legs and backpacks. "Excuse me." I didn't stop until I was on solid ground. I brushed off my jeans, shoved the picture into my messenger bag, then pushed open the heavy theater door.

B Hall looked especially drab after the neon stage, but Jack, halfway to the gym and looking at his phone, might as well have had a spotlight on him.

Since he'd started at Lakehaven on Monday, Jack had been invited onto the yearbook committee and half the school's sports teams, and *in*to EmmaBeth Porter's pants, and those were just the offers I'd overheard.

Meanwhile, I'd spent the whole week fighting the flutter in my stomach that started when he sat next to me in sociology class. And got worse when he smiled at me in calculus. And then he'd showed up at lighting, which meant I'd been staring at the tattoo on his forearm for the last half hour instead of paying attention.

I wasn't just fascinated with his forearms, though, or his deep gray eyes, or the dimple in his right cheek. He *was* ridiculously attractive—not pretty, but good-looking in a chiseled way, his jawline an angle rather than a curve, not a strand of espresso-colored hair out of place—and to a lot of people, that would be enough.

To me, though, there was more. Jack was the new kid, like I was. Like me, he said no to all the invitations. I never saw him talking to anyone for more than a couple of minutes. But *he* seemed so confident about it. It was like he actually . . . didn't care.

I *pretended* I didn't care. About friends. About boys. About having a life. Sometimes I thought I'd actually gotten the hang of it, but then I'd find myself sneaking out of lighting rehearsal because there was a traitorous part of me that wanted to know if this guy I'd been watching for the past week had been watching me, too.

Jack made an abrupt right out the exit to the courtyard.

I should have stopped following him. What was I planning to do, anyway? But when I got to where he'd turned, I heard a voice echoing back into the hall through the plink of raindrops. "Why would he be coming here?"

I stopped short, confused. Carefully, I peered through the propped-open doors. Maybe it was somebody else.

It wasn't. All I could see was his left arm, but it was Jack. His compass tattoo was facing me, north pointing to the ground.

"Have you got any idea when?" he said, and I tried to make sense of it. Unless my ears weren't working, Jack Bishop was speaking with a British accent.

He glanced behind him, and I shrank flat against the lockers.

"No, I haven't seen him yet. Aren't there more important things to worry about?" He paused. "What would the Dauphins want with *her*?"

Her? My hand flew to the front pocket of my bag, where I'd tucked the photo.

"Sir?" Jack's voice changed from agitated to confused. "Certainly," he said. "Level one priority. I understand."

I shook my head. Of course he wasn't talking about me. But what *was* he talking about?

"I'll do it by tonight, then," Jack said after a pause. "Yes, sir."

He must have hung up the phone, because he cursed under his breath, and his footsteps squelched away on the rain-soaked sidewalk.

I sagged against the lockers. The last few words of the conversation played out in my head. *Level one priority. Sir.*

An old teacher of his, maybe. A strict British grandfather. It was none of my business, but the uncertainty in Jack's usually calm voice had unsettled me as much as the accent had.

I tucked a strand of dark hair behind my ear and took out the picture again, studying my face in the dull fluorescent light.

Wait.

I looked closer. This photo was taken in the front yard at my house. I recognized the spiky pine tree.

I didn't remember Lara taking pictures there, and *I* never posted photos online.

And if that was the case, where had Jack gotten it?

CHAPTER 3

very June West!" I jumped. I'd spent too much time thinking about the picture, and now I was about to be late for next period. I turned to find Lara bouncing down the hall toward my locker, her blue-tipped hair swinging. "Dude, thanks for running out on me. What is your problem?"

For some reason, I didn't want to tell her about Jack. "I told you I don't really like heights," I said instead.

I spun my lock, jiggled the handle, and smacked the corner of the door with my palm. It sprang open. Being the new kid in the middle of the year means you get a lot of leftovers. Lockers are no exception.

"And we agreed lighting would be good for that, remember?" Lara pulled a pack of Twizzlers from her backpack and offered it to me. I shook my head. "And then you get to hang out with *me*. If you did set design, you'd have to deal with Amber Leland the rest of the year, and gross."

I grabbed my Ancient Civilizations book. "I'm not going to ditch you for set design."

On the way to Ancient Civ, Lara told me about how Amie Simpson had been suspended for smoking cigarettes with the janitor, and how her date had no one to go to prom with now, and their dinner reservation was blown.

"You should just come," she said, pointing a long red Twizzler rope at the prom committee table. "I know you said you weren't going, but you could be Amie's replacement."

I looked at the prom poster. The theme was A Night in Hollywood. "I don't think so, but thanks."

I didn't do school dances. Just like clubs—and especially like very cute, very intriguing boys—they weren't part of The Plan. I was determined to stick to The Plan here in Lakehaven, Minnesota.

"Your loss," Lara said. "The Olive Garden has unlimited breadsticks."

I tuned out when Molly Mattison came running up to ask if she could borrow Lara's favorite feather earrings.

Was the whole idea of The Plan cynical of me? Sure. Kind of pathetic? Definitely. But I'd realized I needed to stop caring years ago, in a moving truck between Portland and St. Louis. The Plan worked, just like it was working this time. Lara was nice, but we'd never be all that close. I'd done lighting today to get both her and my mom off my back, but I'd specifically chosen the activity so I had an excuse to fail. Thank you, fear of heights.

The thing is, being lonely is like walking in the cold without a coat. It's uncomfortable, but eventually you go numb. Once you get used to *not* being lonely, though, the shock of going back is like having your down comforter yanked off at six o'clock on a Minnesota December morning.

Lara stopped talking and narrowed her eyes.

"What?" I started to say, but then I saw. Jack was walking toward us down the hall. There was no way he'd followed me to my house and taken a picture when I wasn't looking. Lara *must* have taken it.

"He is a ridiculous human being," Lara said.

Unlike every other girl in the school, she had no interest in Jack. She thought he was a snob. "Too J.Crew," she said, and she wasn't entirely wrong. He strutted down the hall with his hands in his pockets, wearing a tailored button-down with rolled-up sleeves, like he'd just stepped out of a photo shoot.

"Yeah," I said. "Ridiculous." I twisted the gold chain of my locket between my fingers and shot one last glance over my shoulder as the bell rang and we hurried into Ancient Civ. A few seconds later, Jack paused in the doorway. His eyes met mine before he took his seat, and I traced lines on my notebook.

Jack was in this class, calc, and sociology with me. We'd been paired up for a project on "Families in America" the past couple of days in sociology, which meant he now knew everything there was to know about my life, from the constant moving for my mom's job to my dad leaving us when I was little. I was still surprised I'd told him as much as I had. He wasn't nearly as forthcoming. I thought he would have at least mentioned posh British relatives who gave him enigmatic assignments over the phone.

"Miss West? Avery?"

I jumped, and my pen slipped off my desk with a clatter. I hadn't even realized that class started.

"Can you answer the question for us?" Mrs. Lindley asked.

"Um . . ." I glanced at Lara. She pointed to her notes, but I couldn't read her pink scrawls. On my own notebook, where *I* should have been taking notes, was a rough sketch of Jack's compass tattoo. I quickly covered it with my elbow.

"The Diadochi, Miss West, from the reading assigned last night. Can you tell us the role they played in the life of Alexander the Great?"

I'd done the reading. I always did the reading. I might not be good at people, but I was good at school. Right now, though, I was drawing a complete blank.

"Alexander the Great conquered a lot of the ancient world. Um, from Greece all the way to India," I said, stalling as I flipped pages, hoping the words would jump out at me.

Mrs. Lindley's lips pursed like she'd bitten into something sour.

"The Diadochi were Alexander's successors," a deep voice said, from three rows away. I turned. Jack was staring right at me. His voice was back to normal, with no trace of the British accent.

Mrs. Lindley quirked an eyebrow in my direction.

"Alexander didn't have a blood heir, so he left his kingdom to his twelve generals," Jack continued. Mrs. Lindley sighed and turned her attention to him.

"Thank you, Mr. Bishop, for demonstrating what happens when we do our homework. This time, I'll forget that you didn't raise your hand. Can you tell us what year Alexander the Great died?"

When Jack had answered all her questions, he glanced back my way.

I turned quickly back to my notes. I wished he hadn't done that. The last thing I needed was another reason to like him. I ripped out the drawing of his tattoo, crumpled it, and shoved it into my bag.

After class, I waited while Lara put her books away. I made a point to not look at Jack, but when I heard footsteps heading toward us as the rest of the class filed out, I knew exactly who it was.

Jack's dark hair had gone a bit wavy from the humidity, and he had his canvas messenger bag slung casually over one shoulder. I fiddled with the lace at the hem of my tank top.

"Hey! *You* left me high and dry at lighting, too," Lara said, poking her index finger in the middle of Jack's chest. "Rude. Both of you are rude."

"I'm sorry about that." Jack's voice was low and rough around the edges, like it was scraping over gravel. "I had to take a call. My grandfather's sick."

Oh. The tension I didn't realize had been building in my chest relaxed. I resisted the urge to ask where in England his grandfather lived—then reminded myself once more that I shouldn't care. Not about Jack's personal life, and not about the fact that even when he was talking to Lara, he was looking at me.

Lara wrinkled her nose in a way that could mean either *I'm sorry* or *eww, old people.* "That sucks," she said. She turned back to me as I hitched my bag up on my shoulder. And then she turned back to Jack when he didn't leave. And to me again. She gave me the most unsubtle eyebrow raise ever. "Oh. Okay. I just remembered I gotta go. Do . . . things. Ave, come over after school if you want, even if you aren't coming to prom. We're doing our nails."

I could have killed her, but I just pulled my hair out from under the strap of my bag and smiled through clenched teeth.

"I think you lost this." Jack handed me my pen as Lara walked away. "It rolled under my desk."

"Thanks."

He walked beside me out of class, slowing his long strides to match mine. He was probably just a little taller than average, but I still had to crane my neck to look up at him. He glanced at me out of the corner of his eye at the same time.

"And thanks for earlier," I said quickly, "but I *did* do the reading. I would have remembered the answer eventually."

"Oh." The space between his brows knitted together. Jack's brows were heavy and dark, and were as expressive as the rest of him was stoic. "I'm sorry. I thought—"

"No, it's okay." I went through the motions of opening my locker again. "I'm just saying I didn't actually *need* to be rescued. But I appreciate it."

He gave me a tiny smile, and it was like sun shining through armor. I busied myself putting my books in my bag.

"Actually, Avery," Jack said, "I need to talk to you."

My calculus book fell the rest of the way into my bag with a thump.

"Can we go somewhere—" His phone buzzed. He let out a frustrated breath. "One second."

While he checked a text, I zipped my bag shut. I didn't care what he had to say, I told myself. I didn't. *I didn't.* My black ankle boots squeaked on the damp tile, and the hall echoed with last-minute prom plans and the finality of lockers slamming one last time before the weekend.

Maybe he was going to ask about homework. Or maybe he'd say something horribly arrogant, Lara could be proven right, and I could truly forget about him.

I hazarded a glance up, and Jack's brows quirked down dangerously as he typed a text. It was the same look he'd had on his face when he'd left lighting earlier.

"Is your grandfather okay?" I asked.

"My—" His eyes narrowed for second, then he nodded. "He'll be fine. But, I was . . . um. Tonight." He shifted, running a hand through his hair. "Lara mentioned you're not going to prom?"

I clenched my fist around the strap of my bag.

"I don't really go to school dances," I said. My voice was an octave higher than usual.

"Oh." Jack and I were mirror images of each other, two islands in a swirling river of people. "I get it," he said. "You move all the time. If it's not going to last, is it even worth the effort, right?"

I looked up sharply. There was no way perfectly put-together Jack Bishop could understand The Plan.

"It's just that—I was wondering—" Jack rubbed the compass tattoo on his forearm with his opposite thumb, like a nervous habit. Then he looked up at me from under his lashes, his gray eyes unbearably hopeful, and I melted into a puddle on the dirty hallway floor. "I wanted to see if you'd like to go. With me."

The rest of the school year flew by in fast-forward. We'd go to prom. Maybe kiss good night. Sit next to each other in class, walk hand in hand down the hall. Have someone who got what it was like to be new when everyone else had known each other since they were in diapers. And eventually, as much as I tried not to, I'd let him in.

I fast-forwarded more. It might be a month, it might be a year, but inevitably, we'd move, and this time I wouldn't be the only one losing somebody.

I closed my eyes. It'd be better for him to ask someone else to prom—a cheerleader, or a choir member, or anybody who wasn't as screwed up as I was. And better for me to forget he existed.

When my eyes fluttered open, I couldn't look at him. "Thanks," I said to his feet. "But I don't think so." I turned and stalked off before he could see the carefully patched-up hole in my heart tearing wide open.

CHAPTER 4

I was so lost in my thoughts, I almost blew through the one red light in Lakehaven on the drive home from school. I slammed on the brakes and came to a stop in front of Frannie's Frozen Yogurt as pedestrians poured into the crosswalk.

I let my head flop back against the headrest. It was fine. I'd be fine.

Saying no was the right thing to do, even though nobody had ever asked me to a dance before. Even though it was *Jack Bishop* asking me. But it was fine.

I rested my forehead against the steering wheel. I wished the light would hurry up and turn so I could get home and this day could be over.

The crosswalk finally cleared, but as I sat up with a sigh and eased my foot onto the gas, one more person stepped out.

I stomped on the brake again, but the guy kept walking, like he didn't care that I'd almost hit him. He was tall, with straight dirty-blond hair a few weeks past a haircut, and so slim I would have called him skinny if not for the tightly muscled arms peeking out from under his T-shirt. He wasn't from here—that much I was sure of.

His gray skinny jeans tucked into half-tied boots, and the bag slung across his chest—that was hard for a guy to pull off unironically unless he was a big-city hipster, and Lakehaven didn't have any of those. And even though I might not know everyone's names yet, I knew every face at school. I was sure I'd recognize one that looked like this.

The guy's eyes swept from side to side, unhurried. They lit on three freshmen coming out of the frozen yogurt place, on a group of cheerleaders holding dry-cleaning bags, on a girl on a bike—and then, on me.

He stopped.

He stood there, right in the middle of the street, a smile stretched across his face. It wasn't a friendly smile. It was a smile like a lion about to pounce on prey, like blood, and hunger, and it tingled low in my stomach and made me push the lock button.

The car behind me honked.

The guy adjusted his bag and strolled the rest of the way across the street, turning to watch me drive away.

When I got home, I pushed the front door closed and snapped the deadbolt shut. The sound echoed in the quiet house.

I wished I *had* gone to Lara's. She had three sisters, and her aunt and uncle and cousins lived next door. Between the shrieks and giggles of the little kids and the adults in the kitchen drinking wine and teasing us about school and boys and college, her house exploded with life.

"Mom?" I called. The only answer was the washing machine's irregular clunk and a low murmur of voices from the TV.

I tossed my bag on the kitchen table and shrugged out of my denim jacket. The story that had broken the night before was still on the news: a car bomb in Dubai had killed nine people, including a Saudi prince.

I clicked the TV off. The news was depressing. My mom was obsessed, which seemed like a waste of time since we couldn't do anything to change what happened.

I wandered the kitchen, opening cabinets, the fridge, and finally pulling pistachio ice cream and frozen Thin Mints from the freezer.

The guy in the crosswalk could have been another transfer student, but I'd think I would have heard about him. Maybe he was somebody's out-of-town cousin. Or prom date.

I set my ice cream on the table and flipped through the pile of mail. I dropped it all when I got to a postcard. Istanbul—a picture of a mosque with soaring turrets. That was new.

I flipped it over and smiled at the familiar precise cursive.

Avery,

Hope this finds you and your mother well. Istanbul is beautiful. You'd love all the color in the markets, the textiles, the lights on the river. Remember the gyro stand you liked near Copley Square in Boston? There's one on every street corner here. The whole city smells delicious.

Charlie says hello.

Much love,
Fitzpatrick Emerson

Mr. Emerson had been our next-door neighbor in Boston when I was eight. It was right after our first move, and the longest we'd stayed in one place since. Mr. Emerson was all gray hair and round glasses, with a big booming laugh and a bowl of jelly beans—the classic grandpa I never had.

I'd always thought life would be easier if we had *some* family. Brothers and sisters as built-in friends, or cousins to write e-mails to, or an aunt to spend summers with—somebody besides my mom and me. Mr. Emerson wasn't actually related to us, but he was the closest thing we had.

I ran a finger over the Turkish postcard stamp and read the message again. Charlie was Mr. Emerson's grandson, and I swear, Mr. Emerson had been trying to set us up since I was a kid. I'd never seen so much as a picture of Charlie Emerson, but every time he wrote, Mr. Emerson told me about his adventures, and said he talked to Charlie about me.

I flipped the postcard over and looked at the picture. The Hagia Sophia. I remembered Mr. Emerson teaching me about it when I was little. About how "Hagia" was actually pronounced "Aya," and its name meant "Holy Wisdom."

I was glad he got to travel now that he was retired from teaching. And I was glad he still cared enough to send postcards. He was the only person over twelve moves who had stayed in touch for more than a couple months.

The laundry room door squeaked open and my mom poked her head out, a frown on her face. "Hi, Junebug. Have you seen my green pen? I swear, I was just holding it."

I pointed to the top of her head, where the pen stuck out of a messy bun. She felt around, sighed, and pulled it out, letting smooth blond waves fall around her shoulders. "You'd think I'd learn, wouldn't you?"

"You'd think." I dipped a cookie in my ice cream and took a bite. My mom wasn't actually the flighty, flustered type. It was more like keeping our lives together crowded out unimportant stuff like keeping track of writing implements. "Oh, you were out of fizzy water," I said. "I got you a case. On the counter."

My mom came over and kissed me on top of my head. "What would I do without you, daughter?"

"Be thirsty and unable to take notes," I replied. I hugged her hard around the waist.

"Hey," she said, a note of concern creeping into her voice when I didn't let go immediately. "Everything okay?"

"Yeah," I said. I hadn't realized just how much I needed a hug. "Fine."

I let go, but she slid down and nudged me to the side so she could sit on half my chair. She glanced at Mr. Emerson's postcard but didn't pick it up, and I wondered if she thought that was what was bothering me. Not that she'd ever ask about it directly. We used to talk about the moves, about how lonely I was, but it got to where it made it worse. Now we talked about everything else, but with undertones so clear, they may as well have been subtitles.

"Was play rehearsal okay?" She looped her arm through mine. *I push you into these things so maybe we can both feel better,* the subtitles said.

I put my head on her shoulder. "It was as bad as I told you it would be. Maybe worse." *I know you didn't actually think I'd stick it out.*

"Sweetie, everyone has a hard time with new things." My mom pushed back the hair that had fallen in my face. "Is something specific bothering you?"

"Um, yes. *Falling.*" I shivered, thinking of the swaying catwalk. "Falling to my death." That one was actually kind of true.

"Oh, Junebug." She sat up and took my face between her hands like she used to when I was little.

Everyone said we looked alike. We had the same thick hair, with just a little wave—though hers was blond—same small frame, same little, round nose. But my eyes were wider, darker—especially with my brown contacts—and my very dark eyes in my very pale face made me look young. Her eyes belonged to someone older than the rest of her, especially with the deep worry lines between them.

"I know you're afraid of falling, but sometimes, you've got to let go." *And I'm not just talking about your fear of heights,* the subtitle read.

I know, and I don't want to talk about it, I sighed.

My mom got up. "Tea?"

I nodded. She filled the kettle with water and set it on the stove. The burner clicked a few times and burst to life.

She took two tea bags from the cabinet and rubbed her forehead with a sigh that echoed in the quiet room.

I stopped scraping the bottom of my ice cream bowl. "Everything okay?"

"Did you see the mysterious new boy again today?" she asked. "Jack, right?"

I winced. She wasn't the only one who could change the subject. "Mr. Emerson's in Istanbul. Cool, right?"

The two mugs my mom was holding clattered to the counter. "Yes," she said, straightening them. "I saw the postcard. Sounds like a fascinating city."

"Mom. What's going on?" There was obviously something bothering her, and it wasn't the postcard.

"Nothing." Her fake smile was back. "It's been a long day. And . . . well, Junebug . . ." She looked longingly at the teakettle, like it might save her, then sighed heavily and sat across from me at the table. "We need to talk."

I knew what she was going to say before she pulled the manila envelope out of her laptop bag.

"A new mandate," I said flatly. I should have known.

I remembered the first time I'd heard the word. My mom was a military contractor—not *in* the military, like she didn't wear a uniform or anything, but she worked for them, doing administrative stuff in cities all over the country. Sometimes she had to scout a location for new offices and the job lasted a few months, and sometimes it would be more of a desk job she'd do from home, and we'd stay longer.

That day, I was nine years old, and we lived in Arizona. I'd cut my hand. When I came inside for a Band-Aid, my mom was on the phone.

"It's not that I want to leave. I hate doing that to her," she was saying, and I stopped to listen. "Of course because of the mandate. Why else?"

When she heard the door slam behind me, she hung up the phone.

"What's a mandate?" I'd asked, and she'd reached in her purse and pulled out a large envelope, exactly like the one she was holding right now. It was her new set of orders, sending us to a new town, a new life. The word *mandate* had hung over our heads ever since.

I should have been relieved to see the envelope now. Especially in the last week, I'd let myself come dangerously close to liking Lakehaven.

The teakettle sputtered, then whistled, and my mom poured water into two mugs. She set the one with the Eiffel Tower on it in front of me and I wrapped my hands around it, even though it was too hot. "Where?"

"Maine. Our new house will be right by the water, and the summers are supposed to be beautiful!" she said, too brightly.

I dunked the tea bag. "When?"

My mom leaned on the counter. "I reserved the moving truck for Sunday."

"Sunday?" I let the bag fall, and tea splashed over the side of the mug. Two days? "Mom! I'm not eight years old anymore. There are things I can't leave that fast. Like . . . getting the records for my AP classes transferred. There's no way a new school will let me into AP at the end of the year without paperwork. And checking the weather in Maine so I can put the right stuff in the right boxes. And—" I couldn't stop thinking about that picture in my bag. Jack. "There are *things.*"

"I'm sorry, sweetheart. Next time I'll try to give you more warning, but right now, it is what it is."

I pushed my mug across the table. If we *were* leaving in two days, maybe seeing Jack wouldn't be violating The Plan. One night wasn't getting involved; it was just letting myself live a tiny bit. "I think I'll go to prom tonight, then."

"No!"

I looked up sharply. The only time my mom ever raised her voice was when she burned dinner. Now she was frozen at the counter, eyes wide like I'd suggested skydiving.

"I have to go out of town for a couple of days, starting tonight," she said quickly. "I'd rather you stayed home."

She sometimes had to take care of things at the home office before the moves, but she never acted this weird about it. "A month ago you were forcing me to go dress shopping," I said.

She picked up a sponge and swiped at the counter. "And you didn't get one, because *you* said you didn't want to go, remember?"

A month ago, I wasn't about to move. A month ago, Jack didn't live here. "I have that old lace dress. The purple one. I'll wear that."

My mom pursed her lips. "I don't want to worry about you while I'm gone. There'll be drunk teenagers on the road. And what if you lock yourself out?"

"I have literally never locked myself out in my life." I ran both hands through my hair. "And prom's at school. I can walk there in twenty minutes if you don't want me to drive."

She tossed the sponge into the sink. "Avery June West, *promise* me you'll stay in tonight."

I must have looked alarmed, because she took a deep breath and let it out slowly. "Pack. Relax. You can go to prom in Maine!" My mom only spoke in exclamation points when there wasn't actually anything to be excited about. "You'll be a senior then. Senior prom's more fun anyway!"

I gathered up my stuff, ignoring her pleading eyes. "Fine."

"Avery, I'm sorry—"

"No, seriously, it's fine," I said through gritted teeth. This was why I never let myself care. It always got ruined, one way or another. I stalked to my bedroom without another word.

CHAPTER 5

I threw myself onto my ruffled comforter. I *wouldn't* go to prom in Maine. By next spring, we'd be in the next place. Always in the next place, in the future—that's when I'd have a life. I rooted around in my bag and found the picture again, and next to it, the crumpled drawing of Jack's tattoo. I smoothed out the crinkles.

The compass was vaguely familiar, like I'd seen it in a movie or something. Now I'd never know. I finished sketching the south and east points, pushing so hard with the pen, I tore a hole in the paper.

My phone dinged.

If you change your mind, I'm still going to prom. Hope to see you there. Jack.

I stared at the message. He wasn't upset. He cared enough to try again. One night. It was *one* night. Why was my mom being so unreasonable?

I want to say yes so much it hurts, I typed in, then erased it. *I'm going to try not to picture EmmaBeth Porter's tongue down your throat all night,* I typed, then wrinkled my nose. Eww. Already unsuccessful. *Kill me now,* I typed, then tossed the phone at my headboard and watched it slither down between two pillows.

I flopped onto my back and stared at the mustard-yellow ceiling. The first couple of moves, redecorating is fun. Changing paint colors, unpacking all your knickknacks. By the twelfth, all the breakable stuff is left wrapped, and the puke color stays on the walls.

Who knows. Maybe my mom vetoing prom was a sign. Jack *seemed* nice, but carrying a vaguely stalkerish photo was weird. And that phone call was weird. The more I thought about it, the more it hadn't sounded like he was talking to a sick relative at all.

But maybe if I had a family of my own, I'd understand not wanting to tell a virtual stranger all about them.

Maybe if my mom didn't move us so much, I wouldn't be such a reclusive weirdo who forced herself to think the worst about everybody.

Maybe, maybe, maybe.

Maybe none of it mattered, since we'd be leaving the day after tomorrow anyway.

I listened to make sure my mom wasn't coming down the hall, then leaned over the edge of the bed and pulled out a shoe box that I'd hidden behind some winter clothes. I opened it and tossed my sketch of Jack's tattoo and the photo of me on top.

I was about to slam the box shut, but stopped. I pulled out the top few mementos—invitations to parties I never went to, a picture of me with a neighbor's family. Rattling around in the bottom of the box was the infinity-sign pinky ring from eighth grade, when I broke The Plan for Missy and Alina and Katy. We called ourselves the Fab Four, and promised to text every single day when I moved. That lasted for about six weeks.

Halfway down the stack, a ripped-out sheet of notebook paper listing everyone I'd ever found on Google named Alexander Mason who could maybe, possibly, be my dad.

He and my mom had dated in college, and when she got pregnant with me, he left. When I was younger, I wondered if one day he would realize he'd made a mistake. That he wanted us after all, and we'd have a normal life, full of smiles and holiday dinners and cheesy, feel-good, cell-phone-commercial family moments. My dad's parents were dead, and he didn't have any other family, but I used to think about how there was a possibility of brothers and sisters if he came back into the picture.

I got over that wish a long time ago. I ran a finger over my locket. I'd taken the one picture I had of him out, and now there was only a photo of me and my mom, protected by the worn gold filigree. The picture of my dad stared up at me from the box. It was small, and blurry, but you could tell my dark hair and pale skin came from him, and I knew I had his eyes. You could almost call my natural eye color deep blue, but that wasn't quite right. Really, my eyes were purple.

When I was younger, kids had teased me that I was wearing contacts to be cool. That normally wouldn't have been a huge deal, but as weird and friendless as I was already, it killed me. But it did give me and my mom an idea. Since I had horrible vision anyway—and, though she'd never admit it, probably because they reminded her so much of my dad—my mom suggested colored contacts. I'd had dark brown eyes ever since.

I jammed everything in the box and shoved it back under the bed—and then opened it once more and snatched out the compass drawing.

Even if The Plan was the right thing to do in the long run, what was one night? One dance. One date with one guy. Tonight could be one tiny memory that wasn't a what-if.

I could hear my mom in the kitchen, opening the cabinets over the sink. I knew the sound of her bundling the silverware, wrapping it in a dish towel, and putting it in the bowl of the blender, the same way she'd always done it. Next she'd pack up the baking stuff and the cleaning supplies, and I'd pack my room and the bathroom and the laundry room. And then we'd pile those boxes alongside the ones we'd never gotten around to unpacking from last time.

I made a decision.

I fished my phone out from between the pillows, typed out a quick text, then jumped off my bed and went to the kitchen. I grabbed some of the broken-down boxes my mom had brought up from the basement. "You're probably right," I said, and her thin shoulders relaxed. "I'll start folding clothes."

The rest of the afternoon, I was a model daughter. I packed my room, vacuumed, and even heated up frozen lasagna for dinner. Then I waited until my mom was safely on her way to the airport, slipped my dress on, threw my hair up with bobby pins, and walked out the front door.

CHAPTER 6

The gym reeked of cheap aftershave and a hungry energy fueled by the crush of bodies and the open backs of dresses and the euphoric faces blinking in and out of the dark. Streamers on the walls caught the strobes and exploded with light, like fireworks, spearing the dark corners of the room.

The swirl of bodies in jewel tones and sparkles and pressed black suits parted around me as I stood at the edge of the dance floor, physically present but not actually a part of anything. I wondered sometimes if they all knew how good they had it: girls in circles with their friends, singing at the top of their lungs, or with their arms curled around their boyfriends' necks. Girls who had gotten their hair done by a big sister, cheesy prom pictures taken by a proud dad.

Across the gym Lara saw me and jumped up and down waving, the spinning lights flashing off the glittery blue tulle of her dress. I waved back, a surprisingly sharp pang running through me at the thought of leaving her, too. I'd tried so hard not to get too close to any of them. I held up a finger to tell her I'd be over in a minute.

I wove my way past the line for the photographer, who was posing a guy's hand on a girl's hip, and pulled at the hem of my dress. I'd gotten it in the ninth grade for a neighbor's wedding. It was pretty, with capped sleeves and scalloped lavender lace, but definitely too casual for prom. I hoped Jack wouldn't care.

If I ever found him, that is. He hadn't texted back. It would be just my luck if he'd turned his phone off and didn't see the message until tomorrow.

Fifteen minutes later, I'd circled the whole gym once, twice. Casually peered onto the dance floor. Walked by the bathrooms and the water fountain. Gotten a cup of punch from the snack table, just in case he was waiting there. Checked my phone five times. Stopped and talked to Lara and her date. Still no Jack.

I traced a pattern on my scuffed leather messenger bag with one fingertip. It was fine. It was probably better this way.

I took one last look at the human-sized papier-mâché Oscar statuettes, felt the bass of the dance track vibrate through my feet, and took a sip of too-sweet red punch. Then I turned to head for the exit—and ran straight into a senior in a yellow dress.

"Sorry . . ." I trailed off when I realized I'd splashed punch all over myself. Perfect.

The girl was staring intently at something I couldn't see, though, and didn't even notice me. The friend she was dancing with was looking, too.

I put down my cup and, dabbing at my dress with a napkin, ducked between two guys in tuxedos and too much cologne to see what was going on. I stopped short.

It wasn't a *what* that was going on, it was a *who*.

Crosswalk Guy.

He leaned against the gym wall, one foot propped casually over the other, his blond hair falling over his eyes. He was a head taller than everyone around him, and had to be at least a year or two older than all of us.

As if to confirm that, he blew a stream of smoke out of the corner of his mouth, then stamped out a cigarette, right there on the gym floor. No wonder everybody was staring. How had he not been caught by a teacher? There didn't seem to be any around.

The guy's eyes continued to roam the crowd. And then they got to me. His face broke into that slow, lazy grin again.

I held my breath as he pushed off the wall at half tempo, so the strobe lights seemed to move entirely too fast. Half the dance watched him watch me. Was he mistaking me for someone else?

A slow song started as he stopped in front of me. "Avery West."

I took a step backward. How did he know my name? He had a light foreign accent—maybe Russian? That would fit with the jaunty blond hair and the high, sharp cheekbones. It made my name sound exotic, like a Bond girl. *Ay-veery*.

"Lovely to see you, sweetheart," he continued, plucking the napkin out of my hand with a frown and dropping it to the ground. "A dance?"

He slipped one cool, sure palm into mine before I had a chance to respond.

"Um," I said. He settled his other hand on my lower back and drew me close. EmmaBeth Porter, dancing nearby, stared from him to me with a look halfway between appalled and so jealous, she could throw up.

I brushed back a strand of dark hair that had escaped its bobby pin and stared up at him. "I'm sorry, I don't think I know you."

"You don't." He smiled. "And even more interestingly, *I* do not know *you*. Why don't you go ahead and tell me who you are, and we can skip this little charade?"

He squeezed my hand.

EmmaBeth and her date had moved toward the stage, where last year's prom court was assembling, leaving me and Crosswalk Guy by ourselves on the far edge of the dance floor. Even though all he'd done was say things I didn't understand, I suddenly did not want to be alone with him.

"I'm not sure what you're talking about," I said, pulling at my hand. He held on tighter, and alarms went off in my head. "I'm going to go—"

"Stellan," came a quiet voice from behind me.

Crosswalk Guy—Stellan—rolled his eyes. "Oh good," he said. "*You're* here."

I ripped my hand out of Stellan's, turned around, and was hugely relieved to see Jack.

He wore a perfectly fitted black suit over a crisp white shirt and a thin tie. He met my eyes for just a second, then looked past me at Stellan. He scowled. Even that brought out a hint of the deep dimple in his right cheek.

"Stellan, get away from her," he said. His British accent was back. "Avery, come here."

I was headed toward him anyway, but stalled at the command. I looked between them. Compared with Jack's slim but solid frame, Stellan was taller, sharper, almost gaunt in that ethereally beautiful way you see on runway models. And while Jack looked like he might punch someone, Stellan wore the kind of patronizing smile adults get when kids are fighting over a toy.

I wrapped my arms around myself. "What's going on?"

"So who is she?" Stellan said to Jack. He unbuttoned his gray suit jacket. "If you weren't here, I'd think I had the wrong girl. She's so . . . ordinary."

I looked down at my punch-stained dress and sale-rack strappy sandals.

"Not that you're not pretty." Stellan smiled thinly down at me. "You are." He turned back to Jack. "As I can see *you've* noticed. And such a little thing. I could snap her in half with one finger."

Jack growled low in his throat, and Stellan laughed. "You make this too easy."

"Excuse me, I'm right here," I said. "And this is really . . ." Bizarre? He had to think I was someone else, right? But then how would he know Jack? "Jack, let's go—"

Stellan stepped between us, loosening his tie. I suddenly realized he wasn't getting comfortable. He was getting ready for a fight. Sharp slivers of alarm pierced my confusion. Maybe it was time to let go of the idea of Jack as a prom date.

I started to inch away.

"What do you even want with her?" Jack said. His voice was low and dangerous, with no trace of the anxiety I'd heard while he was on the phone earlier. "There's no reason for you to be here."

I stopped. The memory of the phone call flooded back. He had asked the caller what they wanted with "her." And when "he" was coming. And had mentioned "tonight."

"Jack, seriously, what is going on?" I said, but my words were drowned out by the electronic screech of a microphone.

"And now, it's time to announce your new prom court!" said a senior cheerleader. On either side of her, last year's court lined up, holding sashes and crowns.

"If it isn't obvious," Stellan said, a lock of blond hair falling in his face, "*we* want her because *you* want her. And we'd like to know why."

Jack stared him down. "Like I said, it's none of your business."

"Ah, but it is our business when Alistair Saxon sends a Keeper to attend high school classes halfway across the world while every other family is using their resources on more essential tasks."

It felt like I was watching TV in a foreign language. I was about to make Jack fill me in when Stellan continued, "So the reason *I'm* here is to figure out why this girl is more important to the Saxons than the mandate."

CHAPTER 7

The familiar word struck me like a slap to the face. "Wait," I said. "Did you say *mandate?*"

Jack glared at Stellan, and Stellan rolled his eyes. "No one can hear us. Relax. And *she* must know about it, so it doesn't matter."

I knew about the manila envelope on our dining room table, but I highly doubted my mom's work orders had anything to do with two strangers fighting over me at the Lakehaven High prom.

"This year's prom queen," said the cheerleader on stage, "Emma-Beth Porter!" Her friends, lining the stage, squealed prettily. A loud "booooo" sounded from where the stoner kids were gathered at the edge of the bleachers, followed by a chorus of laughter.

Stellan put his hands in his pockets in a way that could have been casual if the rest of him didn't look like a tightly coiled spring. "So she has information on the search?"

"The what?" I felt very small looking up at the two of them. It didn't help that they were ignoring me entirely, and that I was at least two steps behind in the conversation. "What's the mandate?"

"Or she's a spy?" Stellan said. "Are the Saxons using American teenagers as spies now?"

"A *spy*?" I looked around. "Is this a hidden camera show?"

"Of course she's not a spy." Jack's mouth tightened in irritation. "She's got nothing to do with the mandate. I was sent to find her because she's related to the Saxons."

I let out a breath. At least that made sense. "Okay, you *do* have the wrong person," I said. "I don't have any family."

Jack looked down. The grim set of his jaw looked like it belonged to an entirely different person than the guy who saved my grade in history class, but his eyes softened. "Yes, Avery, you do."

"I think I'd know—" But I stopped, the tiny locket-sized picture in my memory box springing into my mind. I felt my face go slack.

Jack lowered his voice. "In class you told me you didn't have any family. Maybe your mother doesn't, but your father did."

I had to wet my lips to get words out. "Are you kidding?"

"No," he said quietly.

My vision darkened at the edges, and I went light-headed. I must have looked like it, too, because Jack put a hand on my elbow.

I blinked up at him. Could this be real? My *father* was looking for me? After sixteen years, my father actually cared?

"Where is he?" I said, whipping around. "Is he here? Who are *you*?" Was Jack some kind of private investigator?

Stellan looked up from studying his fingernails and heaved a sigh. "As fascinating as this is, I don't care. My orders are to find the girl and take her, so I'm going to go ahead and do that." He took my arm in a death grip.

"What? No!" I tried to pull my arm back.

Jack lunged for me, and Stellan reached under his jacket. A flash of silver glinted in the low light. I did a double take.

"Oh my God," I whispered. Stellan had pulled out a knife the size of a small sword. I shrank away, but he didn't let go.

"I had hoped it wouldn't come to this." I could hear the smile in his words.

"No you didn't," Jack said through clenched teeth.

"You're right. So much more entertaining this way."

The microphone screeched. "And now, the Lakehaven High prom king!"

I couldn't stop staring at the knife. Jack stepped in front of us. "I'm not letting you take her."

"Oh, right—you'll want to stay for the prom king announcement. Might have a chance at it this year." Stellan started to drag me away, knife to my side.

"Quit it!" I finally snapped out of it and fought against his hand, careful to avoid the knife. "Let me go!"

A few curious sets of eyes turned toward us, and I stopped struggling. As much as I wanted to get away from Stellan, I didn't want to make a scene. I needed to hear what Jack had to say about my father.

"Hey." I pulled on Stellan's jacket. If Jack was an investigator, what was Stellan? He cocked his head down at me, but didn't stop steering me around the edge of the dance floor, past the DJ booth. "If you don't let me go, I will scream and you will get arrested." I hoped I sounded more confident than I felt.

A laughing, jostling group of guys walked by and peered curiously at us. With a sigh, Stellan hid the knife.

The second he did, I ripped my arm away and ran to Jack, who had been following us. He tucked me behind his back and surveyed the exits—the front doors, the emergency exit out the back. "The side doors would be the easiest way to get out," I said, panting. "But are you absolutely sure you have the right person? My father's name is Alexander Mason."

Jack's shoulders tensed.

"What?" I pleaded. "Stop being so cryptic. Just tell me what's going on."

"Avery, I'm—" He glanced at me over his shoulder and eyed Stellan, who typed on his phone as a teacher made her rounds past our corner of the gym. Jack let out a breath and turned around. "I'm so sorry. I know very little about your father. I don't work for him. I work for his family. He's—it appears he passed away, some time ago. His family didn't know you existed until recently. I'm sorry to be the one to tell you."

Passed away. On the stage, the new prom court stood waving, and their faces blurred into one artificially lit grin.

My father was dead. I felt something shift within me, a key turned one click farther in a lock, a compass spun in a new direction. I wasn't a girl whose father had left. I was a girl whose father was dead.

"You're sure?" I whispered.

"That's what I was told."

It shouldn't hurt like he was a real person. He'd been dead to us for a long time. But still, my throat burned with the promise of tears. I hadn't realized how much I still harbored that secret wish of meeting him, and now I never would.

But if Jack was telling the truth, he had family.

Stellan glared daggers at the white-haired teacher who was now chatting about the weather with the very tall and intimidating football coach, not ten feet away from us. I'd be safe for a couple of minutes. I sat down at an abandoned table littered with glitter and streamers and empty punch cups and played with a star-shaped piece of gold confetti. "Do they want to meet my mom, too?"

"I was told to approach *you* specifically." Jack pulled out the chair next to me. "Is it possible your mother wouldn't want you to know about them?"

Yes. It was more than possible.

I'd never made a secret of wishing we had somebody, and she'd never made it a secret that she was bitter about my dad. It must have been easier for her to tell me he had no family than to say I couldn't meet them. Anger bubbled up hot inside me. I half wanted to call her right now and yell at her. Moving for her job was one thing. Hiding a whole family was another.

"You said distant family?" I asked. Stellan was still watching us. I turned my back to him, facing Jack. "Like, how distant? Siblings? Cousins?"

Jack held up his hands helplessly. "There are quite a few family members. I'm not sure which ones are related to you."

"Why wouldn't they just call if they wanted to see me?" A new song started, louder, and I leaned in close to Jack.

"They weren't sure of your identity, so I was sent to verify the information," he said.

And then it hit me. Jack Bishop was at Lakehaven High to spy on me. All this time—sitting next to me in class, talking about our families, that photo—had been *surveillance*. God, he'd probably asked me to prom because the person on the phone told him Stellan would be here tonight. After everything else he'd just told me, it shouldn't matter, but all of a sudden, I couldn't meet his eyes. I didn't want him to see the well of humiliation spilling over in mine.

I stood up abruptly and made my way around the table, running my fingertips over the backs of the chairs. "Then who is *he*?" I pointed to Stellan. "And who is this family that they'd do that rather than *calling*? Or e-mailing? Or writing a letter on fancy stationery?"

"They run your world, sweetheart." Stellan strolled up, slipping his phone into a pocket inside his jacket. I saw that the teachers had left.

Jack jumped to standing. "Stellan." He cast his eyes toward the group of kids dancing nearest to us. "Not now."

"Like, they're in the *government*?" I'd always pictured my dad as a regular guy who ran from the responsibility of being a father, but maybe his family was rich and powerful, and they'd sent my non-rich and powerful mom off with a little hush money so they wouldn't have to deal with his illegitimate kid.

"Hey," a giggling voice said. Three of the prom princesses pounced on Stellan, their sashes proudly displayed against their fake tans and sequined dresses. "Do you go to Brickfield?" Jessa Marin, in a pastel pink gown with wide cutouts at the midriff, batted her eyes and touched his arm.

Jack put a hand on my back and steered me toward the door. I shook him off. "Where are they?" I repeated. "If I agree to meet them, where are we going?"

He didn't answer, and I turned to see him stopped dead, his face illuminated by the cool blue glare of his phone.

"What?" I said.

Stellan watched us over the heads of the three girls as Jack made a call. Over the music, I heard the very faint ding of voice mail picking up. Jack cursed quietly. "Call me back," he said, shooting an uneasy glance at Stellan, then at me.

I crossed my arms over my chest. "What's going on now?"

"I might ask you the same thing," he said under his breath, then slipped the phone into the breast pocket of his jacket. "Let's just go. Quickly."

I twisted my locket around my fingers. "I really don't know if this is a good idea—"

Jack faced me. "Avery, I'm sorry. I didn't mean for it to be like this, but they want to know you. You'll want to know them. I promise, it'll be all right. I'll make sure of it."

If I did this, it wouldn't be because of promises from him. I wished I could call my mom, but I clearly couldn't count on her to tell the truth.

Let myself live a little. Wasn't that what tonight was about? This would be living more than a little. This could change my life.

"All right," I said. I let go of my locket, and my fingertips tingled. "Okay."

Jack started toward the door immediately.

Stellan extracted himself from the girls and came after us.

"Is he going to try to hurt us?" I said, glancing backward over my shoulder. "Should you call the police or something?"

Jack didn't answer, but as we passed the photographer, he slowed and took out his phone again. His eyes darted from the phone, to the gym doors, to the phone . . . to me. "No, he won't hurt you. He'd get in trouble if he did anything to you." He clicked his phone off, then rubbed his forearm with his opposite hand and cursed again, not so softly this time. "Go with him."

I stared at him. "Excuse me?"

Jack scrubbed both hands through his thick dark hair and shot a pained glance at Stellan. "Don't tell him anything."

"What? No way. What did that text say?" I was starting to panic. "He doesn't even work for my family, does he?"

"For you, it's practically the same," he murmured. "The Saxons will be there tomorrow, and I will, too. You'll be fine until then."

He raised his voice as Stellan approached. "If you're going to be this difficult, she's yours," he said. "We'll collect her later."

I glared at Jack. First he'd spied on me, now he was abandoning me? "You can't just *decide* to let him have me," I said. "Tell me where to find my family and I'll go meet them myself. I have a car."

Stellan laughed. "She's funny," he said, and then turned to me, the smile falling off his face. "Listen, if you are who he claims you are, you'll meet them soon enough, and everyone will be happy."

I glared daggers at Jack, whose eyes pleaded with me. It seemed like he was telling the truth about this. If going with Stellan was what I had to do to meet my family, I guessed I would.

"Okay," I said.

"Finally." Stellan propelled me toward the back door.

And then I remembered something. Jack had said he'd see me *tomorrow*. "Where are we going?" I asked Stellan. If we were going as far as Minneapolis or something, my mom really would kill me.

We stepped into the parking lot, and Stellan opened the passenger door of a little black car parked in the principal's space. I got in. "*Parlez-vous français, cherie?*" he said, and slammed the door.

CHAPTER 8

The plane pitched, and I grabbed the armrests so hard, my finger-nails hurt, like holding on would save me if we fell from the sky.

France. We were going to France. In a matter of hours, I'd gone from moving to Nowhere, Maine, to this. Visions of summers in Europe with exotic, wealthy relatives danced in my head. I knew I was getting ahead of myself—they probably just wanted to satisfy their curiosity and send me back home with a souvenir key chain.

But Stellan hadn't taken me to a regular airport. We were on a private plane nicer than any house I'd ever lived in. And not only that, but the second I'd heard we were going to France, I'd told Stellan I didn't have a passport.

He said it didn't matter.

I thought I'd heard wrong, but the fact that I had no passport and was on my way to Europe did. Not. Matter.

I rested my forehead against the cool of the plane window and stared out at the endless blackness, broken only by the blinking white and red lights on the plane's wings.

Stellan was taking me to Paris, Jack had a British accent, and they could get me into another country without a passport. *They run your world*, Stellan had said.

I glanced at Stellan. As soon as we'd taken off, he'd stretched out on one of the ivory leather couches and fallen asleep. He snored lightly, the white T-shirt he'd had on under his dress shirt pulling tighter across his chest with every inhale. One hand rested on his stomach, rising and falling with the easy rhythm of his breath. His other hand clutched the handle of his knife—dagger, sword, whatever it was—even in sleep.

There were other couches, and my seat leaned back so far, I could lie down, but there was no way I was sleeping with the heady combination of anxiety and exhilaration coursing through me. I crossed and uncrossed my legs, and my foot wouldn't stop bouncing.

How had my mom gotten involved with this? An aristocrat's son studying abroad, falling in love with a commoner? Or a powerful politician seducing a young girl, then ditching her when she got pregnant? How had I not known my mom's life was a soap opera? And what, if anything, did the *mandate* have to do with it?

The plane pitched, and I drew a sharp breath. Stellan sat up and rubbed his eye with the back of his hand, the hint of soft sleepiness in his face and the blond halo of his tousled hair making him less intimidating for a second.

I'd expected Stellan to look less epic in the light and without half the prom staring at him like he was a Greek god, but I was wrong. Where Jack was always perfectly put together, Stellan might have cut his mop of hair himself, and he'd slept in his clothes. And still, he was attractive in an almost unbelievable way, like he glowed from the inside.

Well, I didn't care if he *was* a Greek god. I didn't trust him for a second. And that would have been true even if he hadn't pulled a knife on me a few hours ago.

He cracked his neck from side to side, then stood and stretched his arms above his head, raising his shirt to expose a strip of toned midriff.

I averted my eyes, but not before he caught me and smirked knowingly. "We're landing soon. I'm going to clean up," he said, scrutinizing me. "You might want to do the same."

I tucked my feet under my skirt. I knew I barely looked presentable for a small-town dance, much less for meeting with government officials in Paris, but it wasn't my fault. I hadn't had time to change out of this punch-stained dress or wash my face or anything. I was lucky I happened to have a hairbrush and contact-lens drops in my bag.

"What's the mandate?" I said, putting on a veneer of bravado I didn't feel, but that I'd need if I was going to get any information out of him. I'd already run through all my questions once, in the car after we left prom, but Stellan had ignored me and spent the whole drive making official-sounding phone calls in French.

He reached into an overhead compartment. "Nothing that concerns you."

I pressed my lips together. "You said something about a search. Can you at least tell me what you're searching for?"

He retrieved a small leather duffel bag and tossed it onto the seat. "What's everyone always searching for?" With a glint in his eye, he leaned in close to my ear. I tensed. "Treasure," he whispered.

The breath whooshed out of my lungs, and I frowned up at him. He chuckled.

"Is my, um." The word still felt strange. "Is my family from England?" I said.

He took a folded shirt out of the bag. "The *Saxons* are from England; maybe they're your family."

A smile pulled at my lips. My relatives had British accents. "And you don't work for them?"

He reached up one slim arm to pull down the combat boots he was wearing when I first saw him. They hit the floor with two hollow thumps. "I represent another family of the Circle."

I traced the cream-colored leather of the seat through the lace overlay of my dress. "Which is what, exactly?"

Stellan paused, then turned, his hand resting on the overhead compartment so he loomed over me. "The Circle of Twelve?"

I shook my head.

He narrowed his eyes. "They claim you're family, but you didn't know your father, and you don't know what the Circle is."

I pressed my lips shut. Jack had said not to tell him anything. I didn't think I had anything *to* tell, but Stellan had seemed especially curious since the dance, so I wasn't going to risk it.

Stellan shook the creases out of the clean shirt, then stripped off the one he was wearing. I tried not to watch him, but my breath caught when he turned to put his bag away.

A network of scars crisscrossed his back. They were startling, long and slightly raised, but didn't look like any scars I'd ever seen. Not fresh ones, like when Joshua Metcalf had been in that car accident in tenth grade, and not old ones, like the one on my mom's leg she got falling off a horse when she was little.

These were translucent, and they disappeared into two tattoos, both black, made topographical by the scar tissue underneath. One was a sword, starting between his shoulder blades and traveling down his spine. The other looked like a sun, just above it.

I stared at my headrest. The same sun symbol was embroidered onto each seat and etched into the mirror behind the bar and on every door in the plane. It had a large circle in the middle, with short rays coming out of it.

My eyes snapped to Stellan's back, to the scars, to the sun tattoo, to the sword, until he closed the bathroom door behind him with a bang. I slumped back into my seat.

The Circle of Twelve. Maybe they weren't government, but a group of European crime families. A French and British mafia. Was there a French and British mafia? Maybe that sun was their symbol. And those scars were . . . some kind of brand? Or just an old injury.

And there was also Jack's tattoo, which was different. So . . . rival families?

My excited side conceded a little to my nervous side, and I buried my face in my hands, not sure whether to cry or laugh or scream. I decided to take out my bobby pins. My head hurt.

Since Stellan had taken the bathroom, I peered through the rows of crystal liquor bottles to the mirror behind the bar. I felt like a mess, but I *looked* even worse. Besides the stained dress, my mascara had smeared, and my hair was a wreck.

I wet a cocktail napkin and wiped some of the dark rings from under my eyes, then turned to my hair.

The bathroom door clicked open, and I dropped the pin I was holding.

"Jumpy," Stellan said, easing the door closed. "Afraid of flying? I should have brought the big plane instead. Less turbulence."

This was the *small* plane?

Stellan tightened the knot on a slim black tie and reached over me to flip on an espresso maker. "Coffee?"

I stepped aside and side-eyed the espresso cups he set on the counter. I wanted to get him talking. If he wouldn't answer any of my questions directly, maybe he'd at least let something useful slip. "I would have taken you for a vodka-in-the-morning kind of guy," I said, measuring his reaction.

He loaded the machine with coffee grounds. "Why's that?"

"I want to say because your accent sounds Russian and that's the stereotype." I tapped a bobby pin on the sink. "But really, from what I've seen so far, it's just what I would expect from *you.*"

He filled a small cup and set it in front of me with a quick laugh. "*Half* Russian," he said in that light accent. "The other half's Swedish, so feel free to make insulting Viking references, too. Besides, they don't have my favorite vodka on this plane."

He sipped a second cup of espresso and gazed silently out the window at the fingers of pink sunrise stretching across the sky. So much for getting him chatting.

"So you and Jack are what, bodyguards?" I took my place at the sink again, concentrating on the mirror.

He smiled. "Has anyone ever told you that you look like one of those dolls?" he said. "A . . . *kuklachka.* How do you say it in English? With the white skin and the big eyes."

"A porcelain doll." My pale complexion and dark hair would have been enough, but add dark eyes and cheeks that flushed too easily and too often—like I was determined for them *not* to do right now—and that sealed it. He wasn't the first to make the comparison. "Why does the family you work for care about me if I'm related to someone else?" I said, steering the conversation back around.

"A pretty little porcelain doll," he said. "That's you. *Kuklachka.*"

I wasn't sure if he really did want something from me, but if he thought taking his shirt off and acting like we were on some kind of bizarre vacation was going to make me flustered enough to reveal secret information, he was wrong. It was only making me a *little* flustered.

I shook it off and reminded myself that even if he'd been civil since the prom, something about him still made me uncomfortable, which meant it was deeply messed up to let him flirt with me at all, much less react to it. But if he was trying to get me to let my guard down, I could do the same to him.

I yanked out a few more bobby pins, which clinked as I pitched them into the trash can under the sink. The next pin stuck, shellacked in place with hairspray. I pulled harder, and hissed through my teeth when I yanked out a few strands of hair. It wouldn't help to take my nerves out on my scalp.

"Here." Stellan set his espresso cup down on the sink and peered into my mess of hair, his fingers moving mine aside.

I ducked away. That was going a little far. "Absolutely not."

He moved my hands off my head. "It reflects poorly on me for you to show up looking like you've been in a bar brawl."

I twisted away, and he sighed. "I'm not going to hurt you."

"Maybe if I knew what you *were* going to do to me, I wouldn't be so worried you'd stab me with a bobby pin," I said under my breath. Honestly, I wasn't that worried—it did seem like it was his job to deliver me unharmed. I just didn't want to let him think he was getting in my head.

He ignored me and placed my hands firmly at my sides.

I was too exhausted to protest anymore. And who knew? Maybe it'd be good for me to let him think he was getting in my head. Plus he was right—the stuck pin was making it look like I had a wing on top of my head. He worked it out with a surprisingly gentle touch and pushed my hands away when I tried to take over again.

"What am I going to do to you, you ask? Well, I barely know you," he said, freeing the last of my curls and softly tousling my hair for any remaining pins. He looked me up and down in the mirror. "But I'm sure I could think of something. I do appreciate your enthusiasm."

I didn't give him the satisfaction of rolling my eyes, but my inconveniently active blushing mechanism gave away that the innuendo wasn't lost on me. He gave a short laugh, and adjusted an earpiece in his right ear.

We broke through a layer of clouds, and a vast city spread out below. I pushed by Stellan and stared out the window.

If this was real, I was about to meet my family. People who had known my father. For the first time in my life, people who wanted to know *me*. But I couldn't help thinking about Stellan's scars, and the tattoos, and about what kind of people would practically kidnap a girl from her prom to bring her to France, and my heart skipped painfully.

"Please take your seats," the pilot's voice said from the speakers in the cabin. "We'll be on the ground in twelve minutes. *Bienvenue à Paris.*"

CHAPTER 9

Paris looked like a movie of Paris.

Most places don't. All of New York isn't Times Square, and you can't see the Hollywood sign from the beach in L.A. The only place I'd ever been that could have played its movie self was the Las Vegas Strip, which we drove through on our move from Texas to Oregon.

But Paris wasn't just the white dome of the Sacré-Coeur on a hillside in the distance, or the Eiffel Tower—the *Eiffel Tower!*— growing larger every second. It was the details.

The entire city seemed to have been color coordinated long ago, so the gray roofs and cream buildings and wrought-iron balconies all worked in perfect harmony. The bridge we trundled over featured rows of dark streetlamps that looked straight off a movie set, and golden statues at both ends of it kept watch over the Seine. It felt unreal, like a camera crew would show up at any moment and remind me that this wasn't my life.

The car rolled to a stop.

Stellan climbed out and came around to my side. He stood straight now, hair smoothed, suit jacket buttoned, very official. I couldn't help but yank on the hem of my dress. I suddenly felt very small and very out of place and very nervous. I rubbed the gold filigree on my locket as the driver opened my door, marveling that there was a driver opening my door. I felt like Dorothy stepping out the door of her little house into Oz.

A tour bus that had been blocking my view pulled away—and I did a double take at the glass pyramid in a vast courtyard. "The Louvre?" I said, surprised. The building was easy to recognize from pictures.

But rather than walking toward the main entrance at the pyramid, Stellan's boots crunched across the fine gravel toward one of the side arms of the complex. He murmured into the microphone attached to his earpiece and glanced back at me. "Coming?"

I hurried to catch up, the straps of my prom shoes digging into my heels. "Could we maybe go sightseeing later?"

Stellan stopped. "Do I look like I want to play tour guide? We're not sightseeing. There's an informal meeting going on, and I'll have to take you through it. Unknown teenage family members are to be seen and not heard, understood? Or in this case," he continued under his breath, "maybe not even *seen* until you're cleaned up, but I guess it can't be helped."

I hugged the bag over the stain on my chest and followed him. It was a beautiful morning. Paris in springtime—the sayings about it were true. We walked down the side of the Louvre, past tourists taking pictures and eating ice cream on expanses of new-green grass. A group of kids giggled and played tag in what looked like a maze of hedges. I could still see the Eiffel Tower, far in the distance against a sky dotted with clouds.

Stellan stopped at an unassuming set of double doors with men standing at attention on either side. One of them spoke to him in French, then held the doors for us, and Stellan gestured ahead of him. I took a deep, centering breath and walked inside.

The first thing I saw was a machine gun.

I recoiled automatically, but it was just a security checkpoint. The guard holding the gun across his body ushered me through a metal detector, and a stern woman on the other side patted me down. The low hum of conversation and background piano music beckoned from a nearby entrance hall.

The music grew louder as we stepped through a high archway draped in red velvet curtains. People milled around a drawing room covered in more red velvet and gold than a PBS period drama. Even though it was before noon, I felt incredibly underdressed.

This didn't look like a mafia gathering. I supposed government officials could take over the Louvre for a brunch party, though. A gray-haired man with wire-rimmed glasses spoke to Stellan as we walked by. Stellan just gave him a tight smile and gestured down a hallway, but I couldn't help but glance over my shoulder as we moved on. The man looked exactly like Edward Anders. As in, the vice president of the United States. This man was shorter than I would have imagined Anders, but the resemblance was uncanny.

I hurried to catch up with Stellan as he stepped into a smaller drawing room with the same gold-trimmed red velvet brocade on the walls and chandeliers dripping with crystal. I did my second double take of the morning when I saw Padraig Harrington on a bench, deep in conversation with a man wearing a white turban. This time, I was sure it was him. Padraig Harrington was the most famous golfer in the world, nearly as well known for his tabloid antics as he was for the distinctive scar on the side of his face, which was turned toward me right now.

Lara would die. She was obsessed with celebrity gossip. I was still staring when Padraig Harrington looked around the room and caught me. He grinned and gave me a wink. I felt my cheeks blaze.

"Are you going to tell me any more about the Circle?" I said to Stellan. If that was Padraig Harrington, maybe that other man really *was* the vice president. What would that mean? Was this a fundraiser for a French politician? I never imagined being connected to anyone who attended events like this. "Which of these people am I related to?"

Stellan held up one finger until he was finished speaking into the small microphone on his lapel. Even though he'd combed it back, his blond hair fell into his face. "I've just been told the Saxons are arriving tomorrow. My orders are to keep you here until told otherwise."

I deflated a little. If they cared enough to send a private plane, I'd hoped they'd have someone here to meet me.

Wait. "Did you say you're keeping me *here*?" I wondered out loud. "For how long?"

Stellan was already walking away. "You're not going to question everything I say, are you? It's growing tiresome."

I started to reply that keeping me in the dark was also growing tiresome, but I shut my mouth and watched him climb the stairs ahead of me. His slim dress shirt was tucked into still-wrinkled black pants, which, on him, looked like they were meant to be that way. Stellan was different from how he'd been on the plane. The teasing note to his voice was gone. I hadn't gotten anything out of him before; I could tell I really wasn't going to now that he was in work mode.

We wound our way past a series of small rooms off the main corridor. The whole party hummed with power and wealth, but if I hadn't known better, I'd have said people also seemed . . . paranoid. The guests darted glances over their shoulders as they talked, and you didn't have to be a body language expert to see all the strained smiles, the tension in gestures. I couldn't help but wonder what exactly this meeting was about.

Stellan stopped in front of one room, where a line of people waited to talk to a hugely pregnant woman with a pale, striking face and a severe blond chignon.

A slim girl wearing black pants and a black jacket and holding a clipboard appeared from inside. She narrowed her eyes and eased the door partway shut behind her when she saw me. She was probably about my age, but at least six inches taller, and seemed to be part Asian and part European, with wide almond-shaped eyes, a blunt blond bob that was obviously dyed but perfectly highlighted, and heavy bangs. Since I'd just seen Padraig Harrington, I assumed she was a French actress or model, so I was surprised when Stellan said, "I'm taking her to a room on the fourth floor. Are they made up?"

"Of course," the girl said, her voice unexpectedly husky and bored. She made no show of pretending she wasn't giving me a once-over, then frowned and switched to French.

"Avery's a guest," Stellan answered in English. "Distant family of the Saxons, waiting here until they arrive. What are you doing?"

The girl tapped her clipboard. "Keeping track of baby shower gifts. So far we've been promised artwork, highly trained military, next year's Olympics . . ."

"Her *assistant* of all people shouldn't joke about it," Stellan said, glancing in at the blond woman. "It's important for all of our futures."

"Nothing I said was a joke." The girl gave a saccharine-sweet fake smile. Stellan frowned in response, and she rolled her eyes and disappeared back through the door.

"What was that?" I hurried to keep up with Stellan's long strides.

"Elodie wanted to know who you were. It's uncommon to see strangers at a gathering like this."

"She *was* joking, right?"

Stellan laughed once. "I have things to do, so I'm going to take you to your room. Please stay there until I retrieve you."

To my surprise, he didn't lead us out of the Louvre, but farther into the maze of hallways off the front sitting room. "I'm *staying* here?"

"The Dauphins live here, and for the moment, you are their guest. So yes."

"They live here. In the Louvre."

"That's what I said."

Maybe it was better I wasn't meeting my family right now. I couldn't seem to put together a coherent thought, much less a whole sentence. It didn't help that I hadn't slept for even a second last night. I was starting to wonder if this was all a very vivid dream.

With one last glance back at the party, I followed Stellan, keeping a close eye on everything we passed. Paintings and tapestries and bookshelves lined the walls all the way upstairs. I ran a finger over one of the shelves we passed, and my eyes caught a row of books, all a deep purple, each with a different symbol in gold filigree etched into its spine. On the book farthest to the left was that sun from the plane and from Stellan's tattoo. Above it was another symbol, like a starburst with long rays emanating from a dark center, and a phrase in a few languages, including English: *Rule by Blood.* Below the sun, in smaller lettering, and just French and English: *Light in the Dark.*

I slowed and scanned the rest—an olive branch, some kind of wheel, and many others—including the compass from Jack's tattoo, on the third book from the end. They all had the same *Rule by Blood* phrase and starburst, but below Jack's compass, it said *Know the Way.* I did a quick count. Twelve books total.

The Circle of Twelve, Stellan had called them. The Saxons were one, the Dauphins were another, and I assumed other families made up the rest. At least that made a modicum of sense.

A dark-haired older man came out of a room at the end of the hall, nodding at us as he passed, and I slowed. He wasn't famous, but I couldn't stop staring at him anyway. His eyes.

His eyes could almost have been deep blue, but they weren't, not quite. No, they were a dark violet.

They were exactly the color of my eyes.

I had never, ever seen another person with my real eye color. The guy disappeared back into the party. He must be related to me. I had to bite my lip to keep a smile from spreading across my face.

The suite of rooms Stellan showed me to was less flashy than the rest of the house, but the high bed covered in navy brocade and the crystal-and-gold chandelier looked antique and expensive. The air in the room was a little musty, but the pillows were silky and crisp under my fingertips.

Stellan gestured inside. "Rest, wash up. I'll come for you later."

He left, and I found myself all alone, in a suite three times the size of my bedroom in Lakehaven. Probably as big as our entire apartment had been in New York. I crossed to the window and drew back the navy velvet curtains to reveal a view of the Louvre courtyard. Below the window, a long balcony stretched as far as I could see to the left and right, and far in the distance, the Eiffel Tower reached above the Paris skyline.

I stared at it for a long minute, then rooted around in my bag, pushing aside an unopened package of Junior Mints, my least favorite pair of sunglasses, and a library book I'd meant to return on the way home yesterday. I finally found my cell phone. No signal, which I should have guessed, since this was a US cell phone and Dorothy, we weren't in Minnesota anymore. After a quick search around the room, I found a discreet landline tucked away on a desk in the corner, with a card beside it listing country codes for international calls. I dialed my mom's phone. I wouldn't let her force me to come home, but I was starting to feel bad. She was probably worried that I hadn't answered my phone all night. Maybe she thought I'd snuck out to prom and gotten in a car accident, or even that I'd spent the night with some guy.

Not that I meant to spend prom with Jack if the night had gone as planned. Even now that I knew all his interest in me was purely professional, the thought made me blush annoyingly.

No answer on my mom's phone.

I did a quick calculation and realized it was before dawn in the United States, and called two more times in case she was asleep. Maybe her phone was off. Or her battery had died.

Just in case she'd realized I was gone and was home already, I called our house, too, and when she didn't answer there, I called her cell again.

"Hey," I said when her voice mail picked up. "It's me. I'm okay, don't worry. I'm . . . in France. Sorry," I said automatically, but then stopped. "No. I'm not sorry. I really want to meet my dad's family, and I know you probably don't want me to, but give me one day, okay? My phone doesn't work here, so you won't be able to reach me. I'll call you back later. I have a *lot* of questions."

I hung up, shaking a little, half shocked that I'd just said that, and half exhilarated. I'd made it. I was here. She'd get my message and be mad for a couple of days. I'd been lied to for sixteen years. Thinking I didn't have anybody when, really, I had family.

I stared out over the Paris morning and thought the word to myself, over and over. *Family.*

CHAPTER 10

A pounding reverberated in my head and I bolted upright.

Where was I?

Warm afternoon light streamed through the window and lit the crushed-velvet comforter, still indented from my head, and I remembered. After I'd tried to call my mom, I'd taken a shower, and then I'd realized I hadn't slept in twenty-four hours, so I was going to sit down for a minute before I went exploring . . .

The pounding came again. It was someone knocking at my door. "Just a second," I called, my voice thick with sleep.

I rubbed at my dried-out contact lenses and pulled the bedroom door open.

"If I'd known it was shower time, I would have brought a towel." Stellan flicked his eyes over my suddenly too-small white bathrobe.

Heat crept across my skin. I drew the robe tighter and frowned at him to disguise the fact that I was now trying—unsuccessfully—not to think about him in the shower. He was doing this on purpose, I reminded myself. And it still wasn't going to work. "Can I help you?"

His slow smile said he knew exactly what I was thinking. "I

suppose I'll take a rain check on the shower. Now I am taking you to get a gown for the ball. A welcome gift."

I blinked. "For the what?"

"The ball." He'd untucked his dress shirt and rolled up the sleeves, and when he drummed his long fingers on the doorframe, I could see the muscles in his forearms twitch. "Tomorrow night. It's a celebration for the Dauphins' new babies."

"Babies." I remembered the pregnant woman downstairs, who got the Olympics as a baby shower gift.

"Madame Dauphin is giving birth to twins," Stellan said, like it should be obvious.

"And there's a ball that's a baby shower. And I need a . . . gown." Obviously my brain hadn't woken up yet.

"Madame Dauphin likes her guests to reflect well on her." He shot a disdainful glance at my prom dress, now balled up in the corner. I opened my mouth to protest, but honestly, he was right.

"Shouldn't I wait here until Jack shows up? Or the Saxons?"

"Do I really have to tell you this again? Alistair Saxon is supposed to arrive tomorrow. You'll see them soon enough. I have other errands to run, so unless you're wearing that, I suggest you get dressed. You can find something in the closet." He gestured to a door in the corner that I'd found earlier led to a huge, well-stocked walk-in.

He left, and I called my mom again. Still no answer, on either phone. With that on top of the shock of being here that was finally starting to hit me, nerves fluttered in my stomach. I kind of wanted to curl up under the covers and not leave the room until my family got here.

But it wasn't like there was anything wrong with shopping. It could be fun. It was nice of the Dauphins to take me in, and I might as well enjoy the perks while I could, before my mom found out what I'd done and locked me up until I turned eighteen.

I searched the closet for an acceptable ball gown shopping outfit. Ball gown shopping. I smiled. There was a phrase I never thought would apply to me.

I slipped on a navy sundress with white stripes, grabbed a similarly striped piece of taffy from a candy bowl on the desk—I was starving—and headed toward the hall where I was meeting Stellan. I passed a library with the door open a crack. The pregnant blond lady, who I assumed was Madame Dauphin, sat at a conference table with four men. As I passed, a word jumped at me.

". . . about the mandate," one of the men said. I tripped over my sandals.

"Any news?" Madame Dauphin asked.

I flattened myself against the wall next to the doorframe.

"The Mikados claim to have a lead, but it's unlikely," one of the men replied.

"And nothing has come of the Louvre exhibit?"

"Not yet," said another voice. "Cecile, time is running out. If more information on the mandate is not found—"

"Then we choose the union ourselves, and assume the rest are intelligent enough to rally behind us, even without confirmation of the One. We can't let this opportunity pass us by. Meanwhile, we keep searching for the tomb. As much as some of the families want to believe it, the mandate isn't *magic*," Madame Dauphin said scornfully. "This is the modern world. No one's even certain anything will happen."

There were murmurs of assent, then a few moments of silence, broken by a hesitant voice. "And we must have a united front if we expect to stand against the Order. Aren't you particularly concerned about them right now? The recent attacks . . . They seem to know so much. They even found out about the baby girl."

"What are you saying?" another man said. "Do you think information is being leaked?"

There was a loaded pause. The taffy stuck in my teeth was sickeningly sweet.

"It doesn't matter how they're finding out. You heard what Alistair Saxon has been saying. He thinks the Order should be eliminated altogether, just in case," someone else said. "And it sounds like many others are starting to agree."

Madame Dauphin cleared her throat. "And if we vote to do that, it will be made easier by finding the tomb. Shall we return to the matter at hand?" she said coldly. "Monsieur Dauphin has sent some intelligence out of Egypt. If you will turn to page three . . ."

I took this time when everyone would be looking down to creep past the door. I glanced in as I did, and saw another familiar face.

One of the men who had been speaking was the president of France.

The mandate. The Order, whatever that was. Alistair Saxon—someone from my own family. The president of France. *Attacks*.

It didn't sound like they'd been meeting for a fund-raiser. I thought about all the paranoid looks at the party, and it was almost enough to make me forget I was in a limo, driving along the Seine. I tried to shake off worries about politics that weren't my problem and enjoy that I was going dress shopping in Paris with friends of my family. And especially that I was suddenly able to say "friends of my family."

Stellan sat in the facing seat and looked me over, from my sundress to my white wedge sandals. I followed his eyes down to my chipped eggplant-purple pedicure, which looked out of place with these casual-but-obviously-expensive clothes. I tucked my feet back against the seat.

"So, Avery West," Stellan said. "I've been wondering about you. You don't know much about your extended family?"

I looked up from my hands in my lap. "I think we've established that."

"Why were you so willing to come along, then?" Stellan leaned forward. For the first time, I noticed that his eyes were deep blue, with splashes of gold around the irises.

I frowned. "I—"

"What kind of girl abandons everything for people she doesn't know?" he continued, eyes narrowing.

"If you'd stop interrupting, maybe I'd tell you."

"Please do." Stellan splayed his long legs casually into my foot space, and I ignored them with Zen-like control. I couldn't help but wonder again what he was trying to do. He could be one of those guys who saw an uninterested girl as a challenge, but I felt like there was more to it.

"I wanted to meet—"

"Yes, yes, you wanted to meet your family. Your father was a long-lost third cousin twice removed. But that's not all of it. Really, you wanted a change." He folded his hands behind his head. I opened my mouth to chastise him for interrupting again, but then what he'd said sank in.

"A change," he continued with a slow smile when he saw my face. "A way away from 'the ache that is your existence.'"

Zee ache. In Stellan's light accent, it sounded especially weighty, like an ancient prophecy. I leaned forward without really meaning to.

"*Toska.*" He leaned forward, too. "It's a Russian word. It has no translation into any other language, but the closest I've heard is *the ache.* A longing. The sense that something is missing, and even if you're not sure what it is, you ache for it. Down to your bones."

I sucked in a sharp breath.

Stellan rested his chin in his hand and watched me, like he understood things I wasn't saying.

How did he know that? How did he know exactly the way to describe the gnawing hollow in my chest? I sat back and folded my arms like he could see straight inside me. "I'm not longing for anything," I said defensively. "I don't even know what you're talking about."

I scooted as far away from him as I could and leaned against the window. We were stopped at a light, and outside, a group of laughing girls rode bicycles along the cobblestone walk bordering the Seine.

I could tell Stellan was still watching me. *Toska.* The Ache.

Past the walkway, through the flowering trees, I could see people taking photos from the deck of a white barge cruising lazily along the river. The sun warmed my face through the sterile cool of the car's air-conditioning.

"It was Nabokov who coined that translation of *toska*," Stellan said after a minute. I heard the shift as he leaned back into his seat. "Nabokov is—"

I let out a breath. "I know who Nabokov is," I said without turning around. "I've read *Lolita.*"

Stellan kicked his feet up on my seat. "Have you?"

I moved even farther away. "Why not?"

"*Lolita* is not a children's book."

"How old do you think I am?"

"I know exactly how old you are. Sixteen, seventeen next month. June fourteenth."

Now I did turn around. "How did you—"

"Five foot two inches tall." He looked me up and down again, and I straightened automatically. "One hundred and three pounds."

"How do you know—" I tucked my skirt under my legs. "That's creepy. Why do you know that?"

"Could use a little more meat on those bones, if you ask me," he said, leaning across the seat to wrap one slim hand entirely around my upper arm.

"Do not touch me." I jerked away. "So part of your job is stalking? What, did you find my driver's license records?" After everything else that had happened, I shouldn't have been surprised.

"Why would an innocent thing like you read *Lolita*? Into older men?" He raised an eyebrow.

"What is *wrong* with you?" I pulled my feet up onto the seat, tucking them under my dress.

"Ah. Daddy issues, then," he said with a sage nod. "Though I suppose that should have been obvious when you immediately agreed to run off with strange and somewhat threatening men you didn't know."

I felt myself flush. Okay, yes, obviously I did have daddy issues, but it had nothing to do with my literary preferences. I fished for a witty comeback, but I'd gotten too flustered. "You're an ass," I said instead. "I'd read through the whole kids' section of the library by the time I was seven, so . . ."

Stellan rolled his window down a few inches and tested the breeze with his fingertips. Outside, a car smaller than a golf cart zipped past. "So then you read *Lolita*?"

"So then I read everything," I huffed. It was none of his business that imaginary friends were my only friends for a lot of my childhood.

"Everything? Just fiction?"

"Everything." I turned to the window again. How could I possibly make it more obvious that this conversation was over?

Stellan drummed his fingers on the seat. "You know Aristotle? 'He who is to be a good ruler must first have been ruled.'"

I ignored him.

"So that's a no? By 'everything' you really just mean twisted love stories."

I gritted my teeth. "Yes, I've read some Aristotle. And I can see that *you've* read philosophy to give yourself an excuse for pretentious name-dropping."

"Works better on girls than you might think," he said with a wink.

"Ugh." I rested my forehead on the window.

"And I don't only read philosophy." He nudged my hip with his boot. "I enjoyed *Lolita* for the lollipops."

I finally turned and shoved his boots off the seat. We drove by what must have been a government building. High, arched windows were ringed by carved stone garlands, and a row of statues kept watch from the roof. But then again, nearly every place we'd driven by looked like that. It would make a good game. Buildings in Paris: significant national monument or apartment complex?

"What about history?" Stellan said. "How much do you know about Alexander the Great?"

"What does that have to do with anything?" He made me so combative. As hard as I'd tried to ignore him, and even though I knew he was doing it on purpose, he still annoyed me.

I gestured to the outline of the knife hilt on his side. "So, why the concealed weapons? What is there to be afraid of on a weekend of famous people going to balls and meetings?"

He tilted his head to the side. "Even a girl from small-town Minnesota should not be that naive."

"What's the Order?" I said. Two could play at this game. He'd deflect my questions, and I'd ignore his deflection.

The smile slid off Stellan's face. "They're nothing you need to worry about, *kuklachka*." He cocked his head to one side. "Unless, of course, you know something I don't."

The car rolled to a stop, cutting off any more conversation. We were on a wide street, lined by trees in full bloom. Shops paraded down either side, and the Eiffel Tower loomed much closer than I'd realized. The annoyance dropped away and a thrill shivered through me.

Yesterday, I'd never left the United States. Today, I was shopping in Paris. I opened my own door before the driver got there, and followed Stellan out of the car and down the street.

And then we turned up the walk to one of the shops and I stopped, my foot halfway up a step. The tasteful gold lettering on the cream-colored building said PRADA.

CHAPTER 11

A young man opened the doors, his deep-set eyes dark and shadowed behind wire-rimmed glasses. His shoes clicked a staccato beat as he led us past the mannequins standing guard in the front window, across a black-and-white checkerboard floor, and into a foyer thick with the perfume of stargazer lilies and wealth.

"Where is everybody?" I whispered to Stellan. No one browsed the racks of buttery leather gloves, and not a single bored boyfriend read magazines on the white leather couches.

"Madame Dauphin prefers to shop alone," Stellan said. "She has the store closed for her guests as well."

I took a deep breath. Prada, in Paris, was closed. For me. To choose a ball gown. It was ridiculous. And extravagant. And . . . amazing. My father's family and the rest of the Circle were by far the most interesting thing that had ever happened to me.

A few minutes later, Stellan had left to do errands and I stood in an opulent dressing room, all snowy white with splashes of gold and magenta and a whole wall of mirrors. I held my arms out to the sides while a tall girl named Aimee, who had shockingly red hair, cinched a measuring tape around my hips. I remembered buying my purple prom dress off the sale rack at Macy's, and almost laughed out loud.

"Does Madame Dauphin come here a lot?" I asked, pretending to be capable of normal conversation.

Elisa, who was tiny with a dark pixie cut, nodded, and held swatches of colored fabrics up to my skin. "Every week."

"Has she sent other guests in this weekend?" I asked.

Aimee unzipped my sundress and gestured for me to take it off.

"Yes. You are the last appointment of the day. And the only one under the age of fifty," Elisa said, and Aimee swatted her with the tape measure. "It's true! The fashion sense of the other younger ladies must already meet Madame's approval. I don't mean to offend," she said to me, "but you are not a regular guest at the family's events, am I right?"

I shook my head.

Aimee lowered her voice conspiratorially. "Tell us. Who are they? We could never ask Madame Dauphin. Are they only rich, or diplomats, or—?"

"Aimee!" said Elisa, and I pressed my mouth closed. Even if I knew their whole story, I had a feeling I shouldn't respond to that kind of question. It did make me wonder, though. If the Dauphins were in French politics, Aimee and Elisa would know it.

"What dresses are we trying on?" I said, and the questions were over.

Soon, they were slipping gowns on and off me like I was a doll. Gowns that were as much art as clothing. There was a red-feathered dress that was pretty, but shaped weirdly in the hips, and a stiff, architectural cobalt gown Aimee loved.

One dress was black and modern, and a white one with a full skirt was gorgeous but could have been a wedding dress. Elisa was partial to a gray shift, but the top was too sheer, and another dress was short and pink and looked too eighties.

All of them were amazing pieces, but it felt like I was just playing dress-up until Elisa lowered a burnished silver gown over my head.

The dress looked like a glittering stormy night. I pushed my hair off my shoulders to see its delicate, sheer straps, which blended into shimmering raw silk that crossed my chest, then hugged close to my hips. I turned to see the back, open to my waist in a deep V. A small train swished behind my feet.

All of a sudden, I felt like I should be going to a ball.

Elisa giggled, and I realized my mouth was hanging open.

"You like it?"

I nodded. I couldn't find any words.

"We'll keep it aside, then," said Aimee.

They lifted the silver dress off me, and I fought the urge to touch it as Elisa hung it on the opposite wall. The next dress was flashier than what I'd usually choose—gold, covered in intricate beadwork and sequins—and I barely paid attention to it at first. I couldn't take my eyes off the silver dress. But when they slipped it over my head and the light hit me in the mirror, Elisa gasped out loud. I glowed.

The dress was nothing like the silver one. If that one had been storms, this was sunlight. It glowed against my dark hair, and hugged my body all the way down, from the plunging halter neckline to the flouncy mermaid hem. I ran my hands over my hips, and my reflection glittered.

Aimee had been prepping a pink dress with a lace bodice, but she put it back on the hanger. "The gold one. Or the silver. We do not need to try more, no?"

I glanced at myself in the mirror, then at the silver dress again. I shook my head.

Elisa led me to a three-way mirror, where a girl who hardly looked like me stared back in triplicate. They changed me into the silver dress and the girl in the mirror looked more serious, more elegant, then the gold again, and she was glamorous, striking. I pictured myself dancing in both dresses, because that's what you did at a ball, right? Dancing, laughing with the people I'd meet soon. Being introduced as part of the family.

Toska. The word echoed in my head. A change. In who I was, in how I saw myself. Filling that ache that never quite left my chest.

I found myself hoping fiercely that my mom would let me stay for the ball, and even a little longer. Meet the Saxons, find out more about my father's family and the rest of the Circle. To feel like I belonged in this strange, fascinating world. To feel like I belonged anywhere, just for a second.

"You have to choose eventually." Elisa smiled. In the mirror, the sequins shimmered.

The gold dress was perfect for my body type, Elisa said, and I had to admit it was dazzling. But there was something about the silver. It belonged on me. The silver felt right.

Aimee was grinning as big as I was. She unzipped the gold dress and left me to get out of it, following Elisa downstairs to wrap the silver one. I watched it go. I couldn't believe that, just like that, it was going to be mine.

I stood in front of the mirror for a few more minutes, watching the gold sequins twinkle. This was the only time I'd ever get to do anything like this. I wanted to make it last as long as I could.

I was about to step out of the gold dress when I heard footsteps coming up the stairs. "Elisa?" I said. "Aimee?" There was no answer.

In case it was one of the men come to escort me downstairs, I zipped the dress up.

The girls were nowhere in sight, but the man who had let us in stood at the top of the staircase.

"Sorry, I'm not ready yet," I said. I smiled at him, and he reached into his jacket pocket.

He pulled out something that, for a moment, didn't register. It was too discordant with the marble floors, the dresses, the Bach chiming from the speakers. He stepped toward me, and the overhead light glinted off the object.

Then I knew, but I still didn't understand.

It was a knife.

CHAPTER 12

I stood frozen, half in and half out of the dressing room. The man moved slow and steady toward me, the dagger—shorter than Stellan's, but thicker and more menacing—gleaming in his hand. My reflection glittered in his wire-rimmed glasses.

I stumbled back into the dressing room and slammed the door. I snapped the lock shut with shaking fingers, and my heartbeat thundered in my ears.

The store was almost empty, plus it was late afternoon—the perfect time for a robbery. I just hoped he wouldn't come after the gowns that were in here with me. There were only a few, and they couldn't be as valuable as the cash register, or the jewelry, or the merchandise out on the floor.

I held my breath.

The doorknob jiggled hard.

Silence.

Then a crash.

I jumped away. One more crash—a shoulder or a foot slamming into the door. The thin wood splintered down the middle.

I tried to scream, but nothing came out.

He wouldn't be going to that much trouble for these dresses. He must not want to leave any witnesses.

And I was trapped.

"Aimee! Elisa!" I forced out. My voice sounded tiny in the emptiness, and there was no answer. Besides the jagged rhythm of my own breath and the tinkle of the music, the shop was deathly silent. Oh God. He might have gotten to them already.

The whimper that came out of my mouth didn't even sound like me.

One more thud and the man's foot cracked through the center of the door.

I whipped around, frantic, the adrenaline shooting through me bringing the dressing room into focus. The gleaming mirror, the pink velvet armchair. The smattering of crimson feathers from the red dress that had fluttered to the carpet and fanned out like bloodstains. My own reflection, a small girl with dark hair falling over her shoulders in waves, whose wide, panic-stricken eyes didn't match her exquisite dress.

Someone was trying to kill me while I was wearing a ball gown. This didn't happen in real life. But I was pretty sure I wasn't dreaming, and this wasn't an action movie. The door cracked further, and bile rose in my throat.

If this was a movie, I would at least try to defend myself.

A tall vase of lilies sat on a table next to the armchair. I ducked behind the chair and grabbed it, the dreamy scent of the flowers surrounding me as I dumped them on the floor, drops of water splattering my bare feet. I held the vase like a baseball bat.

The man yanked away a cracked section of the door, making a hole large enough to reach through to the lock. The door swung open.

He didn't run at me, didn't yell, didn't glance down the stairs to see if anyone had heard my screams. The cold calculation in his eyes was more frightening than rage would have been. Like the eyes of a hunter. Whatever this was, it wasn't just a robbery.

The heavy vase trembled in my hands. "Get away from me!" I screamed.

He toppled the armchair with a casual swipe of his hand. I brought the vase down as hard as I could. It shattered against the side of his head, and I dodged.

I wasn't quite fast enough. His knife sliced into my shoulder. A scream ripped out of my throat, but I sprinted past him, finally hitting the cold glass of the floor-to-ceiling mirrors on the opposite side of the room.

I clutched at my shoulder. Blood seeped between my fingers and dripped onto the white carpet. The crunch of the hunter's feet on the shards of vase forced me to tear my eyes away from it.

He was between me and the door. He wouldn't miss next time.

I ducked behind the metal garment rack of rejected dresses and pawed frantically through them for anything I could use to protect myself. I found nothing but vibrant silk and beading, so enchanting a few minutes ago, now mocking me with its uselessness.

The man was halfway across the room. As a last resort, I yanked at the garment rack itself to see if I could pull out a pole or anything to use as a weapon. But when I leaned on it, it moved. It was on wheels, and an idea popped into my head. It wasn't a very good idea, but it was the only one I had.

When he was just a few feet away, I gripped the end support and shoved the rack as hard as I could.

It smashed into him. The metal vibrated in my hands, and the whole rack toppled with a crash.

I darted toward the door as a flare of silver snaked out from the mound of brilliant fabric. I dodged the knife, and he missed.

Blood thundered through my veins, propelling me down the stairs. "Help! Aimee! Elisa!" I screamed. "Help!"

Now I wished my shopping trip hadn't been so private. Silent, faceless mannequins gazed up at me from the sales floor. Beyond them, though, was the foyer and the door that led out of the shop.

If I could get outside, I could get away.

That square of sunlight pushed my legs faster. Almost there. *Almost there!*

A few steps from the bottom, my foot caught the gold dress's mermaid hem. I grabbed for the railing, but it was too late. My feet flew out from under me, and I launched through the air. I barely had time to throw up an arm before my head smashed into the ground.

Pain exploded in a thousand glass shards in my brain. I lay on the ground, crumpled, choking. Air wouldn't go into my lungs. *Run!* my mind screamed. *Run!* My body wouldn't listen.

I forced myself to my hands and knees, and the blood running down my arm streaked a perfect river of red between a black tile and the white one next to it. My vision went blurry at the edges.

"Help," I sobbed to no one. "Please." I clawed at the floor and forced myself not to pass out. If I passed out, I was dead.

The clang of heavy footsteps on the stairs turned the pain in my head to wild panic. I crawled to a couch and clung to it, dragging myself dizzily to my feet as the killer reached the bottom of the stairs.

The room spun like a carnival ride. He stood between me and the front door. I scanned the store frantically, and under a staircase in the back, another door glowed like a mirage.

I was afraid I'd collapse if I let go of the couch, but he started toward me from the bottom of the stairs.

I ran.

The back door was a million miles away.

There was a shout, and a display a few feet from me exploded, shards of glass slicing my skin. I screamed and dropped to the ground, scrambling under a table piled with scarves and out the other side. I hadn't even realized he had a gun. Another kick of adrenaline pumped through my aching body, and I pushed my legs faster.

I couldn't tell how close he was now. The only sound I could hear was my own desperate breath.

Then there were footsteps all around, right behind me, almost to me. More yelling.

He'd caught up. He had me.

I braced myself for one last frantic, futile dash, but strong arms grabbed me from behind.

"Let go!" I screamed. "Let *go* of me!" I lashed out against him, dug my nails into his skin, tried to rip his hands off me, but we were falling, on the ground, struggling. If I could grab the gun and point it away from us—but he wouldn't let go.

I was about to die.

No sense of calm came over me, no rush of memories flew through my head. Strangely, the only face that swam in front of my eyes, the voice I heard yelling my name, was Jack's.

I heard a grunt and drew one last breath, squeezing my eyes shut.

Nothing happened.

I was still alive.

"Avery!" My eyes flew open. I *had* heard my name. "Avery! Stop! You're safe!"

I quit struggling. The arms encircling me loosened enough for me to focus on his face.

It *was* Jack.

I hadn't been imagining it. How he'd gotten here I didn't know, but Jack was here, and I was alive.

My face was pressed into his chest. He cradled my head above the floor and held both my wrists in his other hand, trying to keep me from scratching his eyes out. I stared up into his face—flashing silver eyes, mussed dark hair—and for a second, I was back in my calculus class last Monday morning, pretending not to stare when he walked in the room.

"Jack—what?" I choked out. If Jack was holding me, where was the killer? Then I saw the gun in Jack's hand, and, even though I didn't think I'd heard another gunshot, I put together what had probably happened.

He pulled me to sitting and looked me over, taking in the cut on my shoulder.

"Stay here." He let go of me and hurried away, his gun drawn.

He'd saved my life. A dizzying rush of relief washed over me and tears were running down my cheeks and I was gasping. *I was alive.*

I pushed up onto my knees to see where Jack was going, to get him to come back. I didn't want to be alone.

I froze when I saw the head.

The head of the man who had tried to kill me, no longer attached to his body. His head was at my eye level, wire-rimmed glasses still perched on his nose, blood dripping from his severed neck.

I scrambled backward, but slipped and fell in a pool of dark blood, the killer's and my own.

I followed the arm holding the head up to the thin, angular face and shock of light brown hair of a boy about my age, who peered at it with a bland curiosity. He tossed the severed head across the floor like a bowling ball and grimaced at a bloodstain across his chest. "*Merde,*" he said. "This was my favorite shirt."

I got slowly to my knees again, my gold dress soaked through with crimson. The boy stood above me, polishing blood off a huge knife.

He grinned at me, and I stared into his eyes. Purple eyes, just like mine. Then I vomited onto his boots.

CHAPTER 13

Don't do well with blood, I see." The boy helped me limp to the white couch in the foyer.

My knee hurt so badly from the fall down the stairs that I wanted to curl into a ball and cry. But then the throbbing in my head overpowered it. Then the blood still oozing out of my shoulder. Then the body. The headless body on the floor, and the sick coppery smell and the music: the ridiculous chime of the Bach playing over the bloodbath like some kind of twisted parody.

I leaned on the armrest but winced away from a small, bloody handprint—my *own* handprint—which contrasted gruesomely with the white upholstery.

"Why would he try to kill me?" I whispered.

"A mistake, *cherie*. He was Order. Must have thought you were someone else."

Order. Like Madame Dauphin and those men had been talking about. I knew it hadn't felt like just a robbery. But it also hadn't felt like a mistake.

The boy lit a cigarette, then offered me the pack. I shook my head. "You are Avery, I presume. I am Luc."

Madame Dauphin's son. I'd overheard someone asking about him earlier at the Louvre. His cologne was almost strong enough to overpower the scent of blood. How was it possible he was so nonchalant? Celebrities and politicians and ball gowns—fine. That was everyday life for some people. But politicians and Prada and *murder?*

Luc blew a stream of smoke out of the corner of his mouth. "I was looking for Stellan. Where is he, by the way? Luckily, I heard you scream from down the block. Nice lungs."

A commotion sounded from the back of the store, and Jack came out of the other room. He had the other man who worked here, Frederic, in a choke hold, pressing the gun to his side when he struggled, all while nudging Aimee and Elisa along in front of him. I perched on the edge of the couch, but just then the door opened, letting in street noise.

Everyone turned as heavy footsteps came into the foyer, then stopped dead. Stellan's eyes widened as they flicked to the body, to the blood, to me, and finally to Jack, hovering over Frederic and the girls.

He met my eyes. I blinked once, twice, and he came savagely alive. He was across the floor in three long strides, glaring first at Jack, then down at Frederic.

"What's going on?" he asked, and yelled again, in French. "*Ce qui s'est passe?* What the—" He broke off into another language, which sounded like Russian.

"The Order tried to kill Avery." Jack's quiet anger was almost more frightening than Stellan's rage.

"Tried to kill—" Stellan's gaze shot to me. He reached down to Frederic and yanked at his collar, exposing a tattoo on his chest, of a circle split by two lines. Then he pulled out his dagger and drove it into Frederic's chest.

Frederic coughed once, and then his body slackened and fell to the ground, his blood mixing with the stain already spread across the floor.

"No," I tried to say, but it came out as a strangled gasp. Elisa wailed. Stellan ignored us both.

"How the hell did this happen?" he said to Jack. He pulled out the dagger. "How did the Order get in here?"

"*You* were supposed to be watching Avery." Jack hauled Aimee and Elisa up by their arms and moved them away from the spreading pool of blood.

"Like I knew they'd come for her!" Stellan said. "Unless you've been lying about who she is, there is absolutely no reason for this."

Elisa spoke in rapid, garbled French. Stellan pointed the bloody tip of the knife at her.

"Don't!" I found my voice and tried to stand, but had to grab on to the couch to keep from falling. "She didn't do anything."

Stellan whirled on me. The beautiful, arrogant boy I'd been talking to in the car was now a beautiful, arrogant boy with a knife in his grip and blood on his hands. "Why did he try to kill you?"

"What?" I choked in disbelief. Was he angry with *me*? "I have no idea! Why did you kill *him*?"

He stalked across the floor until he towered over me. "Did you not get the *tried to kill you* part?"

"He didn't. The other guy did." I tried to yell, but my voice broke.

"And this one was Order, too."

"So why didn't you question him? Or lock him up? Or—"

I quaked, looking from the headless body to the newly dead Frederic and back.

"You don't reason with the Order," Stellan spat. Blood dripped off his dagger, and he held it like he was about to plunge it into someone else.

Jack pushed between us, his hands on Stellan's chest. "Stop," he said. "It's the Order's fault, not hers." After a second, Stellan's arm dropped to his side, but his eyes never left my face, even after Jack let him go.

Luc stood up, running a hand through his messy hair, his lanky shoulders more tense than they had been a few minutes earlier. "If I may propose a theory. The Order learned we would have family members here today, in whatever way they've been learning of all our movements. They planned another strike. They may even have wanted *me*." He paused and took a long drag of his cigarette, and I thought again of that conversation. The Order. *Attacks*. "It seems our guest was in the wrong place at the wrong time."

From the other side of the room, Aimee piped up again.

"She says these two"—Luc gestured to the bodies with his cigarette as he translated—"came a few hours ago. Said the other branch of the store sent them. The girls thought nothing of it until Frederic tied them up in the back room."

Luc had to be right—the men wanted someone else. But then again, that was what I'd thought at prom.

"Doesn't matter now." Luc put out his cigarette on an issue of *Vogue* on a side table. "Get these girls out of here so we can have someone clean up this mess." He said it like milk had been spilled on the kitchen floor.

My hands started shaking.

Luc flipped through a rack of coral-colored dress shirts. "Would you call these pink or orange, *cherie*? Pink is not my color, but I need to change for dinner. I'm starving."

It took me a second to register what he'd said. "What?"

"There's an adorable bistro around the corner, or that little cafe on Rue de Rivoli," he continued.

Stellan, too, wiped blood off his dagger with nothing more than a scowl. Jack, at least, was covering the bodies.

I blinked. "What is wrong with you?"

Luc pulled a shirt off its hanger and cocked his head to one side.

"People are dead." My breath rasped. "Who cares if the shirt's pink?"

Luc draped the shirt on the rack. His face softened. "*Cherie*, I apologize. This all is new to you. I must appear so callous. You've got to understand—killing Order members is not the same as killing normal people. Even if he hadn't hurt you, if you knew all they'd done to our families, you'd understand."

I shook my head. I wouldn't understand. I didn't understand.

Across the room, Jack dropped a patterned scarf over the killer's head and stood. "You should get cleaned up," he said. I shook my head again.

"There's a bathroom upstairs," he said pointedly. I bit my lip, hard. I could tell he thought I was about to lose it. Maybe he was right.

"Show me?" I whispered. He started to point up the stairs, but I steeled myself. Jack would give me some answers. He had to. "Show. Me."

He frowned, but nodded. On the way to the stairs, he flipped through a rack of floral sundresses and pulled one off its hanger. "Here. Put this on."

I held the dress by the tips of my fingers. "I can't just take this—"

"It doesn't matter." He climbed ahead of me up the stairs.

I stared at the dress. It did matter. It mattered that this dress cost more than my entire wardrobe at home. Probably more than we paid for a month of rent at home. But to these people, it didn't. It didn't matter that there were two dead bodies on the floor downstairs and that I could have been a third. That beheading someone—in one of the fanciest boutiques in Paris—was nothing more than a minor delay of your dinner plans. And that someone had attacked me, right as I learned that I had family who associated with some of the most powerful people in the world, and that it hadn't *felt* like a case of mistaken identity.

Just how much had my mom been hiding? Was it possible that she'd kept my father's family from me because of more than hurt feelings?

Jack opened a door off the hallway.

"Please," I said. He held the door wide open with one arm, peering in like he was making sure it was safe. "Tell me what's going on. Was this really a mistake? Luc said it was nothing."

He looked both ways down the hall, chewed his lip, then finally met my eyes. "Clean up, and then we'll talk about it. But no, it's not nothing. And I don't think it was a mistake."

CHAPTER 14

The blood wouldn't come off, and none of it was a mistake.

There was non-mistake, not-nothing blood everywhere. The dried blood from my hands and the fresh blood still oozing from my shoulder turned different shades of pink as they swirled down the drain.

I glanced at the beautiful gold dress balled up in the corner, bloody, ruined. A whole swatch of sequins was ripped off the front, like a gaping wound. I must have grabbed my necklace earlier, because there was a bloody thumbprint on it, and a smear of red where it lay on my chest.

The shaking that had started in my hands expanded, until my whole body was trembling and I couldn't stop it.

I scrubbed my hands until the water ran clear, and then scrubbed some more.

A rap at the door startled me, and in the mirror I saw Jack slip into the room. The door clicked shut behind him.

He came up behind me at the sink, and I felt him watching over my shoulder. I opened my mouth, but I didn't know what to say. Instead, I held up my hands. My skin was pink and scrubbed raw, darker red stains still under my fingernails. I dropped them back under the tap.

We stood in silence, both watching the water splash over my skin, and after a few seconds, he put his own hands under the faucet, too.

I tensed, but he didn't let go. He ran his thumb down my fingers, one by one. I felt myself trying to say it's fine, I'm fine, I don't need your help, but it wouldn't come out. All I could do was stare at his hands, big and strong and scarred and cradling mine so gently.

"Look away a second," he murmured.

The window next to the sink was streaked with dirt and age, so the Paris I saw outside was as hazy and distorted as it was oblivious to what had happened on this side of the glass. My eyes skimmed over the cream buildings, the cobbled street, the dark ironwork of the Eiffel Tower in the distance, lighting on the bursts of red that slashed the neutrals of the city. A little girl's jacket, a bright store awning, a wide flower bed running down one side of the street.

The cold scraping under my fingernails told me Jack was cleaning them with a knife, which should have scared me but didn't. I watched him in the mirror, his dark brows knitted together, his lower lip caught between his teeth. I hadn't noticed earlier, but a new bruise was spreading under his left eye. When he said I could, I looked back down and the bursts of red on my hands were gone. My heart flared with gratitude.

And then I realized my hands were still in his, and cradled them to my chest. They left wet blotches on the flowered sundress.

He watched me in the mirror. "I'm sorry. I shouldn't have left you alone. You've had quite a shock."

Absurdly, I couldn't stop thinking about his perfect, proper British accent.

"I'm fine." I grabbed a paper towel and turned away from the mirror, from him.

While I was changing clothes, he'd gone to a pharmacy down the street. He held out an assortment of painkillers, and I plucked two ibuprofen from his palm. He handed me a third, and I watched him put the rest in a bag. This was Jack Bishop, Lakehaven High new kid. In a Prada store, in Paris, offering me painkillers after I'd almost been murdered.

A laugh choked up in my throat, and I very nearly lost it again. Instead, I sat on the closed toilet seat and swallowed the ibuprofen dry.

The music still tinkled out of the speakers. Why had no one stopped it? Someone should have stopped it. "Turn off the music," I said.

Jack stared at me, pharmacy bag in hand.

"Turn off the music," I said again. "Please. And can I use your phone?" After a second, he handed it to me and left.

I made myself take a deep breath.

I probably *was* close to going into shock. I had this fuzzy, half-there feeling, the constant replay of the knife cutting into my skin, the smell, the squishing noise as the killer's head hit the marble floor. The thought that I'd seen both Stellan and Luc kill people, which probably meant Jack had killed people, too. That my family killed people. And people wanted to kill them.

I dialed my mom's number, then our house. Both rang and rang, and finally clicked over to my mom's tinny voice on the voice mail again. I couldn't leave what had just happened on a message.

The music stopped in the middle of a note. I almost wished I hadn't told Jack to turn it off. It was too quiet now. My breath echoed, too fast. Too panicky.

No. I was alive. I was fine. I really wished I could talk to my mom. I took deep breaths over and over, in through my nose, out through my mouth.

I sat up straight as the door opened and Jack slipped inside. He spread bandages from the plastic pharmacy bag across the sink.

Would mafia families have somebody bring me bandages when I was hurt? I wasn't sure why I wasn't just asking it straight out: Who are you? *What* are you? Maybe I didn't really want to know. In the space of one day, I'd turned into what I thought I'd never be: a naive, hopeful idiot. Despite my wariness, I'd convinced myself this was fun. I'd spent all day smiling at famous people and admiring Paris and playing dress-up. I was thinking about going to a *ball*. All the while I had willfully ignored the ominous signs I didn't want to see.

I smoothed the pleats of the dress over my knees. I just had to do it. I had to ask. I opened my mouth just as Jack turned, his gray eyes darker than usual, a deep crease between his brows.

"Who are you?" he said.

I closed my mouth. Blinked. "Who am *I*?"

He leaned against the sink, spinning the top on the bottle of painkillers. "I agree it wasn't a mistake. But you don't fit the pattern in any way, and the Order is more careful than that."

"Pattern? Shouldn't I be the one asking who *you* are, since it's so common for all of you to be attacked?" I started to stand, but I felt dizzy. I sat down again, rubbing the knot on my forehead.

"I just want to know if you're telling me the truth," he said, a little more gently. "Are you really as in the dark as you seem?"

I wanted to be calm. I wanted to be rational. Why was this not making enough sense for me to feel rational? I clenched my hands between my knees and spoke in a slow, measured voice. "What are you talking about? What do you think I'm supposed to know?"

"I'm talking about the fact that I was sent to small-town America to gather information about a distant family member. Unusual, but nothing unheard of. Considering everything else that's going on, it wasn't shocking for the Dauphins to send Stellan to investigate. But then, just as we'd gotten it all sorted and I was about to take you to meet your family, I got this bizarre message from my mentor, telling me to put myself on the line to keep you safe."

I squeezed my knees together until my rings dug into my skin. It all made sense—that phone call I'd overheard, Stellan at prom. Even that text Jack had gotten that had made him turn me over.

"And now, I can't reach my mentor," Jack continued. "Fitz. I was on my way here to find out what you know about him, and you're nearly being killed by the Order." He pulled a brown bottle from the pharmacy bag. "You tell me—does that not sound suspicious?"

My mouth felt like sand. "But I don't know you. I don't know the Saxons, or the Dauphins, or your mentor. Why would these Order people care about me?"

"That's the question, then, isn't it?" Jack crouched in front of me with a cotton ball soaked in peroxide.

"Who *are* the Saxons?" I said finally. "Politicians, or . . . something else?"

His eyes were directly on level with mine, but carefully avoiding them. He ripped open a packet of gauze. "Politicians, in a sense, *and* something else."

Like I'd suspected, I guess. "The Dauphins, too? All twelve?"

Jack was so close, I could feel his body tense, but he nodded. With the cotton ball in one hand and a gauze pad in the other, he brushed my hair aside, and I watched his rough fingers slide the strap of the yellow sundress off my shoulder, carefully avoiding the knife wound.

I thought about downstairs, where I wanted nothing more than for him to stay with me. At the sink, with my hands cradled in his. Even now, his body was like a magnetic force. I realized I was leaning toward him, and I abruptly pulled back.

I might be upset, but I wasn't helpless. And I was not going to let myself start depending on anybody now, especially not here. Especially not *him*.

"I don't need you," I said. I reached for the cotton ball. "I don't need you to do this, I mean. I can do it. I'm *fine*."

He held it out of my reach. "This isn't just a scratch. Unless you happen to know first aid, let me handle it."

I glanced down at the cut, and the flap of skin hanging off it. I shivered. "All right," I said, but I sat stiffly while he leaned in again, careful not to relax into his touch.

The wound had mostly stopped bleeding, but it throbbed with every beat of my heart. Jack pressed the cotton ball to it, and I hissed at the bright bite of peroxide.

When he'd cleaned it and smoothed on a bandage, I brushed past him to the sink. I pulled up the strap on my dress, then wet a paper towel to wipe off the blood on my necklace while Jack washed his hands.

"What did the message say?" I finally asked. "The one your mentor sent."

Jack pulled out his phone, pressed some buttons, and handed it to me.

The girl is in danger. Don't take her to Saxons. If the worst happens— follow what I've left you.

"That's it?"

Behind me, Jack carefully unrolled and rebuttoned the sleeves on the clean white dress shirt he'd changed into, and frowned as he rubbed away a slash of dried blood—probably *my* blood—from his neck. I wondered what the people at the pharmacy had thought about that. "That's it," he said.

A pang of surprise and unexpected gratitude swelled in my chest. He'd sent me with Stellan to keep me safe—going against a direct order to bring me to the Saxons—all because of this vague message. Maybe he cared a little bit after all.

I studied the text again. Then I looked at the picture of the sender, and the phone almost fell out of my hands.

Staring up at me was a familiar face, laughing eyes peering out from behind small, round glasses. A face that couldn't be on Jack's phone.

"This is your mentor?" It suddenly felt chilly in the tiled bathroom.

Jack finger-combed his dark hair in the mirror and nodded. "Fitz."

I stared at the picture. "Jack, I *know* him. This is Mr. Emerson."

Mr. Emerson, my pseudograndfather, whose most recent post-card was sitting on my bedside table.

Jack was across the room in a second, snatching the phone out of my hand and squinting at the picture. "His name is Emerson Fitzpatrick."

"When he lived next door to us years ago, he went by Fitzpatrick Emerson."

Jack looked from the phone to me. "There's no way," he said. "You must be thinking of someone else—"

"I'm not." This time, I wasn't even going to entertain the possibility of a coincidence. I stalked to the bathroom door. "How do you know him?"

"He works for the Circle, and has for decades. Which means . . ."

I ran my hands through my hair and leaned against the mirror on the back of the door. "Mr. Emerson was *spying* on me?"

"No." The single forceful syllable echoed off the walls. Jack paced. "He's one of the good guys. I just can't believe you know him." Jack glanced at me, appraising, and I hadn't realized how closed off he'd been until he opened up again. It was like me knowing Mr. Emerson made him feel like we were on the same team. I still wasn't sure.

I stared at a copy of a Monet water lily painting on the wall above the toilet. "You think he's in trouble?"

"He just hasn't answered his phone since he sent that message." Jack stared out the window, fiddling with a basket of fake fruit on the sill. He picked up a lemon and tossed it anxiously from palm to palm. "I've been to his place here in Paris, and he's not there. And he's not answering the phone at his flat in Istanbul."

Istanbul. Like his postcard, from the Hagia Sophia. Jack was saying Mr. Emerson *lived* there, and wasn't just taking a vacation from Boston.

I turned and looked at myself in the mirror. "What does this mean?" I whispered.

I stared into my eyes, still bloodshot and haunted, and it hit me.

"Luc's eyes," I said. "They're purple."

"Yes . . ." Jack turned, letting the plastic lemon rest in his left hand. He met my eyes in the mirror like he heard the question in my voice.

"That's a Dauphin family trait?"

"Many of the Dauphins do have violet eyes, yes." He set the lemon back in its basket.

I swallowed. "I know you said I'm distant family of the Saxons, but I think I might be related to the Dauphins instead. Could that be what Mr. Emerson meant?"

When Jack turned back around, I could see in the mirror that his face was pale. "Why would you think that?" he said.

I turned slowly. I didn't know whether they had lied about who my family was, or had bad information, or why it would change anything, but it was suddenly obvious it did. Cold moved up my spine.

"Avery." Jack crossed the room and loomed over me. "Your eyes." He lowered his voice to a murmur. "You don't mean your eyes are purple, do you?"

I wished I could back away, but the door pressed into my shoulder blades. "Um. I wear contacts, but yeah. My real eye color's a lot like Luc's."

Jack brought his fingers to his mouth, dropped them. Started to say something, but stopped. His Adam's apple moved up and down with a hard swallow. "Your eyes are purple."

I nodded. Something was wrong. Something was seriously wrong.

"Well." He blinked. "That changes things."

"What do you mean?"

"I mean," he said, "I know exactly why someone would want you dead."

CHAPTER 15

"Because they want to hurt the Dauphins?" I said. A car horn honked outside, and I jumped more than I should have. I ducked around Jack. "So I am related to them? And not the Saxons?"

"Shh." Jack opened the door, peered into the hall, then shut it again. "No. Maybe. God. I don't know. To them, to the Saxons, to a different family entirely . . . All I know is that you are much, much more than a distant relative."

I swallowed hard. "But if I have the same eyes as the Dauphins . . ."

"All twelve families of the Circle have violet eyes." He swept all the first aid supplies into the pharmacy bag and stuffed it into his pocket. "That tells us nothing."

I leaned over the sink, staring into my eyes again. "How is that possible—"

"Have you told Stellan and Luc any of this?"

"No—"

"Okay, then. Fitz was right. You're in danger. From a lot of people, and especially the Order. I must have misinterpreted that message. The Saxons won't hurt you, and I'm taking you to them." He plucked my bag off the little vanity counter where he'd set it when he'd brought it from the dressing room earlier. He handed it to me. "Let's go."

I hugged it to my chest. "No." Jack stopped with one hand on the doorknob. "You need to explain exactly what's going on," I said.

Jack ran a hand through his hair, mussing it up, then the other way to smooth it back into place. I could tell he was trying to act normal, but he stared at me with a mix of awe and horror, like I was some dangerous mythical creature. "I'm not the one who should be telling you this. We should really just—"

"I'm not going anywhere." I plunked my bag back down on the vanity, toppling a trio of tiny lotion bottles. "What do my eyes matter? Why would someone try to kill me? What the hell is the Circle?"

After a second, Jack bit his lip and seemed to come to a decision. "All right," he said. "Okay. Avery, the Circle are . . . how to put this. The Circle of Twelve are important to the world. We make things happen."

"So, politicians," I said.

"Not exactly, no." He paced to the window, back to the door, then to the window again, like a caged animal. "Well, most major government officials are members of one of the twelve families, yes. But—"

"*Most*? You rig elections?" My voice rose sharply and Jack shushed me, nodding at the door.

"No," he said. "Well, usually we don't have to. It's advantageous for leaders in government, business, economics, to be ours, but most of them already are, organically."

My shaking fingers twisted the tiny gold cap off one of the lotions, screwed it back on, twisted it back off. A warm rose scent wafted from the bottle. "Business? Economics? What does that mean?"

Jack frowned uncomfortably. "It wouldn't be wrong to say that in our modern world, and in much of history, all roads lead back to the Circle. We're so entwined in society—its history, its present, its future—that even though you don't know we're there, your life would be entirely different without us."

I took a shaky breath and opened the next lotion. Citrus. "Like what?"

He glanced at the door again. "You know World War One, and Two?"

I raised my eyebrows at the stupid question.

"There are twelve families, and together they form the Circle of Twelve. Occasionally, a family will attempt to win more than their share of power. The Hersch family—they're the ones currently in Germany—did just that, and it was the driving force behind World Wars One and Two."

I paused, the lotion cap halfway off. "You did *not* just say the Circle started both World Wars."

He held up a hand. "The *Hersch family* started both World Wars. Not everything each family does represents us as a whole."

I set down the lotion. Having business and political leaders in the families—and even rigging elections—sounded almost plausible, but if he'd been teetering on the edge of the "makes frightening sense" cliff before, he'd just launched himself off.

"Avery!" Luc's voice echoed up the stairs. Jack and I both froze. "We're hungry. Are you ready to go?"

I'd forgotten Luc and Stellan were still waiting to go to dinner, of all things. I cracked the door. "Almost!" I yelled. "Give me one more minute!"

I turned slowly back to Jack. I wasn't sure what would be worse—if he was messing with me, or if he really believed this.

"I think I've heard this conspiracy theory," I said carefully. "New

World Order, right? A small group of really powerful people who run the whole world behind the scenes."

"Yes," he said.

"So . . . you're telling me that's what you are." I could hear the condescension in my voice, like I was talking to a kid playing make-believe.

"That's exactly what we are." He was looking at me like he wasn't sure what I'd do, and I realized he'd gotten himself between me and the door, trapping me inside.

I ran my fingertips over the subtle damask of the wallpaper, letting it ground me in reality. "You know that's not real, right? That's why they call it a *conspiracy theory,* and not a fact."

"And it's very convenient for us that that's what the world believes. Avery, listen. I promise, I'll explain it all. But we have to go before Stellan and Luc—"

This time I was the one holding up a hand. "So you're actually trying to get me to believe one of the families started both World Wars," I said. "And the other eleven . . . participated?"

"Of course." He paced the room again, like a professor lecturing to a class. "The families had to take sides. You know the history of which countries lined up where. You just don't know that each of those countries had a family of the Circle behind it. Trust me, things would have gotten much worse if we hadn't. And it's not only history." He plunged ahead, seeming to gain steam. "Even now, some of the Middle Eastern families . . . Well, they're difficult. And you see how the ramifications of that bleed into the world. Or sometimes, certain families use their influence to modify the stock market. Or banking interests."

"*Modify.*" Now, that made sense. Rich people manipulating the stock market I understood. "So if strapless dresses aren't flattering on a Circle member, they can put halters on the cover of *Vogue* and make them popular instead?" I asked, not sure whether I was joking or not. I glanced accidentally at the bloody gold dress.

"If they cared about that, then yes. Absolutely." Jack rubbed the back of his neck. I could see his compass tattoo through his sleeve.

"This is all insane, you know," I said. "You sound like one of those paranoid people on the Internet telling everyone to wear tinfoil hats. Next you're going to tell me you killed JFK."

Jack looked up. "Not me personally."

My mouth fell open.

"I'm sorry. That wasn't funny. But . . . there were reasons for it." Jack shot me an almost-sympathetic look. "I'm sure it must seem absolutely mad from the outside, but it's the reality of our lives. Of *everyone's* lives," he said quietly. "The world doesn't operate like most people think it does. I'm telling you the truth."

It *did* seem absolutely mad. But I couldn't help thinking about my original suspicions. Mafia, or politicians. Wasn't that kind of what he was describing? Politician-mafia. On a huge, huge scale. I crossed my arms over my chest, only partially to hide the fact that my hands had begun to tremble again.

"So what you're saying," I ventured, "is that Stellan wasn't exaggerating at the prom when he said the Circle runs the world."

"Avery!" Luc's footsteps clomped up the stairs, and I snapped my mouth shut.

Jack started to open the door. "You're coming with me to the Saxons," he murmured.

I ducked in front of him. "Sorry, I'm throwing up," I called down the stairs. "You probably don't want to come up here."

The footsteps stopped abruptly. "Oh," Luc said. "Um. Is Jack still with you?"

I glared at Jack and nodded at the door. He frowned. "I'm sitting outside to make sure she's all right. She's a little shaken up," he called, and I pulled him back inside and slammed the door. We were both right. I was shaken up, and I was *thisclose* to being sick.

"Let's pretend for one second this is true," I said once Luc's footsteps had retreated. The music came back on and switched from Bach to some kind of French hip-hop. "Why would these Order people care about *me*? There have to be a ton of Circle members more important than a teenage girl."

Jack sat on the tiny vanity chair and propped his elbows on his knees. "The Order is an opposition group. They don't think the Circle should have as much power as they do. They've been a thorn in our side for a long time, and they've been ramping up their efforts against us recently."

I made my way to the warped window and stared outside as the afternoon light faded to evening.

Jack took a breath and continued. "Where you come in is with something called the mandate."

The word hit me like a punch to the gut. I closed my eyes, suddenly feeling like I'd been waiting my whole life to hear this. A thrill of fear flared through me. "What exactly is the mandate?" I finally said.

"The mandate . . ." Jack buttoned and unbuttoned one cuff. "If you don't believe the rest of it, you'll find this ridiculous, but the mandate is like a prophecy. Among other things, it gives us a way to subdue the Order."

I stared at him. "A prophecy? You're right. I don't believe you."

"It has a lot of basis in history, and—"

"How?" Now I was the one pacing. "How is this mandate supposed to work?"

"'The rightful One and the girl with the violet eyes . . . ,'" Jack said. "That's the most important line. And the line the Order cares about says, 'the means to vanquish the greatest enemies.'"

"The greatest enemies are the Order."

Jack nodded.

"And that's why they'd want this violet-eyed girl killed, to make that impossible." I'd already started to assume that my mom's mandate and the Circle's mandate were not two different things. That when I'd heard her mention that word on the phone so long ago, she made up that that's what her work orders were called to keep me in the dark about my father's family.

But now I couldn't stop thinking about all the times she got weird. Got nervous. And then we'd move. I'd always attributed her anxiety to work, but hearing this, I had to wonder if she hadn't just been keeping the Circle from me, but had actually been going to a lot of trouble to keep *us* from *them*, and from the Order.

I traced a crack in the tile floor with one foot. "Why would they think I'm the specific purple-eyed girl the mandate is talking about?"

Jack's jaw tensed. "The thing is, very few females get the gene for the violet eyes. Almost everyone who's ever had them is male. A girl with the purple-eyes gene is about to be born, to the Dauphins."

"But . . . ?" I knew a *but* was coming.

"But, until the Dauphins' baby is born, you are the only girl with purple eyes in the world."

I leaned hard against the windowsill. "That's—" I was about to say that was impossible, but really, compared with the rest of this, was it? "Let me make sure I'm understanding," I said, feeling shaky again. "What you're telling me is that, one"—I held up a finger—"you're part of a world-controlling secret society. Two, there's an opposing secret society. Three, you need me, because of the color of my eyes, to stop them, and therefore, they want me dead."

"That would be the simplified version, yes. And now you understand why you have to come to the Saxons. You'll be safe there." He started to open the door again.

"I don't think I want to go to them," I said to my own reflection in the mirror.

Jack rubbed his temples. "I *have* to take you to them. There is no scenario in which anything else would be a good idea, for anyone. You don't understand everything at play here."

I understood that all this time, my mom and I were literally on the run for our lives. For my life. Add that now I'd put myself back in the crosshairs of the people we were running from *and* a powerful group who wanted to use me.

There was one thing I had to ask. "So are you saying my father was *not* a Saxon?"

"Not was. *Is.* Obviously our intel was wrong. Your having purple eyes means that your father is not only living, he could be the head of any of the families of the Circle."

"He's *alive*?" I gripped the edge of the sink. And if they were wrong about that, he might not even know I existed. "Why would the Saxons have thought I was their relative?"

"Intelligence comes in all the time, from all over the world. I don't know where this came from or why it was wrong or even exactly what it said. You'll still be safest with the Saxons," Jack continued. "I promise. And we can contact Fitz and see what he meant by that message."

My father wasn't dead. I let that sink in for just a second before I snapped out of it. Allowing myself to be taken in by the Circle without understanding exactly what I was getting into would be beyond stupid. I had no room to be blindly optimistic anymore.

Jack was standing at the door, like there was no doubt I'd follow him. Yes, I was grateful that he'd finally told me the truth, but it wasn't enough.

I had to get out of here. Get in touch with my mom. Decide what to do next.

But how? Jack would never let me get away again if he had the choice. I glanced at the window. The bathroom was one story up. Too high to jump, but maybe there was a fire escape. I could get him to leave me alone for a second, and run.

And then what? My mom wasn't answering her phone. I couldn't jump in a cab to the airport and fly home without a passport. Maybe I could go to the American embassy?

But the embassy was a government organization. They probably reported to the Circle.

Oh God. Did this mean I believed all of it?

Two sets of footsteps started up the stairs. Too late.

Jack flung open the door. I was surprised to see Stellan in slim dress pants and a button-up shirt, with a jacket slung over his arm. The furious light in his eyes had faded, replaced by a scowling suspicion. Luc was in a light gray suit with the salmon-colored shirt underneath, grinning, and they both smelled too good for what had happened earlier. Behind them, Elodie, Madame Dauphin's supermodel assistant, waited, tapping her foot.

"She's ready to go," Jack said, with a silencing stare at me, "but I'm going to take her to the Saxons' hotel. She needs some rest, and to meet her family as soon as they arrive."

Even with all the guards at the Louvre, I'd have a better chance of escaping from Luc and Stellan and the Dauphins—who knew nothing about me—than from Jack.

"Maybe I should stay with them, meet you tomorrow," I said to Jack. I tried to make my voice breezy. "I already have a room at the Dauphins' and everything. It'll be easier."

His eyes could have set me on fire, but I knew he couldn't say anything.

Luc threw a lanky arm around my shoulders. I couldn't help but stare at his violet eyes. "Stay. You can come out to the club," he said, like the whole world hadn't just changed. For them, I supposed, it hadn't.

Stellan pushed open the door, and he and Jack stepped to the landing. I ducked out from under Luc's arm and he headed out, too, leaving me in the bathroom. If I acted fast, I could slam the door and have some chance of escaping before they realized what was happening.

"Where are you going?" I kept my voice light, but my hand crept to the deadbolt.

"Istanbul," Luc said.

"Istanbul?" I said. "That's a club?"

"It's a *city*," Elodie said from down the stairs. I could tell the words came with an eye roll.

"I know it's a city," I said. Luc chuckled. "Wait. You don't mean you're going to Istanbul, the city. In Turkey. To go to a club."

"Which is why you probably shouldn't go," Jack said. "You're exhausted."

I was, but I was far more desperate. And I'd just gotten an idea.

Istanbul. Half in Europe, half in Asia, home to some of the world's most impressive art and architecture. Mr. Emerson's last postcard to me was from Istanbul. Jack said he had an apartment there. If I couldn't reach my mom, maybe I could find him. The two of them were the only people in the world I trusted right now.

My hand fell away from the door.

"The plane's supposed to leave in half an hour and we're grabbing dinner on the way," Luc said, "so if you're coming, let's go."

"If she's coming, we have to get her a dress," Elodie called up. "Something more interesting than what they've got in this store."

I stepped out onto the landing and let the bathroom door swing closed behind me.

"Istanbul sounds great," I said, ignoring Jack's death glare. "Let's go."

CHAPTER 16

Somewhere between shopping at Prada and clubbing in Istanbul, the rest of the adrenaline had worn off and reality set in. I plucked at the bandage on my shoulder while Luc talked to the club bouncer. Hundreds of people stood in a line that snaked away underneath a white version of the Golden Gate Bridge. I watched them all, paranoid. If the Order could find me at Prada, they could find me here.

Somehow, I had actually come to believe what Jack said about the Circle. It made no sense, but that's why it was the only thing that did. I was standing here in a very expensive dress, after having flown across Europe in a private jet, and I had to get away from some really powerful, really motivated people who wanted me dead.

And that was if Stellan or Luc or Elodie didn't figure out who I was and lock me up first.

I'd also realized on the plane that I had no idea where Mr. Emerson—I couldn't start thinking of him by a different name—lived. Not an address, not even a phone number. As soon as I had a second alone, I'd have to Google him and see if I could find anything.

"If you pick that bandage off, it's going to get infected," Elodie said, and I jumped. My reflexes were still set on fight-or-flight.

"It's fine." I crossed my arms.

Elodie went back to studying her tangerine fingernails. "You got *stabbed*. Who knows where that knife had been?" With her light French accent and her throaty voice talking about stabbing, she sounded very femme fatale.

Stellan came up beside us. In contrast to his pointed-but-light-hearted banter this morning, he had barely talked to me since Prada, but he *had* spent the whole plane ride scrutinizing me. He couldn't know the truth yet, but I could tell he hadn't bought Luc's "wrong place wrong time" explanation for my drawing the Order's attention. He'd put two and two together eventually. I had to be out of here before he did.

"She's right, *kuklachka*," he said. Even the nickname had lost its playful edge. "The Order—and their weapons—are nasty things. It's a shame for a random *innocent* to get mixed up with them."

I tensed, but gave what I hoped was a noncommittal shrug and busied myself picking at invisible lint on my dress. A Herve Leger bandage dress, Elodie had called it. From afar I would have called the color champagne, but up close, it was white, shot through with shimmering silver and gold threads. It was the exact dress Krissy Silver had worn to the Grammys a couple of months ago—Elodie said she'd chosen this specific dress because the singer and I had the same pale complexion and dark hair. I wasn't sure whether it was supposed to be a compliment or not.

Elodie had paired the dress with four-inch copper Louboutin heels—all the girls at my school in New York had been obsessed with Louboutins, and I never would have expected to have a pair on my feet. We'd stood at the bar mirror in the plane while she teased my hair into wild bed-head waves, all the while making it clear that she was playing stylist only because she didn't trust me to do it properly on my own.

Elodie wore a faux-leather minidress, and had pinned her blond bob half up. Her dangling earrings shimmered when Stellan murmured in her ear, and then she glanced at me and her almond-shaped eyes narrowed. I pretended not to notice, but my stomach flipped nervously.

I was saved from further questioning when Luc gestured, and I followed the three of them past the line and inside.

Mr. Emerson was fascinated by the history of Istanbul, and had taught me about it when I was younger. It had been called Byzantium when it was first founded, then renamed Constantinople when Constantine took it over. It was such an important city politically and geographically that it had been conquered and claimed by empire after empire ever since. It wasn't officially called Istanbul until really recently, in the 1930s.

Istanbul had always been a crossroads city. A crossroads between Europe and Asia. A crossroads of Christianity and Islam, like the Hagia Sophia itself. A crossroads between ancient and conservative, like that museum, and modern and anything but conservative, like this club.

I squeezed the shoulder strap of my bag, wondering what kind of crossroads the city would be for me tonight.

Luc and Stellan disappeared into the crowd. I considered doing the same—I didn't really want to be alone right now, just in case the Order *had* followed me, but I didn't particularly want to be with Elodie, either. And I really needed to look up Mr. Emerson. But it'd probably look suspicious, so I followed Elodie across the dance floor, breathing the humid, heavy air that comes from too many bodies in too small a space. She and Luc had cracked a bottle of champagne on the plane, and even though I hadn't had any, I wasn't sure it was possible to feel entirely sober in a club. Between the lights and the unbuttoned dress shirts and the glistening bare shoulders and the driving beat of the music that got under your skin even if you weren't dancing, I was swaying by the time we got to a tall bar table where the lights flashed a little less brightly.

I took inventory of the club—for anyone who looked sketchy, for my eventual exit, for suspicious glances from Stellan. I found him near the dance floor, already being flirted with by a gorgeous, dark-skinned brunette. As I watched, he searched the room and met my gaze. His smile faded.

"As you can see, you're not special." Elodie was staring at him, too.

I leaned on the table to hear her over the pulsating techno mix. "What?"

"He has a list of conquests a mile long. The whole *innocent* thing you have going on is just a novelty." She took a compact out of her bag and touched up a nonexistent imperfection in her lipstick. "He'd corrupt you for fun."

Even though that was *far* from why I'd been watching him, heat shot to my cheeks. I couldn't suppress a flash of what Stellan *corrupting me* would entail. Maybe Elodie liked him and all this animosity was because she thought I was trying to steal him.

"That's really, really not—" I paused, trying to make it as clear as possible. "I'm not interested in him in that way. At all."

Elodie rolled her eyes and the copper on her lids shimmered. "*Everyone's* interested in him in that way."

Before I could answer, an arm went around my shoulders. "What are we talking about, girls?" Luc said, grinning widely. He'd ditched his jacket, popped the collar of his pink shirt, and found a green glowstick necklace.

"The unfortunate attack this afternoon," Elodie said, smiling sweetly at me.

"Aw, El." He squeezed my shoulder. "We're having fun now, remember?"

Luc was the only one who'd bothered to ask how I was doing after Prada. He sat by me on the plane and chatted about movies and Paris and the club we were going to, and I could tell he was trying to get my mind off it. His kindness made how quickly he moved on from *killing* someone even more disconcerting.

And I couldn't help glancing at his eyes, like I'd been doing all evening. They were so much like mine.

"It's time for me to do my job," Elodie said. My ears perked up. I'd assumed they were here to dance.

"Already?" Luc pouted. He bumped Elodie's shoulder with his own. In her towering heels, she was taller than he was.

"We don't want him seeing me with you. I doubt he'd recognize you, but . . ." Elodie leveled a cool stare around the room. The bottom of a tattoo peeked out from under the hair at the nape of her neck. It looked like Stellan's sun symbol.

"I know." Luc kissed her on the cheek, and she wiped a thumb across her face with a pretend scowl. "Be safe," he said.

"It's perfectly routine."

"Then I expect you back by the time we leave, new clue to the mandate in hand," Luc said with a wry smile.

I covered the sharp breath I drew in with a cough.

"I'll be right back," Luc said to me, and slipped his arm through Elodie's.

They walked away, and after I made sure no one was watching me, I perched on one of the tall bar stools and pulled out my phone. On the plane, Stellan had turned on my international roaming and entered his, Elodie's, and Luc's phone numbers—and my number in their phones. In case something happened, he said, but it was probably so he could keep track of me. Now I was about to pull up Google when I saw I had a missed call from my mom's cell phone. Thank *God*.

I dialed my voice mail and plugged my free ear with my finger to drown out the music. "Avery. Sweetheart." My mom sounded understandably tense. "Yes, we do have a lot to talk about, and I wish I could have told you sooner. Please stay right where you are and be very careful. I'm coming to get you."

No. I held the phone in a death grip. She thought I was in France, which meant she probably knew where the Dauphins lived and was headed there. I dialed her number, only to get an immediate chime on her voice mail. "This is Carol West," her tinny voice said. "I'm not available . . ."

I cursed under my breath. She couldn't go to the Dauphins'. She might be in danger from the Order, too—or she could get recognized by my father, whoever he was.

"Mom," I said, "don't—" I was poised to leave the whole story on the message, but stopped. What if Stellan had done something else to my phone, like bugged it? I glanced around the club and lowered my voice. I didn't trust anybody anymore.

"Mom, don't come," I said simply, my voice tight. "Call me back. Or I'll call you. Just *don't come* to France."

The voice mail picking up on the first ring meant her phone was off. She might be on a plane already. If so, I wouldn't be able to reach her until morning.

I looked over my shoulder again. Besides a couple of guys wearing too much hair product who smiled smarmily at me from the next table, no one was watching me. I Googled "Emerson Fitzpatrick."

Too many results, none of them him. I added "Istanbul" to the search. "Emerson Fitzpatrick, volunteer docent at the Hagia Sophia," it said, with a photo of his smiling face. I pictured the postcard. It was like Mr. Emerson was trying to send me clues about who he really was.

But there was nothing else. No personal phone-book entry or anything. I hunched my shoulders over the phone and pulled up a map of Istanbul. If I had to, I could get to the Hagia Sophia, hide until morning, and find someone who knew him. Maybe he'd even be there. If I was going to do that, though, I should probably not try to escape the club quite yet. I'd rather not camp on the street for longer than necessary.

I looked up to find Stellan strolling toward my table. A spasm of adrenaline shot through me, and I stuffed my phone into the bottom of my bag. This was the first time we'd been alone since Prada, and I had a feeling that I wasn't going to like what he had to say.

"All by yourself, little doll?" Stellan set down a glass of something clear and leaned his elbows on the tall bar table. He didn't raise his voice, but the smooth, low tones of his accent easily undercut the electronic beat of the music. "I'm surprised. Aren't you afraid something else might happen?"

Yes. My fists clenched on my bag and I forced myself not to look over my shoulder. That was one good thing, I guess—I had less of a chance of being killed with Stellan nearby.

I gave him a tight smile. "No," I said. "Not worried. Luc said it was an accident."

The DJ, silhouetted against a spill of neon lines cascading down the wall, pumped a fist in the air. Stellan watched him. "I suppose it *is* impressive how easily you got away from that Order operative," he mused. "Maybe you don't have anything to worry about."

I touched my bandaged shoulder. If that had been getting away easily, I wouldn't want to find out what "hard" looked like.

"And at least you understand now why I need a weapon for a weekend of meetings and parties." Stellan's face was half obscured by shadow, half flashing neon blue. I searched for his knife and saw a bulge under the right side of his slate-gray jacket, and another on the left. He saw me looking and flicked the jacket open. A gun.

I swallowed. "Why do you need both? A gun seems pretty effective."

"It takes more effort to kill with a dagger." He rebuttoned his jacket. "You have to do it on purpose. Guns make it too easy."

I was surprised he'd care about that. "It didn't seem very hard for you to kill Frederic at Prada."

Stellan swirled the drink he hadn't so much as sipped and gave me a thin smile. I couldn't help but remember the rage in his face at Prada.

I folded my arms across my chest. "I still don't know why you killed him. I know you don't care about *me* that much."

"Ah, but I do care about being punished for something happening to our *guest*."

Oh.

Stellan pulled out the other bar stool and sat. My feet dangled, but his rested solidly on the floor.

"What's Elodie doing?" I said, because I didn't want to talk about killing anymore.

"There's a wealthy businessman here in Istanbul with an ancient Greek art collection. She's infiltrating."

That explained the trip to a club on the other side of the continent. I wondered how often Elodie had to "infiltrate." That was one disadvantage of being ridiculously beautiful.

"Didn't you say she's Madame Dauphin's assistant?" I said. "Is this a normal part of the job?"

Stellan strummed a stack of cocktail napkins with his thumb. "There are no female Keepers. Sometimes a task comes up that's better suited to a girl."

I felt a sting of indignation. "So guys do the important work, but you bring in girls when you need to seduce somebody? Don't you think that's a little sexist?"

Stellan gave me a one-sided smile, and my jaw clenched in anticipation of the offensive thing about to come out of his mouth.

"Sure, a little," he said.

I was surprised into silence for a second. "But she looks hot doing it, so it's okay?"

"I suppose she does, but that's not the point. It's true she'll have an easier time getting in than I would, but Elodie's doing this job mostly because she knows more about art *and* bypassing difficult security systems than anyone else in our family."

"Really?" I looked for signs he was joking.

He just smirked. "Who's being sexist now?"

At that moment, Luc swept back in between us and clapped his hands. "On with our evening?"

Stellan stood. "I'll be patrolling." He shot a lingering glance at me, and I watched him disappear into the crowd again.

Luc offered his arm, and I slid off the bar stool. He spotted someone across the club and waved enthusiastically. "Liam and Colette are here," he said, dragging me through the crowd toward the half-moon bar bordering the dance floor. Behind it, glowing magenta waterfalls hid nooks carved out of the wall, and behind each waterfall, a girl danced in silhouette, dry-ice steam rising at her feet.

"You said Elodie's looking for a new clue to the mandate?" I yelled as I followed him.

"For deciphering the lines about the One. You know." He waved a hand in the air as he steered us around a couple making out to a techno remix of "Somewhere Over the Rainbow."

As in, *the rightful One and the girl with the violet eyes.* "What exactly do you mean, deciphering?" I called hesitantly, because I *didn't* know, and even if I was planning to escape, it'd be nice to learn what my fate was supposed to be.

Luc turned and jerked me to a halt in the middle of the dance floor. His brows arched practically to his hairline, and with his light brown hair styled in an exuberant bouffant, he looked like an anime character. "You don't know?"

Uh-oh. "I just—I haven't really been around—"

"Does that mean you don't know about the mandate at *all*?"

I thought about lying, but that wouldn't do me any good. I shook my head. "Just a tiny bit. My mom wouldn't tell me anything."

We stared at each other for a tense second, then Luc smiled the smile of someone letting a few drinks take the edge off his worries. He wagged a finger down at me. "Don't let anyone hear you talking like that, *cherie*. It's odd for *anyone* in the Circle to be so uninformed. But I understand your predicament."

I exhaled.

He took my arm again. "We're trying to decipher the mandate because we're looking for something. Something very important."

He pulled me to a stop and his eyes danced, daring me to ask.

"What is it you're looking for?" I said.

He paused dramatically, then leaned close to my ear. "Treasure."

CHAPTER 17

I pulled away and frowned. That was what Stellan had said on the plane. But I thought he'd been joking. "Treasure?" I said skeptically.

"Treasure!" Luc threw his arms wide, face raised to the disco ball. "Wealth! Power!" He twirled, circling behind me, and whispered, "Death."

I whipped around. Luc laughed out loud, reading the surprise on my face. The low light threw the angles of his face into sharp relief. "And it's the Circle's birthright, what with it being in the tomb of our predecessor."

"Who is . . . ?" I could tell he was waiting for me to ask.

"Alexander the Great, of course! In his tomb is everything that made him who he was. It'll make the Circle that much more powerful, and the families of the union infinitely so." He grinned and tapped the end of my nose. "It's so deliciously odd that you don't know this, *cherie*. Your adorable little face is priceless right now."

Luc swooped my hand up and held me formally, like we were waltzing at a garden party instead of to trance music at a club. "Liam and Lettie can wait for a minute. I see you have more questions."

"So the mandate's like a worldwide treasure hunt for the tomb of Alexander the Great?" I said, keeping up with his steps to this unwaltzable music, in these ridiculous heels. *One* two three *one* two three.

"Yes and no." Luc twirled me. "The mandate is like a prophecy. It comes from an ancient book the Circle has had for ages—the Book of Mandates. It's a series of predictions. Many of them have come true. 'By the follies of one and the loyalties of the rest will the world burn a second time.' That'd be World War Two. There was one about World War One. The Crusades. They've been accurate all through history. This one talks about the union between 'the rightful One and the girl with the violet eyes.' That's the most important line, anyway. And now that there's going to be a girl with violet eyes—my baby sister—we're just figuring out who the *rightful One* is."

Someone bumped me from behind and sent me careening into Luc. "Sorry," I said. My throat was starting to hurt from yelling over the music. "What do you mean, figuring out?"

Luc brought my arms around his thin neck, and my forearms glowed green from his neon necklace. "The language on who the One is, or which family he comes from, is vague, but it's believed that only the *rightful* One—the single correct person—will trigger the prophecy's fulfillment. The Book of Mandates is the main source of the predictions, but there were other writings of the Oracles that got lost over time and never made it in, and they've been found all over the world—in museums, or at archaeological digs, or in family memorabilia—all throughout history. We're hoping to find something that gives us more specifics on the One. And if we don't, since we have the girl, my family will choose the One for the union ourselves and hope for the best. So, to make a long story short and answer your original question, Elodie is seeking something more about the mandate."

It made me feel a tiny bit better to know they still had to find something else before using the girl. "And the treasure in the tomb is more than money?"

When the next song started, they turned on a black light. Luc gave me a wide grin, and his teeth gleamed like a Halloween decoration. "Much more," he said. "The mandate says it will make whoever has it *invincible*."

That tugged at my brain, and I remembered our Ancient Civ reading from last week. It was hard to believe that class, where Jack had covered for me, was only yesterday. It felt a million years away from designer dresses and ancient prophecies.

The section about the Diadochi I'd forgotten that day said something about invincibility. Our book referenced a prophecy from an oracle saying that whichever of the Diadochi—Alexander's successors—was in possession of his body would never be conquered. They'd be *invincible*. Vying for his body—and his tomb—was the cause of centuries of war between the Diadochi.

"Wait wait wait," I said. "The Circle are the *Diadochi*? Alexander's successors?" The most powerful people in the world two thousand years ago had descendants who were secretly the world's most powerful people *today*? And the prophecy we'd learned about in history class was part of the Circle's mandate? No wonder Jack had known how to answer Mrs. Lindley's question.

"Smart girl!" Luc patted me on the head like a dog learning a new trick. "Where do you think the word for *twelve* comes from in so many languages? *Dodici*—'twelve' in Italian. *Duodecim. Doce. Dodeka*. Sound like Diadochi, right?"

"Oh wow," I whispered.

Luc grinned wider. "Then you'll really be impressed with this. The twelve months of the calendar. Inches in a foot. Hours in a day. Zodiac symbols. The 'twelve' aspects of those all came into being around 300 BC, just around when the Diadochi took over."

I glanced around the club. I couldn't believe he was saying all this so openly, so loudly, in such a public place. Someone could overhear. But so what if they did? No one would believe it. *I* barely believed it.

"So the Order's after the treasure, too?" I said, because the rest of this was too much to contemplate.

"Again, yes and no. They want the riches in the tomb, yes. But besides wealth and power, the tomb is also rumored to contain a weapon. The mandate says it's so powerful that it will 'vanquish the greatest enemies.'"

Like Jack had said at Prada.

"And so they want the treasure *and* to keep this mysterious weapon from the Circle." I was starting to get it now. "What is the stuff about the Order attacking the Circle?"

Luc's arms tightened around my waist. "The newest assassination yesterday—the oldest son of the head of the Sony Corporation in Japan, in that awful hotel fire? Horrible."

Assassination?

"And the Russian prime minister's son. I did not know Sergei well, but the plane crash was a tragedy. Malik Emir's death, too. He was a good man. A friend." Luc's eyes glinted. "I hate that the whole world thinks it was just militants killing an unimportant Saudi prince."

Something about the death of a Saudi prince had been on the news last time I was at home, right before my mom told me about the new mandate. "You *knew* him?" We were barely dancing now, swaying just enough to not stand still. We'd ended up just below a stage, and a mass of arms waved above us. I suddenly felt very small. "The Order killed him?"

Luc nodded. "Since we don't know who the One is, the Order is trying to take out anyone that could be him."

That's why he had said at Prada that the Order could have been after *him*. "So is everyone in every family a possibility? Are they planning to kill them all one by one?"

"I suppose any male member of the families is a possibility. Like any act of terrorism, it's partially a scare tactic," he said. "And partially blackmail. If we agree not to carry out the union, they stop killing us."

"Oh my God," I whispered.

"I know," Luc said. He untwisted my arms from around his neck and led us away from the ever-more-crowded center of the dance floor. "And of course we can't allow the news to report it as anything more than accidents."

"Yeah," I said vaguely. The fact that they could dictate what the news covered hardly surprised me.

"It appears the Order is going to more effort now because of my mother's pregnancy," Luc continued over his shoulder. "We hoped they wouldn't learn that one of the twins is a girl, but it's leaked."

Maybe they learned about it the same way they learned about me, however that was. If they were going to that much trouble to kill people who might *possibly* be the One, they wouldn't let *me* go for sure. My dress, or my skin, suddenly felt too tight. I watched the revelers around us out of the corner of my eye. So it was true. Both these groups who started wars and assassinated world leaders had very good reasons to want *me*.

I found myself looking around for Stellan. Because I was afraid of him, or because I was afraid of everyone else, I wasn't sure.

Luc grabbed a neon-blue drink off a waitress's tray. "Now do you understand why I'm not mourning a couple of dead Order members?"

Disturbingly, I kind of did. And I was starting to think more and more that maybe hiding out for an extra few hours on the street was better than staying here waiting for the Order to find me, or for the Dauphins to figure me out.

I glanced around for an exit, but Luc took my hand. "Let's not talk about it anymore." He leaned in conspiratorially. "I'm tired of it, love. Let's have fun." His grin looked more forced than it had earlier.

I studied the layout of the club again as we made our way across the dance floor. There were the front doors we'd come in through, and another door nearby that seemed to lead to the back of the club. When we got to the bar, Luc let go of me.

"Did you see we got Clancy Campbell?" someone with an American accent said.

"Yeah, yeah. We've got our eye on a thirteen-year-old from Brazil," said Luc. Out of the corner of my eye, I saw Luc shake hands with the guy and clap him on the back.

I leaned on the bar, pressing my palms to the cool, glossy surface. Breathe. Think. I didn't see any immediate threat. I shouldn't run off yet. A steaming pink trough ran down the center of the bar, and I passed my fingers over the dry ice, letting the cold pull me out of my head.

"That's not going to win you Champions this year," the American guy said.

Luc chuckled stiffly. "Want to bet?"

"You just want to win back Guam."

"It was my favorite," Luc whined. "And that bet wasn't fair."

Guam? I turned around and my heart stuttered yet again. Luc wasn't talking to a random friend named Liam. He was talking to

Liam Blackstone. And . . . yes. There at the bar, ordering something pink, was Colette LeGrand, her famous curves on display in a cleavage-baring boho lace dress. Luc's friends Liam and Colette were Liam Blackstone and Colette LeGrand. *Li-ette.* At least, that's what *Us Weekly* called them when they were on the cover every other week.

"Oh, this is Avery," Luc said. "She's a relative of the Saxons, and since we're all playing nice this weekend, she's come out with us."

I forced a smile in Liam's direction. I wasn't used to seeing him in clothes. He mostly did movies where his abs were the main character. "So you play . . . fantasy soccer?" Guys at every one of my schools had been into fantasy football. What a bizarrely ordinary thing for Luc and one of the world's most famous actors to be talking about.

"I wish." Colette LeGrand slipped an arm under Liam's jacket. Her light, lilting French accent was even prettier in person. "They have bought the teams. Their little game takes up *all* Liam's time."

Of course they owned professional sports teams. That could be the most normal thing that had happened all day.

"Jesse knocked us both out last year," Liam said. He must have meant his younger brother, who was the lead singer in Shadow Play, Lara's favorite band. "He has Man U."

Colette LeGrand pushed her wavy auburn hair behind her shoulder and rolled her eyes like, *see what I mean?* I gave her a tight smile, still a little shocked to be talking to people I'd only seen on screen and in tabloids, but I couldn't help being wary of them, too. As far as I knew, anyone could be a spy.

We stayed at the bar for a few minutes, and I made sure to stand so I could see the whole club. Colette complimented my dress and I fished for something normal to say, finally settling on how her curls looked so perfect all the time—when I let my hair dry wavy, it was a frizz ball. While she told me, I studied Liam, who was laughing over a video on Luc's phone. He and Colette both seemed to be acting normal, and I relaxed just a bit, looking around more widely. I noticed how Luc was already looking a little tipsy. And how he was paying no attention to me at all anymore—in fact, he seemed to be shooting surreptitious glances at the bartender. The bartender who was very cute, and also very *male*. I watched him for a second, and yes, that was definitely a little smile on his face when he caught the guy's eye. And then I remembered how I'd seen him eyeing the people sitting next to us earlier. Now that I thought about it, there hadn't been any girls at that table. And Luc was definitely a little more . . . vibrant than the other guys. Oh. I turned away so no one would see my sudden grin. Not that it was any of my business, but I couldn't believe I hadn't seen it before, and for some reason, even more than Luc being nice to me, seeing this glimpse of what I assumed was a secret made me feel just a little better about being here with them. Like they were just people after all, going about their own lives.

Or Luc was, at least, I reminded myself, searching for Stellan again.

Colette looked around. "Our booth's open. Let's sit." She slipped an arm through mine with a smile, obviously trying to make me feel comfortable, and I could see why she and Luc were friends.

"Why did you two come out tonight, anyway?" Luc said as we slid into the dark leather booth. Liam's sandy-blond hair gleamed in the booth's low red lights, and Colette lit a cigarette and blew smoke up at the ceiling, pursing her trademark full lips. "It's dangerous for any of us to be out in public."

Colette shrugged. "You're here."

"I have a reason to be. Plus, I'm less recognizable than you, *and* I have my Keeper with me. He has knives." Luc pouted. "And guns."

Colette peered over the crowd at Stellan, who was headed toward us but stopped halfway down the bar, looking at his phone. "He certainly does have 'guns' . . ." She gave Luc a wicked grin.

Liam cleared his throat.

"What? Can't a girl look?" Colette batted her eyelashes and kissed him noisily on the cheek. Liam rolled his eyes good-naturedly.

"Did any photographers see you arrive?" Luc said.

"A couple." Colette played with her pendant necklace, which I now realized was an aged copper version of the Dauphins' sun.

Luc's cheerful face clouded over.

"I like to live dangerously, Lucien," Colette teased. "Anyway, Liam is only a second cousin of the Fredericks, and I'm the same to you. *You're* in more danger than we are."

Luc raised a finger at a waiter for yet another drink. He turned to Liam, who was watching not entirely subtly while, next to our booth, a girl with a green pixie cut danced with a girl in a long pink wig, tracing a finger over the dragon tattoo covering her back.

"I hear one of your Keepers was terminated," Luc said.

Liam snapped back around and frowned. "Yes. Xan was a good man. I wish my uncle hadn't needed to punish him so harshly."

I looked around at all their somber faces. "What did he do?"

"Went against a direct order." Luc swigged his drink.

I leaned my elbows on the shiny black tabletop. "They fired him for going against one order?"

A glance passed between the three of them. "Fired is one way to put it," Colette said carefully.

Wait. They weren't saying the guy got *put to death* for going against an order? Before I could ask, Stellan emerged from the crowd. He nodded to Liam and Colette, then looked at the drink in Luc's hand when Luc hiccuped.

Luc narrowed his eyes and downed the drink in one gulp. "Gonna go smoke." He slid out of the booth and flopped onto a stool at the end of the bar.

"What's wrong with him today?" Colette asked. "He's been acting strange."

Stellan watched Luc light a cigarette. "He's been having a hard time with the babies coming and the mandate and all."

The three of them started talking. At the bar, Luc rubbed a hand over his head, mussing his hair. I scooted out of the booth, too, pulling down my dress, which wouldn't stop trying to inch up, and slipped onto the bar stool next to Luc.

"Hey," I said. He didn't look up, and I studied the sharp curve of his jaw, his angular, lanky frame. Besides the eyes, he looked nothing like me. But what if the Dauphins were my real family? If Monsieur Dauphin was my real father? That would mean Luc was my half brother. I felt a wave of affection for him.

"Everything okay?" I said. It was like the couple extra drinks had flipped a switch in him. He stared at his glass with big, miserable puppy dog eyes.

"*Cherie,* you're so lucky." He wasn't even trying to talk over the music anymore. I could smell the sour liquor tang on his breath even over the cigarette. "You, Colette, Liam. You get the perks without the . . . *devoir.* Without the anxiety."

"Are you worried about not being able to interpret the mandate?" I said.

"That, and everything." He pawed at the back of his neck. "This thing. This tattoo." He was slurring now, and pulled clumsily at the collar of his shirt. "This tattoo is so . . . heavy."

I could see the edge of the sun, in the same place as Stellan's, at the top of his spine.

"Even more than my blood," he mumbled, "this *thing* is the weight of my family—of our whole territory!—on my back. Literally."

He snorted with drunken, derisive laughter at his own joke, but just as quickly, his face fell.

"What does it mean?" I asked gently.

He stubbed out his cigarette in an ashtray, and the last bits of smoke curled up toward the lights over the bar.

"Everybody in the Circle gets their family's tattoo on their seventeenth birthday. Family members, of course, but also the Keepers, the house staff . . . everybody." He traced his tattoo with a fingertip, like he knew the lines by heart. "They are a physical sign of our *fidélité*. They mean unwavering loyalty. To the death."

"To the *death*?" So I'd been right about the guy who worked for Liam's family.

He nodded blearily. "As in, we swear to die for the family, and we recognize that treachery can be punishable by death. When you hold as much responsibility as we do, there has to be incentive to stay in line. There are plenty of stories."

I stared at the tattoo. Just like Stellan's. And Jack's. I thought of Jack, desperate for me to come to the Saxons. "Like what?" I said.

"All kinds of things." A rowdy group of guys leaned on the bar right next to me, calling for drinks. I scooted even closer to Luc, who hardly seemed to notice. "Grant Frederick is not . . . tolerant. His Keeper might have refused a kill order, or he might just have talked back when he shouldn't've," he said, starting to slur his words together. "And there're more. Like the Rajesh Keeper who leaked information to a media outlet we don't control. Or the Emir Keeper, who had a relationship with a family member. They got caught . . . you know. *Together*. He was terminated immediately."

My thoughts flashed back to Jack asking me to prom. If being with a family member was grounds for termination, it *really* must have meant nothing.

"Some families are more harsh than others, of course," Luc went on, "but you don't want to test it. And for family members, the tattoos are a constant reminder of our place in our family. And in the world." Luc swirled the ice and lime wedges in his empty glass. "And yet, despite all that power, I can do nothing. Not to stop the Order, not to find clues to the mandate, not even to stop my new baby sister from being married off."

"Married?" That was an abrupt change of subject.

Luc chuckled again, but it was a hollow sound. "Of course, no one finds it odd to be betrothed to an infant. They're all at our home groveling to my parents for the chance. I find it repulsive, but it's what the mandate says, so we will do it."

I wasn't listening anymore. My heart pounded in my ears, off the beat of the music.

Married. The mandate. Betrothed.

The rightful One and the girl with the violet eyes. Their union.

Suddenly, Luc wasn't the only one swaying on his bar stool.

CHAPTER 18

Luc stared at me, waiting for an answer. "Because *union* in the mandate means 'marriage,'" I clarified, hoping I'd misinterpreted. "Right? The girl with the violet eyes marries the One, once you figure out who the One is."

"*Merde.* Why do I say thissthings?" Luc slurred. "I should not talk this way. The mandate, it is good. And, it is *destinée,*" he said, putting air quotes around the word. "'Their fates mapped together.'"

Their fates mapped together. Another line of the mandate—it had to be. I'd been practically kidnapped and almost killed, all so I could be *married off* like a princess in a fairy tale?

I felt myself starting to shake again. It was like the shock had been waiting just under the surface since Prada, held back by a thread that had just snapped. I clenched clammy fingers on my bare thighs.

Luc belched and set his glass down. The music broke into a hard beat, and everyone on the dance floor jumped up and down in unison, hands in the air.

So I was to be married to whoever the Circle decided was the One. If they didn't figure out the mandate, it sounded like the

Saxons would marry me to whatever son they had available. The Dauphins would choose someone to unite me with, if I was their family. If I wasn't, they might kill me so I wouldn't take their baby girl's birthright.

My mom had always known about this. Suddenly, I knew exactly how she must have felt. Trapped. Hunted.

I glanced behind me at the booth where Stellan still perched, talking with Liam and Colette. Colette gestured with a cigarette, her big sleepy eyes laughing like she didn't have a care in the world, even though they'd been talking about a staff member's "termination" a few minutes ago.

The music swelled too loud, and the cigarette smoke was too thick.

"Whasswrong?" Luc squinted one eye.

I scrambled off my bar stool. "Bathroom," I said, and fled.

I shoved past bodies writhing on the dance floor, dizzy from the lights and the heavy bass and the heat. There had to be an emergency exit somewhere.

Stellan appeared by the bar, a head taller than everyone else.

In the second I stood frozen, watching his face come in and out of the lights, he turned and saw me. He must have read something in my face, because his eyes narrowed. I spun on my heel and darted toward the back door I'd seen earlier, shoving it open hard.

The steam hit me first, so heavy it felt like I could drown in it. It took a second for my eyes to adjust to the dim pink light. The room was a long, narrow cave with recesses along the wall. In each one, a steaming fuchsia waterfall splashed down in front of one of the dancing girls I'd seen from the bar.

A short woman with an earpiece and a scowl yelled something

and grabbed my arm, propelling me to a waterfall that was missing a girl.

She thought I was one of the dancers, late for her shift.

I was about to rush back out and find a real exit, but the door opened. Stellan peeked in. I could go with him. Pretend I got lost on my way to the bathroom. But after seeing me run just now, he wouldn't let me out of his sight again.

I leapt onto the pedestal and caught my balance on the slimy stone wall. I let my hair fall in my face and swung my hips to the music, which was muffled like I had cotton in my ears. *Keep walking,* I urged him with my mind. *You were wrong about seeing me come in here. Just keep walking.*

I hazarded a glance over my shoulder. Stellan strolled down the row, an outline in the steam.

Right behind me, his footsteps stopped. I glanced back once more, and his eyes bored into mine.

"What are you doing?" He reached for me.

The next song started, and a plume of sparks erupted behind me, blocking him. If I wanted to get away, it was my chance. I ducked through the waterfall, gasping as it doused my hair and ran down my shoulders.

I was standing on the end of the bar, hundreds of surprised faces turned up toward me. I dashed the water out of my eyes and looked around frantically, and, after a silent moment, whistles and catcalls erupted from all around. I tried to climb down onto a bar stool, and an overly tanned playboy type looked all too happy to set down his martini glass and grab me by the waist. He set me in the center of his group of leering friends, and I swatted a couple of grabby hands as I pushed out of their circle.

An exit sign glowed in a back corner. I dodged a waitress with a tray of shots and hurried toward the door as fast as I could without drawing even more attention. The door opened on a dark street, and cool air rushed over me.

I pushed it closed and ran. I bypassed hiding places that were too close and sprinted into a narrow alley across the street and around the corner. A nest of sleeping cats streaked away in flashes of gray and white and orange, and I huddled behind the Dumpster where they'd been, panting, dripping wet, shaking.

I heard an echo in the quiet night as the door opened and, a minute later, slammed shut again.

I let my head fall back against the cold brick wall and clutched my locket and oh my God the Circle and the mandate and the union and getting married and I was in so far over my head I could barely see the surface. I sucked in gasp after gasp of air.

A year and a half ago. I was fifteen and we were living in New Orleans. The emptiness was bad that year. Lane was a senior with blue-black hair and a lip ring he sucked into his mouth when he smiled. I was wary, sure, but I thought he was bringing me into his group of friends until he had me alone at his apartment and I said no, even though all the "army brats" were supposed to be slutty. He told me to let myself out. A year earlier, Kansas. Mila Anderson and her friends asked me to sit at their lunch table and invited me to a party and walked arm in arm with me down the halls until they finally ditched me at the liquor store in the middle of the night when they realized not every teenager from New York had a fake ID.

Way earlier. Five years old. Chicago. Two neighbors dared me to steal blue speckled bird eggs from a nest on the fire escape. I climbed out, they slammed the window shut, and it stuck. The ground was so far away, I hadn't liked heights ever since. I'd huddled against the stucco wall and clenched my locket in my fist, and then my mom was there. She scooped me up in her arms and saved me. I remembered exactly how she smelled that day, like lavender and sunshine. Like home.

Now I'd flown halfway across the world on a whim, like a gullible idiot, only to find out my family would take advantage of me in a second if they discovered who I really was. Even my own father probably would, if I could ever find him.

I took one last panicked breath, blew it out through pursed lips, and then let my locket fall out of my hand. I was alone, in a wet cocktail dress and stilettos, in the middle of the night, in Istanbul. Maybe giving in to the panic and running wasn't the brightest idea, but it was done. If I was going to fall apart, I'd have to do it some other time.

Across the street, an engine roared to a stop, and I pressed back farther into the shadows. Getting ready to run again, I peeked out and saw a motorcycle at the curb outside the service entrance. Its rider pulled off his helmet.

It was Jack.

CHAPTER 19

My legs were carrying me across the street before I could stop myself.

"What are you doing here?" My hands still trembled, and now I'd added anger and wariness to the toxic brew.

Jack whipped around and took in my wet hair and what I just realized was a wet white dress. I crossed my arms over my chest. His eyes widened a little, but he didn't look as surprised as he should have.

"Get on." He handed me a helmet and gestured to the seat behind him.

I pushed the helmet away. "You were planning to marry me off?"

He dropped his arm with a sigh and got off the motorcycle. "*I* personally wasn't planning to, but yes, that's what the mandate means. I was going to tell you, but you went off with Stellan after Prada." He looked irritated, which made me even more irritated.

I pushed my damp hair behind my ears. "So are you here to kidnap me for the Saxons?"

"Avery, God, no." He paused. "At least, not immediately—"

"Great. Perfect." I stalked away into the dark, my heels clicking on the asphalt. Jack followed. "Leave me alone," I said over my shoulder.

Then I looked back toward the club, toward the dead end, toward the deserted, unfamiliar street. I swallowed.

"I know you're mad." Jack held out his hands like a peace offering. "I'm sorry I couldn't tell you everything immediately. There was a bit of a time crunch, if you'll remember. But I'm assuming you came to Istanbul to find Fitz. That's where I'm going, too."

He took one step closer, and I took one back. A garbage truck stopped down the empty street and lifted a Dumpster with its mechanical arm. "How did you find me?"

"With a tracker I put in your bag at prom," he admitted without hesitation. "It's how I found you at Prada, too."

I threw up my hands. "That's supposed to make me trust you more?"

He ignored me, glancing back at the club. "From the looks of you, I'd say you're trying to get out of here, so let's go." He stalked to the bike and extended the helmet again. "I've already saved you twice when I should have been going straight to Fitz, so I'd really like to get there as soon as possible."

I flinched like I'd been slapped. "Go, then. I never asked you to *rescue* me."

Even as I said it, though, I knew it would be stupid to let him leave. Jack was by far my best chance of getting to Mr. Emerson.

He set the helmet on the seat of the bike and walked back into the halo of the streetlight. "Listen," he said. "I'm sorry. This is difficult for both of us, but I am telling you the truth: I'm not going to force you to do anything. I still think going to the Saxons is the best plan, but . . ." He palmed the back of his neck. "I haven't even told them who you are yet. Okay? They still think you're distant family and that I'm currently retrieving you from a night of clubbing. For now I want you to come with me to Fitz's, make sure he's okay, see what he meant about you, and then we'll talk through the next steps. That's all."

His boots echoed on the asphalt as he turned back to the bike. He hadn't told them? And . . . "Did Mr. Emerson actually say he was in trouble?"

"No. But he's still not answering his phone, and he left me some strange messages." Jack's jaw clenched in the way I was coming to realize meant he was upset. If it really was possible Mr. Emerson was in some kind of danger, that had to take precedence.

"Tell me one thing." I shifted my weight uncomfortably. "My father. You're sure you don't know anything about him?"

Jack hesitated. "I'm not sure of anything."

He frowned in the direction of the club. I watched him tap his fingers on the motorcycle's ignition.

Going with Jack was the best of my limited choices. We'd talk to Mr. Emerson. He'd help me get back to Paris to find my mom. And maybe she'd be able to tell me something about my dad.

"I believe you," I said. "I still don't trust you, but I believe you. I am only coming with you so we can make sure Mr. Emerson is okay, and so I can talk to him. Just so we're clear."

"We're clear," he said.

I took the helmet out of his hand, shoved it on my head, and climbed on the back of the motorcycle.

Istanbul at night was all color, like Mr. Emerson had said in his postcard. Bloodred lights along the river to our left, glittering streets rising to our right like the city was climbing a hill. The cold white gleam of a mosque's dome in the distance, neon storefronts not yet closed for the night.

Straddling the motorcycle in this short, tight dress wasn't easy, but

Jack had shrugged out of his jacket and laid it over my lap. My hips pressed into his, and my arms wrapped around his waist, awkwardly at first, mostly because of the annoyance still lingering between us, but also because I wasn't used to quite so much Other Person's Body touching mine. I could feel the muscles in Jack's chest contract when he turned, and smell his boy smell between his shoulder blades. It made me think back to when he was just a boy I liked. That seemed so far away, and still too close.

Jack swerved around a truck piled high with fruit, and I tightened my grip. I'd imagined riding a motorcycle might be like riding a really fast bike, but it wasn't. Every time he accelerated, it felt like we might fall off, but I'd dig my fingers in and then we were flying, the rushing air around us dragging against my clothes, my hair, my skin.

We stopped at a light, and the smell of sizzling meat turning on a spit in front of a nearby restaurant wafted past.

"Why do they think *union* means 'marriage'?" I said loudly. It was quieter when we weren't moving, but the helmets muffled our voices. "Could they be wrong?"

"They're fairly certain about the translation," he said.

"'Fairly certain' is not a good enough reason to ruin someone's life." To ruin *my* life.

Jack turned around, and his helmet smacked mine with a hollow thump.

"Ow. Sorry." I jerked back and so did he, and I was suddenly even more acutely aware of the ridges of muscle I could feel through his thin cotton T-shirt. I balled my hands into fists, but that was even more awkward, so I let my arms hover, not quite holding on, not quite not.

"Sorry," he said again. I inclined the ear hole on the helmet to hear him. "I didn't mean to be insensitive. It's just that it's all been abstract before now. In the original Greek of the mandate, the word is *gamos*. It translates to 'union' . . . but it also translates to 'marriage.'"

Oh.

The light changed and I had to grab on to him again as we took off, flying down a wide street flanked by rows of shops and restaurants. At the next light, people strolled across the street, and I met the eyes of a girl in robes that covered her from head to toe, wrist to ankle, so just her glittering eyes showed. Then I saw the Louis Vuitton bag slung over her shoulder, and I couldn't help but smile at what to me seemed like a curious contrast but to her was just normal. Even more than Paris, being here felt *foreign*.

Over the rumble of the bike and the distant low beat of drums and some kind of string instrument, I said, "Where exactly did the Book of Mandates come from?"

Jack leaned back, careful to keep his helmet away from mine. "Oracles were important in Alexander's time—like, have you heard of the Oracle of Delphi?"

I shifted on the seat, pulling down on my dress. "Yeah."

"That oracle, others, various seers—they made hundreds of predictions," he continued. "The ones about the future were collected and became the Book of Mandates."

I looked out over the river, where two lit boats passed each other, their reflections rippling in the dark water. "What's the story of this particular mandate?" I said.

The light turned again before he could answer, but after just a few blocks, we got stuck in traffic at a busy intersection. The patio of a nearby bar was filled with well-dressed people laughing and smoking tall hookah pipes, and the sweet scent floated through the night air.

"Before Alexander died, he'd instructed the Diadochi to split his kingdom," Jack called over his shoulder. I was starting to notice that he slipped into professor-speak when he talked about history, like it took effort for him to talk like a normal seventeen-year-old. "But he surprised them. Instead of declaring that he left it to all twelve of them equally, he said, '*Krat'eroi.*' In English, that means, 'To the one who is the strongest.'"

The traffic moved a few feet, and the bike rumbled as Jack inched us forward. He raised his voice to be heard over a portly man in a long robe, selling the mirrored blankets draped over both his arms. "Since then, the Circle has ruled together, as a group of twelve, but the individual families have never stopped trying to determine the one who is the strongest."

He said it like it had capital letters: The One Who Is The Strongest. And then it hit me, and goose bumps rose on my arms. "The One. Like in the mandate."

Jack inclined his head. "Exactly," he called.

"People as powerful as the Circle just don't seem like an ancient cult group who'd believe in a prophecy," I said.

"We're not, exactly." We hadn't moved in a couple minutes and Jack sat up taller to look over the traffic before settling back down with a sigh. "But we leave no stone unturned when it comes to new avenues of power, and finding this tomb would be more than anything we've ever had. It's supposedly far more than just wealth. It's what made Alexander who he was. Whether that means a weapon, or some kind of instructions from him—we don't know, but it's meant to be huge. And with so many of the mandates having come true, we have to try. Plus," he went on, "fulfilling the union—being the One—is so significant, it'll make both the families a dominant force in the Circle no matter what, even if the tomb is never found. So if no one finds more about the mandate, the Dauphins will just pick somebody for a union with the baby girl and try to make everyone accept him as the One, so both families will gain that power."

Like Luc had said. So even if they didn't figure out who was the One, it was true I wasn't off the hook.

The light changed, and we took off again. This time, we turned onto a less crowded street. Jack touched my hand like a warning, then sped up until the lights on the river smeared past. We didn't stop again until we'd pulled up at a block of apartment buildings.

Jack offered me his hand, and I slid off the bike as gracefully as I could.

He stashed both helmets in a compartment under the seat as I attempted to smooth my hair, and we crossed the street toward a modern white high-rise.

"Does the Order fit with the Alexander stuff, or are they separate?" I stepped over a cracked section of sidewalk, careful not to get my heels caught.

"They go back as far as we do," Jack said distractedly. He pulled his phone from his pocket and checked it, and we turned up the walk to the apartment building. "Alexander had a child who would have been his heir, but the boy died young. Some people—mostly those who were in cahoots with Alexander's mother, Olympias—thought the throne should be passed to a member of his extended family. They disliked the Diadochi, so they set out to take them down. They became the Order, and they've grown to hate us more than ever. The Circle do what we feel is best for the world. The Order thinks there should be more autonomy."

As awful as the Order was, they might have had a point. Jack would never speak badly of the Circle, but the notion of such a small group of people controlling so much of what happened in the world still seemed wrong somehow. Probably. I still knew so little about them, I wasn't sure what to think.

Jack ushered me into a sparse but tasteful lobby, and my heels clicked hollowly on the tile.

As we headed to the stairwell, I looked around at the ferns, the seating area, the bank of mailboxes.

Mr. Emerson checked his mail here. Here and in Paris. My sweet pseudograndfather, who let eight-year-old me try on his reading glasses and spent countless flour-covered afternoons teaching my mom and me to make biscuits and cakes and homemade pasta sauce. Who talked with little Avery about books way too old for me, and never treated me like a kid.

Who had known what I was, and the danger I was in, for years. Suddenly, I was a little nervous about seeing him. What did it mean? And what had his text to Jack meant? I didn't doubt he had my best interests at heart, but I couldn't believe the first time I was going to see him in years would be in this context. Assuming he actually was here and everything was okay. I'd feel a lot better once we saw him, for a lot of reasons.

"You said he's your mentor?" We started up the stairs and I thought about taking my heels off—they were killing the backs of my feet—but it couldn't be that far.

"He's a tutor for the Keepers." Jack paused one landing up to wait for me. "I keep forgetting you don't know any of this. Stellan and I are called Keepers. Technically, Keeper of the Keys. It grooms us to be Keeper of the Watch later. The Keeper of the Watch is the family head's right-hand man. He's security, he's an adviser, he helps run the estate."

I nodded. And they were all men, as Stellan had said. In the world of the Circle, even though a purple-eyed girl was so valuable, women generally seemed to be good for marrying off, having babies, and being staff, unless they happened to be needed for something very specific, like Elodie was tonight.

Jack slowed when he realized I was falling behind. "Sorry, it's a fifth-floor walk-up. Anyway, each family has a tutor for their Keepers. That's what Fitz is, but over time he became more of a mentor to me."

Knowing Mr. Emerson, I wasn't surprised.

Jack knocked at a door on the right side of the hall, and when there was no answer after a second knock, he produced a key, slid it into the lock, and swung the door open.

The first thing I saw was blood.

CHAPTER 20

Jack pushed me back into the hallway and pulled a gun from his waistband. "Stay here."

I stared at the blood, a hand clapped over my mouth. The scene from Prada replayed in my head. All the blood. The killer's blood. My blood.

Mr. Emerson's blood.

I ducked inside the apartment, pulled the door shut behind me, and locked it. "Mr. Emerson!" I started to yell, but the words died on my lips when I realized the blood was dry. This hadn't just happened.

Next to the stain, a cell phone was smashed to pieces. I looked around frantically, but at first glance, the room looked just as pristine as Mr. Emerson's apartment had always looked, with the same clean lines and dark colors he favored when he lived in Boston. Not even the magazines on the coffee table had been disturbed. So there wasn't much of a struggle, but they'd hurt him, and now he was gone. Oh God, who would *do* that?

"Fitz!" I heard doors opening all over the apartment. Jack stomped back into the room a second later. "I told you to stay outside," he snapped. "It could have been dangerous."

"It could have been dangerous in the hallway, too," I retorted. "Who did this?"

"The Order. It's got to be, hasn't it?" Jack sat down on the firm gray couch with his head in his hands, stood up, and sat down again. "I should have known. I should have gotten here faster." His eyes were wild as he seized a pillow and whipped it against the wall.

I recoiled. "Hey. Stop." I sat next to him and grabbed him, forcing him to look at me. The muscles in his forearm clenched and un-clenched under my own shaking fingers. "Think. Where would they have taken him? *Why* would they have taken him?"

The heavy rise and fall of his chest slowly regulated. "I haven't got a clue where. As to why . . ."

He cut his eyes to me and I felt like I'd been slapped. Of course.

"It's not your fault," Jack said, pressing his palms over his eyes. "I didn't mean—"

"They took Mr. Emerson to get to me." I raked my hands through my tangled hair. "So, what, they want me to turn myself in? Wouldn't they have left some kind of ransom note?"

Jack nodded. "I was just thinking that. Or . . ." He sat up straighter. "That text he sent."

He was right. I remembered it word for word. *If the worst happens—follow what I've left you.*

"He knew someone was after him," I said. "The text says he left us something. You, I mean. He left *you* something."

"Us." Jack got up from the couch. Only when I noticed how cold my thigh was did I realize our legs had been touching. "I think it's pretty obvious now that we're in this together, whether we like it or not."

I took a deep breath, then got off the couch, too.

Where would you leave a ransom note? It was nowhere obvious. I stalked across the room and flipped through a stack of papers on a modern, dark-wood side table, then studied a bulletin board that had a flyer for a poetry reading and another for a wine tasting, but no note. Next to it was a shelf full of books and vases and picture frames. A little thrill of wrongness stabbed through me, seeing all Mr. Emerson's things from his apartment in Boston.

Jack looked under a stack of magazines on the coffee table, then knelt by the dried blood, inspecting the phone.

I headed toward the kitchen, but stopped short at a shelf. I picked up a small paint-by-number picture of a sunset, with colors that were obviously not meant to fill the spaces. Between the oranges and reds and yellows, splashes of purple and blue and black.

I ran a finger over the little painting. I'd added those other colors because all the sunsets I saw weren't just orange. They had dark spots, too, which made the sunsets even more brilliant. Mr. Emerson had loved it, so I'd given it to him when we moved away.

I swallowed hard. What if we couldn't find anything? What if I couldn't help him? Would I turn myself in? They'd kill me. But if I didn't, would they kill him? I pressed my fist to my mouth.

"Avery?" Jack's voice jolted me back to the present, and I realized he'd been talking to me. "Anything?" he said, and I could feel him watching me, wondering what I was doing.

I shook my head and put the painting back on the shelf. In the kitchen, an empty coffeepot and a clean mug sat on the counter, along with one white bowl on a dish rack. No note, no sign of struggle in here.

"I'm going to check his office," Jack called.

I blew out a deep breath and made one last sweep of the room— and saw something lodged under the coffee table.

A clock. My heels clicked as I hurried across the room. Its face was cracked, and a bloody streak ran across it.

"Jack," I called.

He came back to the living room. I ran a finger over the hands under the bloody glass. They pointed to almost 6:00.

"It probably stopped when they—" Jack swallowed, looking at the bloodstain on the floor. "When it broke." He took the clock and set it on the coffee table.

"I know. If it was five forty-seven a.m. here, what time would it have been in Lakehaven? What time did he text you?"

Realization dawned on Jack's face. He pulled out his phone. "Nine forty-three p.m. Minnesota time." I could see him doing the calculations in his head. "Just a few minutes before this clock stopped."

"If he sent you the text right before this happened," I said, "whatever he left for you has to be here."

"You're right." I could hear the renewed hope in his voice, and we pressed on down the hall, doing a quick inventory of everything we saw before we ended up at an office.

A row of books—history, philosophy, poetry—lined the back of the desk, straight and tidy between their bookends, and just in front of them, three pens sat in a perfect row like soldiers at attention. Also on the desk was a day planner, askew and open to a ripped-out page.

Mr. Emerson wouldn't have left his planner like that by accident.

I went straight to the desk and picked it up. "January thirteenth. Does that mean anything to you?"

Jack shook his head. I looked at the pages nearby. Dentist appointment. Dinner at 7:30.

"Maybe he just ripped out a random page, like to leave a note.

Which would mean it'd have to be around here somewhere." He looked down the hall and paused. I understood his hesitation: even though we were searching for clues, going into Mr. Emerson's bedroom felt like trespassing. I swallowed and headed down the hall anyway—and stopped short in the doorway. The door had been splintered to pieces around the knob.

Jack's eyes went big, and he rushed past me into the room. I inspected the door more closely. It didn't take an expert to tell the door had been locked from the inside and forced open.

"Look." Jack was crouched on the ground, holding three photos.

I hurried across the room, and he handed me a hammered-copper frame with a picture of himself and Mr. Emerson inside, then one of Stellan, of all people. And then . . . a small, folded shot of me.

"These frames are usually in his living room." Jack paced the room, methodically scanning a bookshelf, an art deco dresser, and a bedside table.

"Why does he have a picture of Stellan?" Stellan looked younger and more serious than he did now, and his hair was a lighter blond.

Jack's lips pressed into a hard line. "Fitz sometimes works with the Dauphins, too," he said shortly, and turned away.

"This one is me," I said quietly. I was nine. We'd been cooking, and I was half covered in flour.

I turned the photo of Jack over in my hands, looking for a note, a clue, something. Like on the clock, there was a smear of red across the glass. I wiped it with my thumb and started to stand, but stopped. "Blood," I said.

Jack turned from peering through the slatted blinds. "What?"

"Blood." I jumped up. "Right there. On the floor."

It wasn't easy to see on the hardwood, but droplets of blood led away from where we were standing. One trail led to the bedroom door. The other led into the closet.

We rushed into the closet, following the blood to a safe hidden behind a rack of shirts, a streak of blood marring one crisp white sleeve.

"Do you know the combination?" I said, breathless.

Jack nodded, and spun the lock as I hovered at his elbow. The safe popped open.

Inside was a folded piece of paper with a smeared red thumbprint across its front. The planner page. I grabbed it up, opened it, and read:

Find the three things before anyone else does. Tell no one. My curated collection. Follow from there.

Then, like it was an afterthought:

They're wrong about the mandate.

CHAPTER 21

The *mandate?*" I said. "Wrong how?"

Jack leaned over my shoulder, staring at the note. "I haven't got a clue."

"Maybe they didn't take him just because of me." The guilt loosened its grip. I turned, pushing past Jack out of the claustrophobic closet. "Maybe it's more. What could he know about the mandate? Something about the One?"

Jack followed and took the note. He held it up to the light, twisting it from side to side. "Fitz would have told me if he knew something like that."

I perched on the edge of a white ottoman. Just how many secrets did Mr. Emerson have? "What exactly does the mandate say? The whole thing."

Jack didn't take his eyes off the note as he said,

The rightful One and the girl with the violet eyes.
The One, who walks through fire and does not burn.
The girl, born of the twelve.

Their fates mapped together become the fate of the Circle.
Through their union, the birthright of the Diadochi is
  uncovered.
The riches of Iskander, the power of Zeus, the means to
  vanquish the greatest enemies.
The One, when it is his, becomes invincible.

I drummed my fingers on the ottoman. "Again?" He'd said it so quickly, the words had blurred together, like he'd recited it a thousand times.

He repeated the mandate, enunciating this time.

"Wrong about the mandate," I repeated. "The girl with violet eyes doesn't seem like it could be wrong. What about the other lines?"

Jack rubbed the back of his neck. I could tell he was still trying to wrap his mind around *anything* about the mandate being uncertain. "'Vanquish the greatest enemies' seems obvious. We know what the union is."

"At least you *think* you do," I said. It would be great news for me if that was what was wrong.

Jack gave me a sideways glance. "As I said, it's highly likely our interpretation is correct."

I slipped out of my shoes and stretched my feet against the cool hardwood. "What the Order cares about is the One, right? They're trying to kill him right now. What does it say about the One?" I tried to forget I was talking about a person I was supposed to *marry.* "There's the 'walk through fire' line."

"That could mean any number of things," Jack said, pacing, "but it's accepted to mean a proverbial trial by fire. The One who is the strongest would be able to make it through difficult times."

"We're supposed to find three things," I said to myself. "I wonder if it could be clues about the mandate. About the One. And that's what he thinks they're wrong about."

Jack just shook his head. "If he knew something about who the One was and kept it a secret . . . I just don't know why he'd do that."

I didn't either. "For now it doesn't matter what he means by 'wrong about the mandate,'" I said. "He said to follow what he left. We can think about the mandate stuff if we find anything, but we have to follow his clues first."

Jack's eyes darted to me. I could see the hesitation in them. I knew he really should send me to the Saxons. The longer he didn't turn me in, the more trouble he'd be in if they found out. But telling them would mean they'd want me there right away and we wouldn't be able to help Fitz.

I found the compass points on his tattoo. As Jack stood right now, the north tip of the compass pointed right at me. There was something beautiful about it, but now that I knew what it meant, it seemed sinister, too. With consequences like those in play, could I actually trust him?

"Do you think the curated collection means the Hagia Sophia? He volunteered there, right?" I said, watching for his reaction.

Jack tapped his thumb against his lip for a few seconds, and then dropped it and squared his shoulders with a long exhale. "Yes. We should start there."

If nothing else, I did believe he was worried about Mr. Emerson and would do anything to help. I'd just have to keep my guard up. I nodded and worked my aching feet back into my shoes.

Jack had been pacing from the mirrored closet door to the leather armchair sitting on a sheepskin rug, but now he hesitated in front of me. "I understand how you feel, you know. About the mandate. About all this."

I looked up. "I'm not even worried about that right now. I just want to help Mr. Emerson." I looked down at my hands, folded in my lap. "And I don't think you could possibly know how I feel about it."

He offered me his hand to help me up. "For someone in the Circle," he said, "the union would be a huge honor. For you . . . this isn't your world."

He flicked his eyes to mine, and those old butterflies in my belly gave the slightest flicker of their wings. He let go of my hand.

I swallowed, then rubbed my face. My fingers came away smeared with mascara, and I realized I'd probably looked like a drowned mess this whole time.

"I'm going to wash my face before we go," I said. I needed a second to not think about all this.

Jack nodded. "I need to borrow a shirt from Fitz anyway," he said, rolling his shoulders. The shirt from Prada was a little tight, and stretched taut across his shoulders. The butterflies flapped harder, but I shook them off. What was wrong with me? How could I possibly be thinking about how good he looked in a tight shirt right now?

Jack gestured to the attached bathroom and disappeared back into the closet. I paused at the dresser, where he'd set the picture of him and Mr. Emerson. Mr. Emerson's eyes sparkled from behind his glasses, and even Jack's expression was a little less serious than I was used to. They were standing at what appeared to be the base of a snow-covered mountain.

"How old were you in this picture?" I said. It was so strange that Jack had known Mr. Emerson at the same time I had—it was like we'd been living parallel lives.

"It was my fourteenth birthday." Jack's voice was muffled. "Fitz always said birthdays were the most important holidays, and I could do whatever I wanted if I was with him."

Mr. Emerson had said that to me, too. For my ninth birthday, he'd taken me and my mom to see *The Wizard of Oz*, my favorite movie, at this tiny independent theater that served macaroni and cheese while you watched. It was my favorite birthday of all time.

I stepped into the bathroom but glanced back in time to see Jack's white button-down shirt hit the floor in the doorway. I stared at it for a second too long, then turned on the sink and splashed cold water on my cheeks.

"If I'd wanted to lie on the couch and watch television all day, he would have let me," Jack went on. "But when I turned fourteen, I wanted to climb Mont Blanc."

I dried my face and dug my contact drops out of my bag. I put a drop in each of my tired eyes. "That's in the Alps, right?"

"The peak of the Alps. He told the Saxons it was a training trip. He said he would have taken his own grandson if he'd had one. It was worth it, even if the sunburn lasted for days."

I could see the edge of the picture out the door. Both their noses were bright pink, but Mr. Emerson wore a huge smile.

Jack walked out of the closet, tugging a clean white V-neck T-shirt over his head, and my fingers paused partway through raking my hair back into a ponytail. Then my gaze found the ridges of muscle above his hip bones and I turned back quickly, concentrating hard on twisting my hair tie.

Still, out of the corner of my eye, I could see him study me. He pulled a black blazer from the closet, and held up a cream one for me.

"You should put this on," he said.

I looked down at my skimpy dress, and realized that we were

very much no longer in a club. "Yeah," I said, holding out my hand. "Muslim country and all."

I could swear he blushed. "It's pretty progressive here, actually, but it's just that you're, you know." He studied his shoes, but waved a hand in the general direction of my body. "And that dress is . . . and we're trying *not* to draw attention . . . and I guess it would be respectful . . . Never mind."

He shoved the blazer in my hands.

The last time I'd seen him anything less than perfectly poised was when he was asking me to prom. Was it possible that invitation hadn't been *entirely* fake?

"Thanks," I said. I pulled the blazer on and rolled the sleeves so they wouldn't cover my hands.

Jack leaned over the sink. It felt weirdly intimate, washing up together. I'd done this at sleepovers, of course, but Jack washed his face differently, less carefully. Like a *guy*. I tried not to stare at the way he splashed water everywhere, at how he ran wet fingers through his hair, at the drops of water resting on his eyelashes.

I looked into my own eyes in the mirror again. "Why the eyes? If the Diadochi were his generals, and not relatives, how do the families all have purple eyes?"

"It is odd, genetically, but the prevailing theory is they were all distantly related to start with, and interbreeding over the years concentrated the gene for the eyes."

I handed him a clean towel. Jack scrubbed his hair and it stuck up in all directions. For some reason, right then, I realized why what he'd said about that picture seemed off.

"Wait. You said Mr. Emerson would have taken his grandson hiking if he had one. But he *does*," I said. "His name's Charlie."

Jack stopped still, and slowly lowered the towel. His dark hair hung damply over his forehead. "Did you say Charlie?"

The famous Charlie Emerson. "He used to tell me stuff about his grandson." I backtracked to the dresser and picked up the picture. "We were about the same age, and it's like he wanted us to be friends from afar . . ."

Like a few years after we moved away, Mr. Emerson's Charlie update was about how they went on a long hike for Charlie's fourteenth birthday, and they both got sunburned.

I looked at photo-Jack's pink skin. Real Jack opened his mouth to say something, then closed it again.

No.

"Is your favorite ice cream pistachio with frozen Thin Mints, by any chance?" Jack finally said, tossing the towel on the sink.

It had always been my favorite, and Mr. Emerson said my suggestion had made Charlie a convert. "Is your favorite movie *The Godfather*?" I countered.

"Yes. I—"

I set the picture down with a bang. "*You're* Charlie Emerson?"

He walked past me into the bedroom, a stunned look on his face.

"How? And how did you not realize who I was, if he told you about me?" I went on before he could answer.

"Jack is my middle name. I—" He cleared his throat. "Charles was my father's name. But I already knew Fitz before I started going by Jack. He calls me Charlie. He never showed me your picture. He said your name was *Allie*."

Charlie Emerson was real, standing in front of me, and he thought my name was Allie. "He said you were his grandson."

"He said you were his great-niece." Jack turned around. "I can't believe I'm meeting the girl who thought the first *Godfather* movie was the best. So many people prefer the second, and are obviously wrong."

"What? No! The second was so much better. He told you I agreed with you about the first?"

"He did."

"So did you even like my sundae?"

He bit back a smile. "I've always been partial to coffee ice cream."

My mouth dropped open.

"I'm sorry!" he said, almost laughing. "Looks like Fitz lied to us."

A laugh escaped my throat, and the moment of lightness felt so unexpectedly good, I could have cried. "I can't believe you're— we're—"

Voices came from the other side of the wall, and Jack's head snapped up.

"It's the neighbors," I started, but Jack put a finger to his lips.

"They're speaking English," he said.

Of course. It hadn't sounded strange to me, but here it would. These were people who didn't belong in this building.

The voices stopped nearby. From down the hall, Mr. Emerson's doorknob jiggled.

Jack grabbed the note and handed me the pictures to stuff in my bag, and we ran out of the bedroom.

"It's gotta be here. We must have missed something," came a voice from the hall. The knob jiggled louder. "Didn't you leave it unlocked?"

"It's the Order." Jack made a move toward the door, drawing his gun from his jacket.

I grabbed him. "What are you doing?"

"Capturing them." He shook me off. "Torturing where they're holding Fitz out of them. Whatever it takes."

I was surprised and a little disturbed at the anger simmering in his eyes. "We can't," I whispered. "Mr. Emerson said very specifically for us to find this stuff, and not to let anyone else get it. If we get caught ourselves . . ."

Jack hesitated. He glanced back at the door and ran a hand over his face. Finally, he put his gun away. "You're right. I just . . ."

I nodded. "I know."

"But they're out to get you, too." I could see the logical side of him take over again. "We can't risk them figuring out who you are. Let's go." He glanced around the room and hurried to a small window. He wrenched it open. For some reason, I hadn't considered this would be our way out of here.

He started to climb through, and I hurried to him. "Is there any other way?" I peered out at the four stories to the ground below, fighting vertigo.

A crash from down the hall. They'd kicked in the door. Jack swung both feet onto the fire escape, and offered me his hand. "Not if we want to get out of here alive."

CHAPTER 22

Jack tugged me along the rickety fire escape and adrenaline thrummed through my veins, shooting everything into high focus. The crisp bite of the night air, the acrid scent of incense wafting from another apartment. One of my stilettos sank through the metal grate, and I stumbled, then peeled off my shoes and threw them over the railing, watching the iconic red soles flip end over end. I tried not to notice how long it took them to hit the ground.

"Doing okay?" Jack called over his shoulder.

"Fine," I said through clenched teeth, making sure not to look down. We were running on the sidewalk. On firm ground. On the track at school. Not fifty feet in the air. "I'm fine. It's fine."

The fire escape swayed ominously with each leap we took down the stairs. We ducked under a neat row of wet socks on a clothesline and were just one story up when a shout came from the apartment window. Jack shoved down a rusted metal ladder, which fell with a clang and a sway that was not at all reassuring—then dropped off altogether.

Jack cursed.

The shouts from above got more excited. Two people leaned out the window. One was pale with a shock of red hair, and the other had darker skin—and a shiny black gun in his hand.

"We'll have to jump." Jack swung himself over the edge, then let go. He crumpled when he hit the ground, but rolled and popped up in an instant. "I'll catch you," he shouted.

No. I couldn't. Running along the fire escape was one thing. Throwing myself off it was another. I clung to the railing, searching frantically for another ladder, another staircase.

"Oi, little girlie!" the one with the gun called. I barely had time to register relief that he didn't know who I was before he continued, "I'll give you ten seconds to bring whatever you took from this flat back up here, or I'll have to knock you off that ledge and take it myself!" Even from here I could see him grin like he was enjoying this.

Not good. Really, really not good.

"Jump!" Jack yelled.

A bang ripped apart the night.

A rush of cold air flew past my shoulder, like when you're standing on the sidewalk and a bus drives by too fast. I winced, and the bullet hit the ground at Jack's feet, raising a cloud of dust. Jack danced out of the way. The only thought in my head was that I wouldn't have had time to have a thought if he hadn't missed.

"Avery!" Jack's frustration had turned to panic.

"Just go!" I yelled. "Hide! I'll get down on my own!"

"Are you insane?" he yelled back. "I'm not leaving you."

I sucked in a lungful of cool air.

Above me, the guy started to climb out the window.

"Jump!" Jack shouted again.

Even if he wasn't going to leave me, there was no way I was trusting him to catch me. Ten feet away was a support pole that ran to the ground. I hurried toward it, trying to ignore the sound of footsteps banging on metal.

"No!" Jack yelled. "Jump!"

I lowered my legs over the edge, awkwardly in the short, tight dress. Jack was still yelling. I couldn't tell if the footsteps were still coming closer. I ignored them both and wrapped my legs around the support like a fireman's pole. I squeezed my eyes shut and, with a whimper, let my grip go a little at a time until one hand, slick with sweat, slipped. A sharp piece sticking out of the pole sliced into my thigh.

I fell.

"Jack!" I screamed, and then his arms were around me and we fell with a thud, but he cradled me so nothing but my elbow smacked the ground.

I scrambled off him just in time to see the dark-skinned guy raise his gun again. "Watch out!" I dove into Jack, driving us out of the way as another shot missed us. We barreled into a cluster of trash cans with a metallic crash, then scrambled behind an abandoned couch every cat in the neighborhood must have used as a toilet. Both men disappeared back through the window.

"Thanks," Jack panted.

"You too," I gasped.

Only then did I feel the sting on the inside of my thigh, just above the knee. A river of red ran down my leg and dripped onto the asphalt. I hissed through my teeth.

"Here." Jack dug around in the pockets of his blazer until he found a tissue, and pressed it to the wound.

I grabbed the tissue from his hand and held it in place as he yanked me to my feet. I limped along beside him out of the alley, barefoot.

"There!" a familiar voice yelled, and I whipped around to see four men rounding a corner down the block.

We ran toward Jack's motorcycle, parked at the curb. He got on the bike and I leapt on behind him, pressing myself into his back as we shot away from the curb and into Istanbul traffic. Cars whizzed around us in every direction, their headlights and taillights performing an elaborate waltz to the music of their horns. I clung to Jack like my life depended on it, because it did.

It only took a few seconds to realize we were being chased.

Jack cut off a truck. The bike wobbled, and I slid precariously on the seat. I dug my fingers into Jack's chest and he grabbed my leg, fighting to keep me upright. I gripped the bike hard with my knees, and when we balanced again, he sped back up. The wind whipped so hard in my face that I buried it in the hollow between his shoulder blades. I could feel his frantic heartbeat against my cheek and under my palms at the same time as he sped around a traffic circle, flaunting the rules of the elaborate dance by cutting across all five lanes only to fly back out the way we'd come in. Behind us, a screech and a crunch, and, when I glanced back, a pileup of cars.

The car following us careened around the wreck.

Jack drove up onto a sidewalk, scattering pedestrians, then turned into a dark alley. The cobblestones under us shook the bike so hard, my teeth chattered together, and then we were flying onto another street where two sleek white trams were going in opposite directions. Jack gunned the bike, and we flew straight toward them.

"Jack," I said. No. He couldn't be trying this. This was suicide. My fingers bunched in his shirt. "Jack!"

At the very last second, we shot between the trams, close enough for me to lock eyes with one of the conductors. Then we were out the other side and the trams formed a barrier.

Jack ground the bike to a stop in an alley. We jumped off, and I swept strands of my ponytail out of my mouth as we ducked through a low doorway, emerging in another world of color and sound and—I choked—smell.

It was a market, a huge one, with low, arched ceilings over stalls selling scarves and rugs and gold and silver trinkets and mounds of colorful spices all wedged into a space that seemed too small to hold them.

Even though it was late, hundreds of people still browsed and bargained. Two shopkeepers sitting cross-legged on the floor of their booth under hundreds of colored lanterns glanced up from their tea as we passed, Jack helping me limp as fast as I could.

Down a narrow side aisle, I saw the source of the smell. Dead fish hung all along the back of a stall.

Jack dragged me toward the fish and I gagged, but it was the only deserted stall around. We ducked in and crouched behind the sales counter, and I inspected my leg again. The bleeding hadn't slowed at all, and my tissue was soaked through, my leg slippery with blood.

"We've got to elevate it and keep pressure on it," Jack whispered. "Here."

He produced a knife and slit his own shirt at the waist, ripping off a long strip. He propped my leg on his knee and wrapped the shred of cloth around my thigh, tying it in a knot.

I nodded as I tried to catch my breath, incredibly aware of my bare leg balanced across his lap, and of what that was doing to my very short dress. I tucked the blazer around me as well as I could. Jack peered through the cold glass case of fish heads and innards, and I followed his gaze. "Do you see them?" I breathed.

And then I did. We'd almost been quick enough. Almost, but not quite. A group of men in turbans carrying a rolled-up rug passed the entrance to our aisle—and behind them were all four guys from Mr. Emerson's apartment, staring right at us.

The one who seemed like the leader saw me and grinned. I jumped up. My leg screamed as we dashed out the back of the stall, parting the—thankfully dried—fish like the bead curtains I had on my closet door when I was thirteen.

Footsteps pounded behind us, but at least they weren't shooting. Yet.

Jack grabbed my hand. We raced around a corner, and my heart sank. Dead end. I wheeled around, but it was too late. The leader came into view not ten feet away. This close, I could tell he wasn't too much older than us. He had short, spiky dreads and cinnamon-colored skin, and a dark scar bisected his face from below one eye to his chin. When he saw us, a lopsided grin curved the scar into a grotesque dimple.

Jack yanked me behind him and pulled the gun from his jacket.

The redhead and the other two followed Scarface, guns drawn.

"Give us whatever you bloody kids took from that safe," Scarface said.

Frantically, I searched for something, anything that would give us a few seconds. Shooting in this crowded place would be a disaster. If we could just get out of their line of sight, we could disappear. This place was a maze.

The shopkeeper at the next stall stood plastered against a rack of jars, his eyes wide. Steps away from him, I saw it. His stall had a rickety wooden roof, held up by poles tied to the ground. If I timed it right, and if I could get the Order guys under it, I could crash the roof on them and we'd get those seconds.

"Give me the note," I whispered to Jack.

"We can't let them have it," he said through clenched teeth.

"I have a plan." I pulled him to the side so the stall was between us and the Order.

"You'd better be right," Jack murmured. "Inside left jacket pocket."

I reached around him and stuck my hand in his pocket, feeling around until I found the scrap of paper. He kept the gun trained on the men as I pretended to trip and grabbed the support rope.

"Okay," I said, holding out the note and letting my voice waver like I was afraid they'd shoot us. I nudged Jack, gesturing for him to lower the gun. "Here. Take it."

All four of them darted toward us, and when they were a couple of yards away, I yanked the cord. The stall trembled—and as the red-head reached toward me, its entire top collapsed. His fingers grazed my arm as I jumped out of the way.

What I hadn't realized was that the top of the stall was more than a roof. It was a spice stall, and the top must have been used for extra storage. Bags full of spices tilted and tipped, and finally fell. Red and yellow and cinnamon brown and saffron orange rained down in fragrant cascades. I sneezed once, twice, three times, trying to keep a hold on Jack's back, wiping at my eyes with my other hand.

In the second it took for the men to realize what had happened, we were sprinting down the next aisle, and my heart leapt in triumph.

We didn't try to outrun them this time. Jack ducked into the tiny bit of space between two tentlike shops and pulled me after him, yanking the fabric closed to cover our tracks. We fought off the rippling white canvas, staining it orange and yellow and red on our way to the center of the bazaar.

Finally Jack stopped, so suddenly that I slammed into him.

"Do you think they're—" I started, but he put a finger to his lips and cocked his head to the side. The fabric billowed into us from both sides, and I clamped my mouth shut.

"I think we've lost them," Jack whispered, and I realized it was true. *We* had lost them. Me and Jack. Me and Charlie Emerson. We had done this together. I couldn't have done it without him, and he couldn't have done it without me. We, the two of us, had just jumped out a window. And ridden a motorcycle. And gotten away. I kind of liked that word. *We.*

Jack glanced down at me and his eyes were shining, but not with worry like they so often were.

"You—" He cut off and bit his lip.

"What?"

"Nothing. You're—that was great. Really good." He was panting as hard as I was, the red-yellow-orange dusting his shoulders and across his chest.

I couldn't help but grin. And then I muffled another sneeze in my elbow.

A smile pulled at his lips. "It's the spices. They're almost in your eyes." He reached up to my face but stopped, like he'd thought better of it. "Um." He gestured to my eyes.

I wiped my face and looked back up at him. The dimple came out in his right cheek.

All of a sudden, I realized we were pressed so close between the two fabric stalls that we were practically in each other's arms.

"Come here." Hesitantly, he took my face between his hands. He ran his thumbs under my eyes, along my cheekbones, the tip of my nose. "There you are," he said, in that perfect accent. "All better."

I waited for him to drop his hands, but he didn't. I suddenly realized how infrequently Jack met my eyes. He watched everything else so closely, not missing a detail, always prepared, but he hardly ever looked at *me*. Now his eyes, dark and stormy at the edges, fading to a glowing silver in the middle, held mine, the softness in them crowding out his hard edges.

I could swear he moved a little closer, or maybe I did.

I licked my lips, almost unconsciously, and now he wasn't looking at my eyes anymore; he was looking at my mouth. And now I was looking at his, and his lips parted, and my heart sped up to a flutter—

The fabric billowed again, and we both startled. Jack's hands fell away from my face. "Right," he said. He backed a step away, concentrating a little too hard on fighting off the white canvas.

"Yeah. Right," I echoed. I pulled the blazer tight around me. Had we really just almost kissed? I looked at his mouth again, and quickly away. This was just the adrenaline talking. Nothing else.

Plus, the words *punishable by death* still echoed loud in my head, and the thought of Liam's Keeper, and the Emirs' Keeper, and all the others who had undoubtedly suffered the consequences of going against their families. Jack wasn't just risking his job by not turning me in—he could be risking his *life*. But he was doing it for Mr. Emerson, not me. Wasn't he?

"What now?" I said quickly.

Jack cleared his throat. "I guess we go to the Hagia Sophia. I would say we wait until morning, but the clock's ticking. The Saxons don't care if you're partying in Istanbul and I'm keeping an eye on you, as long as I—and by extension, you—am back in time to prepare for the ball tomorrow."

I adjusted my bag. "So, what you're saying is that we have twelve hours or so to figure out what Mr. Emerson meant and how it relates to this thing the most powerful people in the world have been trying to find for centuries."

Jack ran a hand through his hair. "Right."

I blinked. "Then we'd better get going. I'm sure you have connections that could get us in even though it's the middle of the night, but I was thinking maybe we shouldn't draw attention to ourselves."

He cocked his head to one side. "I was thinking that exact same thing. If anyone in the Circle knew what we were up to, they'd be on us in seconds, and they wouldn't be happy. But how—"

I glanced down at my dress. "I have another idea."

CHAPTER 23

We sat at the end of the wide, tulip-lined walk to the Hagia Sophia. The postcard hadn't done the massive structure justice. It glowed orange gold against the night, its four minarets pointing to the sky like sentries.

Behind us, its twin, the Blue Mosque, gleamed like a mirror image. With their manicured lawns and palm trees lit from beneath, the scene struck me like something you'd see at Disneyland.

I wished we were at Disneyland.

I prodded carefully at the new bandage on my leg. We'd picked up butterfly bandages, painkillers, and flip-flops on our way out of the market, and Jack had shown me how to close the cut, musing that I really would know first aid by the time we were finished. His touch was more tentative on my thigh than it had been on my shoulder earlier.

Now he checked his watch. "Three thirty-two," he said, and we watched a pair of security guards stroll past the Hagia Sophia's front entrance, then continue on their route.

He sat a careful distance from me—a distance that said he was still thinking about what almost happened in the market, too. I couldn't help but look at his mouth again. Jack had the kind of mouth that makes you overly aware of your own—full, soft, almost pouting. He caught his lower lip between his teeth, and I pressed my own lips together and turned away.

The cold of the stone fountain's edge bled through my thin dress, and I shivered, wrapping my hands around the warm, foil-wrapped kebab we'd bought from a street vendor on the way here. It was hard to think about eating right now, but I hadn't eaten in forever—since back at home, maybe?—and the incredible smell wafting from the kebab Jack was already eating was making my stomach rumble.

I started to peel back the foil on mine, but my phone vibrated. I jumped to scoop it out of my bag. I'd assumed my mom would be on a plane until the morning, but I couldn't stop hoping. It wasn't her, though. It was Stellan. This was the eighth time he'd called.

I tossed the phone back into my bag. "Why is Stellan so worried if the Dauphins don't know who I am?"

Jack tensed, just like he did every time Stellan's name came up. It was obvious the two of them had a complicated history.

"You're his assignment, even if he thinks you're just a houseguest," he said tersely, taking another bite. His white shirt, with its mutilated hem and spices smeared across the chest, looked orange in the streetlight. "He's in line for a position in Russia if he proves himself. He can't slip up at all."

"Russia? Near his family?"

An ice cream vendor pushed a cart down the street, tinny music blaring from his speakers.

"Near his sister. His parents are dead."

Stellan hadn't mentioned that. The more I learned about the Circle and the Keepers, though, the more I wasn't surprised he didn't have a normal, happy childhood. He'd clearly thought about the concept of *toska* way before we met. *Something's missing,* he'd said. *You ache for it down to your bones.*

I could tell Jack didn't want to talk about Stellan, but I couldn't help asking how his parents died.

"There was a gas leak, and their building blew up. Stellan and his sister survived," Jack said. "That's why he came to the Circle later than usual . . . Long story."

Wow. *That* was awful.

"Was it the Order?"

Jack shook his head. "Accident."

"Why do you hate the Order so much?" I said. It had been weighing on me since Mr. Emerson's apartment. Jack had looked ready to rip someone's head off with his bare hands. That was more than anger over Mr. Emerson.

Jack rubbed a hand over his face. "Alistair Saxon wasn't meant to be head of the Saxon family. His older brother was. Almost twenty years ago, the Order killed him and their father, and it caused a lot of upheaval. The Saxons' animosity toward them is . . . special. Even before the recent attacks."

So Jack had been trained to hate the Order. And it wasn't unjustified.

We sat in silence for a minute. Finally Jack took another bite of his food, and I followed suit. My eyes fluttered shut in ecstasy at the spicy lamb and warm flatbread and the creamy, minty sauce. I'd had no idea I was this hungry.

"How long have you been with the Saxons?" I asked, taking another bite.

Jack finished his kebab and folded his foil wrapper in half, and in half again. He didn't answer for a second, and I wiped my fingers on a napkin. Maybe this was an off-limits topic.

He unfolded the piece of foil and cleared his throat. "I've been with the Saxons from age four."

I stared at him. I should have assumed it had been a while—he would have been about ten when Mr. Emerson started giving me Charlie updates—but the thought of the Circle training little kids shocked me. Especially training them to be Keepers. I'd seen Stellan kill someone, and the way Jack handled a gun made it clear he was very comfortable with it, which I didn't like to think about. Their *training* obviously involved a lot more than a kid should be exposed to. "Four years old?"

"Yes." Jack stared straight ahead, elbows on his knees. The breeze rustled the palm trees.

"Why . . . ?" I trailed off, already regretting the question. Whatever the answer was, it couldn't be good.

"My mother died giving birth to me. My father gave me up." He must have anticipated my next question. "It's good money, and my father never wanted kids anyway."

I opened my mouth, and closed it again.

Jack sat up straight, and wiped at a spot of blood on his shirt. My blood. Again. "Everyone who works for the families is related to them. Usually in-laws . . . not in the direct bloodline. Enough for us to have an ingrained loyalty, but not enough to make it inappropriate to be employed by them," he said, like he had to justify his life to me. Explain choices he didn't even make for himself.

"You don't have to feel sorry for me," he said defensively, even though I hadn't said anything. He crushed the foil in his fist. "I've never wanted for anything."

I choked down a bite of lamb that had gone dry in my mouth. If he really believed that, he'd led an even sadder, lonelier life than I had.

"Saxon took me in when no one else wanted me," he said. "He's the closest thing to a father I have. Him and Fitz. But it's enough."

He stood and crossed to a nearby trash can. I watched his back.

Jack was so confident, and strong, and mature, and if you didn't look closely, there was nothing about him to suggest the little boy he used to be. But I could see it. It was in his eyes or in the set of his shoulders. In those rare seconds when he was less guarded, there was something a little lost.

"I've never had a father," I said when he came back. "I don't even know what it's like to kind of have one."

"You don't know anything about him at all?" Jack said after a second. "You haven't seen a photo?"

I grasped my locket. "One picture, but it's really old and fuzzy." I sat up straighter. "He seemed to look kind of like me. Dark hair, dark brows. Do any of them look like that?"

Jack rubbed his jaw with one thumb. "I don't know. I mean, most of them have dark hair."

I bottled up the thoughts of my dad and put them away. I'd let my desperation to know something about him override my good judgment once, when I said yes to coming to France, and I wasn't going to let it happen again. And right now, my good judgment still said to help Mr. Emerson, then get as far away from the Circle as I could, as fast as I could, whether I'd figured out who he was or not.

Jack checked his watch again and glanced from the guards, to the other side of the plaza, to a group of drunk tourists meandering in the street. Occasionally, spray from the fountains misted our backs.

The duo of bored-looking guards crossed in front of us again, then disappeared around the side of the building. Like clockwork, another guard strolled to the front doors, said a few words to the sentry posted there, and continued on his rounds. If our calculations were correct, this would mean the door guard would be alone for the next thirteen minutes.

"Ready?" Jack said.

I nodded and put on his sunglasses. The gold-rimmed Aviators were way too big for my face, which was perfect.

Jack stood and marched toward the doors. After a minute, the guard peered around him at me, and I held my breath. We were counting on an American pop star being famous enough all over the world for this random security guard to recognize her.

Jack waved me over. Heart knocking against my rib cage, I walked up to the doors, feeling very, very small as I took in how big the building really was. I tried not to show it. Krissy Silver would think she was entitled to be here. She had had six number one Billboard hits last year alone—or at least, that's what they said at the awards show where she wore this dress. Elodie had said I looked like her, and it was true enough—Stellan probably would have called her a porcelain doll, too. I could only hope the guard agreed. I thrust my shoulders back and put a bored, haughty look on my face.

The guard peered at me dubiously from behind unruly brows that hung down into his eyes. I gave him a condescending smile.

Jack told him in Turkish that I was only in town for the night, and that I was very religious and wanted to see some of the Christian frescoes. "You can let us in, can't you?" I said, batting my eyelashes until I realized he couldn't see them behind the sunglasses. I didn't look enough like her to take them off.

Jack translated, and the guard responded gruffly, scratching his mustache. I held my breath. The guard reached into his pocket.

I grabbed Jack's arm, ready to run, but he put a steadying hand over mine and nodded to the guard's hand. A cell phone.

"He wants a picture for his daughter," Jack said. "And an autograph."

I let out a breath through my teeth, and smiled nervously for the photo. We'd be long gone by the time his daughter told him I was a fake.

"Let's go inside," I said pointedly. Jack spoke to the guard, and he unlocked the doors.

I shivered as we stepped over the threshold. As warm as the night was, the inside of the building was cold in that way stone structures sometimes are, like they don't want to let warmth in.

The guard followed us. That wasn't part of the plan.

His excited chatter echoed in the cavernous space, and Jack shrugged hopelessly and translated. When Istanbul was sacked by Sultan Mehmed in the fifteenth century, he was so awestruck by the Hagia Sophia that, rather than destroying it, he converted what had been a church into a mosque. Since it became a museum in the 1930s, restorations had uncovered some of the Christian murals that had been plastered over with Islamic art, so both were represented.

We crossed the threshold into the central room, and my eyes were drawn upward. As huge as the Hagia Sophia looked from the outside, it was nothing compared with the inside. The dome was so high above us, and so wide open, I felt dizzy. The largest cathedral in the world for almost a thousand years, the guard said.

Like the rest of Istanbul, you could tell it was a crossroads. The spears of moonlight through the windows glinted off a mural of Jesus edged in gold leaf, and above it, giant circular medallions adorned with golden Arabic letters looked too new and modern in the ancient building, like someone had Photoshopped them on. I pushed my sunglasses onto the top of my head to get a better look at a second story running along the sides of the main nave, barely visible through high archways.

The guard turned back around and I smiled at him, but he frowned.

My sunglasses. I shoved them back onto my face, but his hand was already moving to his radio. In a blink, Jack had his hand to the guard's neck. He crumpled to the floor.

"What did you *do*?" I whispered.

Jack lowered him to the floor. "Nothing permanent. He'll wake up with a headache in ten minutes. Let's go."

Without the guard's voice, it was eerily quiet, making the empty space seem even more cavernous. I slipped out of my flip-flops and dangled them from my fingers so they wouldn't clap against the floor and give us away, and we hurried along the dark edge of the museum.

"So what is Fitz's curated collection?" Even my whisper seemed to echo.

"He must have put together some pieces. Here." Jack stopped by an information board listing the current exhibitions. "First floor . . . *Ming Dynasty Bronzes*. Probably not."

I ran my finger down the board to keep my place in the low light. "Art deco, Japanese calligraphy . . ."

"What about that one?" Jack said over my shoulder, and his breath stirred my hair. My neck tingled, and I ignored it.

"*France in the Napoleonic Era?* Seems more like we'd be looking for ancient Greek stuff."

"Look." Jack reached across me to point at the board, just below where I'd been looking.

"*Curated by volunteer docent Emerson Fitzpatrick.*" I scanned the rest of the listing. "North gallery."

CHAPTER 24

We ran by the passed-out guard and up a wide, dark flight of stairs. I stumbled, and Jack grabbed my arm to steady me, and then his hand traveled down to mine and closed around it.

"Would he really have left something important in such a public place?" I whispered. I turned my hand to meet his and our fingers threaded together, a warm spot in the dark. Our footsteps synced as we ran up the steps.

"If it's something the Circle's interested in, leaving it in plain sight might be the best way to hide it," Jack whispered. "They've already checked the collections of every known museum in the world. He could have slipped something new in after they checked this one. It's genius, actually."

"If we can figure out which thing from the collection he's talking about." A faint light shone ahead, and we emerged on the second-story balcony I'd seen from the ground. I took my hand back, and it felt cold. "They're looking for other stuff about the mandate, right? Like, other books?"

"Or artwork with a new mandate or something more about this

one inscribed on it . . . It could be anything. And for all we know, this is something different from the mandates entirely."

Jack nodded his head left, and I went right. The only illumination was moonlight streaming in from the windows overhead, so I had to lean close to see what was in the glass case on each pillar and on the matching informative plaque. A porcelain bust, a decorative plate, a necklace.

"Anything?" Jack's whisper echoed in the quiet.

"No." After the next few pieces, I let out a frustrated sigh. "How are we supposed to know—" I stopped short.

On the next plaque, in the bottom right corner, was something that hadn't been on any of the others. "What the . . ."

Jack hurried across the room, his steps hushed.

"What?" he whispered. He leaned close, studying the thick gold band on a pillar under the glass. But it wasn't the bracelet I was interested in.

"That symbol," I said.

He squinted at the plaque, and I remembered something. I still had my house keys in my bag, and a tiny key-chain flashlight on them. That would have been useful this whole time.

"What is it?" Jack said again. In response, I plucked my locket from my chest. I shone the light on it, then on the plaque.

There, on the plaque for item J-13, *Copper Bracelet*, was the symbol from my locket. I'd always thought it looked like a Celtic knot, but I'd never seen this exact one anywhere else—until now.

Jack took the locket from my hand. "Where'd you get this?"

"My mom gave it to me when I was little," I whispered.

He let the locket fall back to my chest, then grabbed the flashlight and shone it on the bracelet. It was encrusted with jewels in the shape of some kind of winged creatures, and—

"An inscription," he whispered. "That has to be it."

What Mr. Emerson was expecting us to do with a bracelet, I wasn't sure, but if there was an inscription, we'd probably find out. "Okay, how are we going to get it?"

"It'll be alarmed," Jack said, circling the pillar.

I looked inside. I didn't see any trip wires. "See anything?" I said.

Jack checked the next pillar over. "This one has an obvious security setup. Maybe Fitz left the bracelet without an alarm on purpose."

I glanced in the direction of the stairs, expecting a guard's boots to come clomping up them at any moment. "Try it?"

Jack nodded.

I grabbed the foot-wide cube of glass.

To my surprise, it lifted off easily. Jack grabbed the bracelet and pocketed it.

I set the glass back down with a low *thunk* and held my breath. Nothing. No alarm. A smile tugged at the corners of Jack's mouth.

And then the darkness exploded with a shriek of a siren. It was so shrill, I clapped my hands over my ears, but I still knew what Jack was saying.

Run.

We ran down the same stairs we'd come up, but halfway down, pounding feet and shouts turned us back. Before we made it ten feet down the gallery, shouts came from that direction, too.

Jack grabbed my hand and we froze, spotlighted by the squares of moonlight on the floor. Trapped.

The shouts reached the top of the staircase.

Jack took off again, pulling me with him. We were headed to the railing overlooking the main floor.

I stopped, tugging on his hand. "I'm not jumping off there. There has to be another way."

He yanked me close, his face inches from mine, eyes flashing black. "Trust me."

He climbed over the railing and hid behind a pillar. Trying to do it my own way hadn't worked out so well on the fire escape, so even though everything in my body said not to, I took the hand he offered and trusted him.

Twenty feet away, a second railing would have kept us safe, but orange construction tape told me why there was no railing here. I just had to not look down. If I didn't look down, it'd be okay. Just don't— I looked down.

There was nothing at all between us, huddled on a foot-wide ledge, and the cold marble floor three stories below. I clutched at Jack with both hands. One of his feet cartwheeled in the air.

I bit back a scream and squeezed my eyes shut, and the next thing I knew, my face was pressed into Jack's chest, feeling his heart beat frantically, and one of his arms was locked around me. "Don't move," he breathed into my hair.

I wasn't planning on it. Seconds passed that felt like hours while the voices circled our hiding spot and flashlight beams played over the walls and the floor below.

A set of heavy footsteps stalked to the railing a few feet away. Jack's fingers tightened on my back, and I curled farther into him, making us as small as possible.

I opened one eye in time to see a flashlight beam raking across the floor far below, and sweeping quickly toward us. I felt Jack's whole body tense.

Not quite believing I was doing it, I let go of Jack. I took one step away, then another. He followed, and right before the light hit us, we were around the other side of the pillar, hidden.

Jack held out his arm again, and I sank into him gratefully.

The voices had finally retreated, and I'd almost started to breathe when a gunshot reverberated through the cavernous space. I jumped so hard, I nearly fell again.

Jack leaned around the pillar, trying to see.

More shouts, in a language I couldn't understand. The sound of something heavy hitting the floor. Another muffled gunshot. Glass breaking.

"Here! This case is empty," yelled a new voice with a thick and recognizable British accent. Jack cursed under his breath. Somehow, the Order had followed us, and they'd just taken out all those guards. They weren't messing around.

"All right, kids," another voice called. Scarface. "Let's all of us be logical now. I don't know who you are, and I don't care, which means I don't care about putting a bullet in your meddling little skulls. We know the old man knew something. We just want to know who the One is."

He paused like he actually thought we'd respond. I looked up at Jack and widened my eyes. That really *was* what Mr. Emerson meant. He knew what the whole Circle—and the Order—were searching for.

"All right, then," he said. "I'll make this easy. Give us what you took here and from the old man's flat, or he dies."

Jack drew a tight breath. I squeezed my eyes shut.

Would they really kill him? No. I was pretty sure. They'd keep him alive for information, or for bargaining. Or, if they found out, to trade for me.

I clenched my teeth hard, but shook my head up at Jack. He squeezed my shoulder, and I knew he agreed. Mr. Emerson specifically didn't want them having it, so we wouldn't hand it over. At least, not yet.

"Gonna check downstairs again," said the voice I knew was the redhead. "The Commander'll kill us if we lose this stuff to a couple of kids. Like, he might literally kill us."

The Commander? I raised my eyebrows at Jack, and he shook his head.

"We're not going to lose it," Scarface retorted. "Chaz, take the front entrance. Jer, find the old man's office. I'll look downstairs."

We waited until we couldn't hear their footsteps anymore, then I whispered, "Let's go."

Jack put his hands on my waist and lifted me over the railing. He vaulted over after me, and this time we reached for each other's hands at the same time as we sprinted down the stairs and out the first emergency exit door we saw.

CHAPTER 25

A few blocks away, Jack collapsed against a brick wall on a dark street, and I leaned beside him, panting. Somehow, we'd done it again. We'd gotten away, and we had Mr. Emerson's first clue. I didn't mean to, but I started laughing, at the adrenaline, at the relief, at the terror, at the ridiculousness of it all.

Jack stared at me for a second, then his mouth twitched, and then he was grinning, and I was laughing so hard, there were tears running down my cheeks.

They said intense situations could bring people closer than knowing each other for years. I suddenly understood what that meant.

Everything felt sharper, stronger, more intense, too clear, like it had after Prada. Like almost dying made me realize how very alive I was. Right now, I was so alive, it hurt. The tears took a minute to stop after our laughter died out.

I leaned my head back against the rough stone wall and looked up. My favorite constellation hung low in the sky above the Istanbul skyline. Its real name was the Pleiades, but I always called it the tiny dipper, because it looked like the mini version of the Big and Little Dippers.

The myths said the Pleiades were seven sisters, daughters of Zeus. Orion loved them all, but Zeus wouldn't let a lowly hunter have them, so he made his daughters into stars. They said Orion loved them so much, he still followed them across the sky every night, and sure enough, the constellation Orion hung in the sky, not far from the tiny dipper. They looked lower on the horizon than they did at home, but they were still there.

I'd always loved the stars, and the tiny dipper in particular, because no matter where I was, no matter where we moved, it was always the same. The last time I'd seen it was in Lakehaven, about a week ago. Or maybe a lifetime.

Jack took a deep breath beside me.

"How do you think they found us?" he said just as I said, "What's your star wish?"

"What?" he said.

"What?" I said. "Sorry. Yeah. I have no idea how they found us."

Jack was quiet for a second, and when I glanced over at him, he was looking at the sky, too. "What's a star wish?" he said. A garage door down the block ground open and a white car drove out, its headlights blinding me for a second as it went by.

I was about to say we should get back to the clue, but Jack was still looking up at the stars. "Someone I knew used to say your star wish is the thing you want the most in the world," I said. "The one thing you always wish. On stars, on birthday candles, when the clock says 11:11."

He tilted his head like a question.

"You don't have one?" I said. I pushed off the wall, the uneven brick cool under my hands.

He shook his head and crossed his arms over his chest, his eyes still on the sky.

I crossed my own arms. "I don't have one either," I whispered.

"Why?" he said after a second.

"Because it's worse to wish for something that's never going to happen and be disappointed than to never wish for anything at all," I said, studying my chipped toenail polish.

"Is that why you said no to prom?"

I looked up sharply. His eyes went wide like he was just as surprised to have said it as I was to have heard it. "I mean," he said. "I didn't mean—never mind. Sorry."

He pushed off the wall and stuffed his hands in his pockets. "So, your—um. How are you doing? I never asked if you're feeling okay after everything? Learning about all this in one day, and Fitz, and the Prada mess . . ."

I couldn't help but smile at his rambling. And wonder.

"I'm fine—" I started to say automatically. But I wasn't. As much as I said I was "fine," I almost never meant it. I was such a liar.

"No," I said. "I'm not fine. It sucks." God, that was freeing. "I come here thinking I have family, then I almost get killed, find out I'm going to be used for some insane ritual thing, and someone who matters more than most of my actual family is kidnapped. It's been a pretty crappy day, actually." I bit my lip. "So no, I'm not fine."

The word echoed in the quiet night air. I stalked down the street. Don't care. Don't want. Don't get attached. I'm *fine.*

Jack caught up with me. Without a word, he held out his hand. I stopped and stared at it.

I wasn't longing for anything, I'd told Stellan, and it was true, in a way. But maybe that was exactly what I was missing. *Letting* myself ache for something, even if I wasn't guaranteed a happy ending. It wasn't like I'd never wanted things, but I'd always tried to hold it back. I'd always forced myself to remember what a bad idea it was.

But I couldn't keep doing that. I *did* care. I *did* want. I wanted to save Mr. Emerson. I wanted to hear my mom's voice. I wanted Jack to say *we* again. To be part of a "we" at all. To meet my father, my family, even though I knew I shouldn't want that. Just like I shouldn't be noticing the flush on Jack's cheeks, and shouldn't be remembering how much safer I felt on that ledge when his arms were around me. All the wanting was rushing over me in a wave.

I grabbed my locket and twisted it. The little picture inside of me and my mom, just us, alone always. We were fine. It was *fine.* I punctuated the word with a yank on the necklace—and felt a *snap.*

The necklace came off in my hand, the delicate clasp twisted and broken.

I stared at the pretty gold filigree. It had been around my neck almost my whole life. I felt so light all of a sudden. I stuffed the necklace into my bag and took Jack's hand.

Toska. Wanting something you might not even understand. How was it that other languages could express things so much better than ours? And how had Stellan, of all people, seen that about me when I didn't even know it about myself?

Jack walked next to me, his hand wrapped solidly around mine, until my breathing calmed. Pretty soon we were out of the quiet residential area and onto a bigger road with dried gum splotches all over the sidewalk and storefront after barred storefront. A rat scurried across the road in the orange glow of a streetlamp. I cleared my throat and wiped my eyes with my free hand. I hadn't even realized they were wet. "I wonder how the Order found us. They didn't get close enough to plant a tracker."

"I was wondering the same thing," he said. "Maybe our phones somehow? I thought they'd have to know our numbers, but there's lots of tech out there."

"That's not good. Does that mean we should get rid of them?" Now our linked hands swinging between us felt awkward. I used the excuse of getting my phone out of my bag to extract mine.

Jack pulled his phone out of his pocket, too. "Probably, since they could be tracking us right now."

I shot a paranoid glance over my shoulder, but there was nothing but the occasional car speeding by, taking advantage of the sparse early morning traffic. We stopped at a tall office building with a fountain running along its front wall.

I typed out a text to my mom about not having my phone anymore, then reluctantly handed it to Jack. That phone had been with me through our last three moves.

"Sorry," he said, and hurled both phones so they shattered against the fountain's edge and fell into the water.

"I hope it's the phones," he said after a minute. "I hope it wasn't that they got him to talk."

I didn't want to think about that. "If they got him to talk, they'd know everything. They wouldn't need us anymore."

Jack nodded. From not too far away, a low, melodic chanting echoed across the quiet city. "Call to prayer," Jack said, and looked at his watch. "Is it really almost five thirty? We should probably get going with this."

I nodded. "So the bracelet is the first of the three things?"

Jack pulled it from his pocket and studied it. "Seems that way."

"Can I see it?" I plucked the bracelet from his palm. It was heavy and warm in my hand, decorated with a winding vine of words that ran between two rows of small jeweled insects.

"I think it's in French. What does it say?" I asked.

Jack took it back and read, "*He watches over our lady, above the sacred site. Where he looks, it will be found. When it is found, my twin and I will reveal all, only to the true."*

I rubbed my eyes. I was starting to realize how tired I was. "So it doesn't sound like something about the mandate at all. It sounds like a clue, like maybe it's directing us to the next of the three things."

Jack squinted at the bracelet. "But it says 'when it is found,' like you first have to find something to decipher."

I felt a flare of exasperation at Mr. Emerson for sending us on this chase rather than just putting the things in the safe and leaving a note about what they meant. But I immediately felt bad. Anybody could have opened the safe. He'd never have us do something this risky if it wasn't important.

I watched Jack's hands turning the bracelet over and over again, and ran through the clue in my mind. Suddenly, something clicked. "Or," I said, excited, "like the 'he' is the next clue, and what he's look-ing at is the third. We have to assume this is pointing us *somewhere*, right? Maybe if we figure out the 'he,' we can see where."

Jack stopped fidgeting. "You're right."

"'Our lady,'" I said. "Do you think that refers to the Virgin Mary? There's probably Virgin Mary artwork in the Hagia Sophia. And maybe there's some other artwork above it? Watching over it?"

"We don't know it's in the Hagia Sophia. There's Virgin Mary artwork *everywhere*. I mean, maybe it's not even in Istanbul." Jack sighed. "The inscription is in French, so . . ."

We started walking again. The scent of incense and the low, sul-try strains of sitar music drifted out from an open window at the back of a shop.

"The bracelet looks old," I thought out loud, pulling the blazer tighter around me against a sudden briny breeze. "Even the engraving. It's not like Fitz did it himself. Whoever engraved it assumed the next point would be around for someone to find. So it's probably more permanent than a museum piece."

Jack turned the bracelet over in his hands, and I watched it flash in the headlights of a passing car.

"Translate it again?" I said.

He said it in English again, then said, "In French: '*Il veille sur notre dame, au-dessus du site sacre. Où il regarde, il se trouve. Quand il est constaté, mon jumeau et je vais révéler tous, pour le vrai.*'"

"Wait." I replayed the words in my head. "Notre-Dame. Like the church in Paris?"

"'*Notre dame*' just means *our lady*. It's not capitalized like it would be if it meant the church . . ." Jack rubbed the back of his neck. "But Fitz's apartment in Paris is close to Notre-Dame."

"That's something, I guess, but if he didn't write the clue, it shouldn't matter."

"You're right. But . . ." Jack's face screwed up in a frown, and I could see the wheels turning in his head. "Wait. I just remembered something. The insects all over the bracelet. Do they look like they could be bees?"

They were small and winged. I couldn't tell much beyond that. "I guess."

"We got this from a Napoleon exhibit. Bees were Napoleon's symbol. He wore them on his clothes, decorated his residences with them . . ."

"A symbol he wore and decorated with? That sounds familiar." I gestured to his tattoo.

"Oh," he said. "Yes. Napoleon was a Dauphin, but he liked to differentiate himself from the others in the Circle, so he used bees as a symbol of his own along with the Dauphins' sun symbol."

"What does it have to do with the inscription?" I said.

Jack took the bracelet back, read the inscription again, shaking his head. "Of course. You know how I told you it said 'the sacred site'? *Sacré,* with an accent over the *e,* means 'sacred.' *Sacre* without an accent, like it is here, means 'coronation.' It actually says 'the coronation site.'"

"So?"

"So, Napoleon was crowned at Notre-Dame."

My heart skipped. "Notre-Dame. We're going back to Paris."

Back to Paris meant back to the Circle. Back into the clutches of this hugely powerful group who would lock me up in a second if they discovered who I was.

But it might also mean finding my mom, if she really was headed there. And it meant being closer to whichever of the Circle was my family.

I looked up at the sky. "I used to have a star wish," I said.

Jack looked up.

"My father. I wanted him to come back more than I wanted anything else in the world. My mom told me he left us when I was a baby, but still, he was every wish when I was little."

We'd made our way back to the water. A lone fisherman leaned on the railing over the river, his rod propped beside him.

"You said Alistair Saxon and Mr. Emerson were almost like fathers to you." I hesitated. "What's it like?"

Jack ran his thumb over the jeweled engraving. "Not like I exactly have had the normal experience, either, since my real father had no interest in me, but in my mind, it's the feeling of having someone you know is always there for you. Who wants to protect you."

For a second Jack's steely exterior chipped, and I could see another small hint of the person underneath, one more piece to the puzzle of who he really was. And for one more second, I allowed myself to admit that I was kind of starting to like that person. And that, in addition to my own fears about going back to the Circle, I was worried about him.

I glanced up at the bruise under his left eye. He got it somewhere between the prom and Prada, and I was willing to bet it was a punishment for letting me go off with Stellan. And he'd gotten a couple official-sounding calls through the night, like they were starting to get suspicious.

"Luc told me what 'terminated' means," I said. "And about what happened to the Fredericks' Keeper, and the Rajesh Keeper, and the Emirs'."

Jack tucked the bracelet into his jacket.

"Saxon wouldn't . . ." I went on. "If you were caught with me. *Helping* me, I mean . . ."

He cleared his throat. "The Emir family don't allow their Keepers as close to them as many families do, but Rocco was different. He was in their inner circle. He was known for being the best at what he did. And still, the second they found out . . . They say Emir made the daughter who was caught with him pull the trigger herself."

I swallowed. "But not every family is like that."

Jack rubbed a thumb over the tattoo on his forearm. "I'm aware of the consequences of everything I do."

When it was clear he wasn't going to say anything more, I blew out a long breath. I guess it was his choice. "If all of the Circle is going to be at the ball," I said, "do you think my father will be there?"

"Yes," Jack said without hesitation.

I curled my hands into fists and watched the first hints of sunrise glint off the Istanbul harbor. "Let's go to Paris."

CHAPTER 26

I yawned and squinted into the morning sun, then rooted around in my bag for my sunglasses. It was a languid, hazy morning in Paris, the kind of morning that should be used for a stroll through a garden overflowing with tulips, followed by a picnic along the cobblestoned river walk by the Seine. As we walked over the bridge to Île de la Cité, where Notre-Dame rose against the blue sky, the crowds below made it obvious that half of Paris had the same idea.

I hugged Mr. Emerson's blazer tighter around me. As tired as I was, I hadn't been able to sleep much on the small private plane Jack had waiting in Istanbul. I'd had to ask him how many planes each family had. All he'd said was "Enough."

He hadn't slept, either. He'd taken off his blazer and hung it in the plane's closet, then changed into a clean shirt he had stashed there, but that was all the concession he'd made to getting comfortable. He'd spent the whole trip hunched over the bracelet and Mr. Emerson's note.

The whole flight, he'd caught me staring at him almost every time he'd looked up. Our eyes would meet for a split second, and then I'd go back to pretending to be asleep. I wasn't sure why, all of a sudden, I couldn't stop thinking about him. Maybe because my brain was too worn out to worry about real, horrible, dangerous things anymore and somehow, without me quite realizing it, Jack had come to feel safe.

Now he glanced down at me again. We both looked away, but I felt his eyes come back to me immediately. Even through his clean shirt, I could still smell the spices on his skin.

I trained my eyes on Notre-Dame. "'A vast symphony in stone,'" I said, drowning out my thoughts.

"Victor Hugo," Jack said, and he didn't look down at me again. Instead he scanned the square. His head snapped around when a scream sounded from across the road, but it was just a little kid with map-toting parents.

Notre-Dame was much more impressive in person than it was in photographs, its square facade decorated with windows and arches and statues and so much detail, it would take years to see it all.

"Did you know the cathedral might be gone now if it weren't for *The Hunchback of Notre-Dame*?" I said. "It was falling into disrepair by the mid-1800s, and the book brought public interest back to it. That's when they did a lot of the renovations that made it look how it does now."

Jack nodded. "It's when they added some gargoyles, and did lots of restoration on others." He pointed to the stone creatures hanging off the facade. I wasn't surprised he knew about that. *The Hunchback of Notre-Dame* was one of Mr. Emerson's favorites; "Charlie" must have read it, too. "It wasn't long after Napoleon was crowned, actually. As you might imagine, France—and the Dauphins—had a lot on their minds at that time, but Notre-Dame has always been meaningful to them. It was built to commemorate the Circle's early cooperation with the Catholic Church, and built here because this area was one of the Circle's first settlements in northern Europe. This is the historical center of Paris."

As I stared up at the church, bells pealed out from the tower, announcing that it was 10:00 a.m. We didn't have much more time. And—I glanced around. The mention of the Dauphins drove home that we had been anonymous in Istanbul, but people here knew who we were. The whole Circle was no more than a mile away at the Louvre.

"Is it safe for you to even be seen with me here?" I asked once more.

"See how the door on the left-hand side is different?" he said. I guess that was my answer.

The door he pointed to had a triangular carving over it that the other two arched doors didn't have. "It symbolizes the Circle watching over the common people without them realizing it."

"So do you believe it?" I said. "That the world is a better place because of the Circle?"

He didn't hesitate. "Of course." It was amazing how much he seemed to trust them—the Circle as a whole, and the Saxons specifically. Seemed to me like setting yourself up for a fall. "You don't, I guess?" he said.

Honestly, I didn't know what I believed anymore.

He steered us toward a line of tourists that stretched from the entrance. We waited for a few minutes, and Jack tossed a euro into the hat of a street performer singing opera. After everything we went through last night, strolling inside behind a family with two crying toddlers felt almost too easy.

Inside, the church hummed with the sound of hundreds of people all trying to speak quietly. School groups perused artwork, camera-toting tourists took pictures of the stained glass, old ladies lit candles. Jack stopped alongside them and dropped a few coins into the collection box, then lit a candle himself, nestling it among the tiers of dancing orange flames that lit the dark foyer.

He cocked his head and I followed him. "We'll start with the Napoleon angle, I figure," he murmured. "The clue said 'above the coronation site,' which is at the altar. So we'll check around and above there."

We got as close as we could to the altar, but the area directly around it was roped off. Its main focus was a giant golden cross looming over a marble pietà, and there were innumerable nooks and crannies around it where a clue could be hidden. Jack circled behind it while I stood near a British tour group and inspected it as best I could from the front, then the sides. I pointed down one aisle and headed to search it, and Jack nodded and took the other.

"'He watches over our lady,'" Jack said when we came back together, having pored over every inch of this part of the cathedral. "Could we be misinterpreting it? It doesn't say that something *is here*. It says 'watches over.' Fitz knows this church. I don't feel like he'd send us somewhere we can't look properly."

A guard walked by, listening to his walkie-talkie, and we got quiet. "Is there a statue that's watching?" I murmured when he passed. "Or guarding?"

Jack squinted toward the back of the church. "There are a couple paintings that could fit."

Minutes later, we'd checked paintings of the Crucifixion, of St. Peter curing the sick, of St. Paul preaching to a crowd. Inspected any statue that seemed to be looking down over the nave. Nothing. I fell onto a chair in a multicolored ray of sunlight from a stained-glass window. Jack sat beside me, unbuttoning his blazer. He rested one arm over the back of my chair and one to the other side. He sighed deeply and stared up at the ceiling for just a second before he went back to scanning the church. He never let his guard down for more than a moment.

"Maybe we should try them again," I said. "We might have missed something."

"It's possible," he conceded, but he showed no signs of getting up again, so I settled into my chair. Jack didn't move when my shoulder blades rested against his arm, so I didn't either.

I stared up at the grandeur of the church: tapestries, gold leaf, chandeliers. My eyes kept being drawn to the stained-glass window above us.

"See how there are twelve major sections?" Jack said, jutting his chin at the window I was admiring.

I nodded, counting.

"They represent the twelve families. And just there, in the center? This is one of the only churches in the world to incorporate zodiac symbols."

"Which there are also twelve of." I remembered Luc mentioning the Circle's connection to them.

I'd read my horoscope every morning since I could remember, just for fun. The last one I'd read, on the morning of prom, had said something like, *The new moon prompts you to take impulsive action to satisfy your needs.* I had had no idea how true that would end up being.

"What's your sign?" I said. I could see him as a Taurus. The strong, silent type.

"Pisces." He sat forward and rested his elbows on his knees. "February twenty-third. What's yours?"

"Hmm. Calm, rational, self-sacrificing. Both emotional and logical," I said. That actually fit better. It was both sides of him: the poised, proud exterior and the more sensitive parts underneath. "I'm Gemini. June fourteenth."

"Gemini. Extremely independent." Jack buttoned and unbuttoned his cuff. "Quick witted. Inquisitive to a fault." He gave a tiny smile. "Sometimes dual sided or indecisive."

"Oh really?"

"One of the cooks is into all that astrology stuff," he said, and I could swear his cheeks got pink.

Astrology buff was *not* a part of Jack I would've expected to find. Especially not the kind of astrology buff who thought *I* was the dual-sided and indecisive one out of the two of us. Yes, I might have let excitement override caution to come to France in the first place, but I wasn't the one asking a girl to prom, then making it clear she was just his assignment, then going out of his way to take care of her. Would he have turned me in if we didn't have Fitz's clues to follow? Why did I keep caring so much?

But then again, why not? Wrong or not, maybe I could actually admit to myself that I wanted him to care.

We stood up to let a tour group pass in front of us.

"We'd better get back to it," I said awkwardly. "I wonder if we're missing something. Like, if 'watching over' could mean it's on the balcony." I gestured to a second floor that ran the length of the cathedral on both sides. "Is there anything up there?"

"Not artwork or statues, as far as I know."

A chubby tourist with a camera walked by. "We gotta take a picture of the gargoyles," he said in a thick Southern accent. "Like in that one movie."

Jack's eyes went wide. "The gargoyles. I didn't like coming to church. Sometimes Fitz would bribe me by promising me we could go up to the bell tower . . . with the gargoyles." A little smile crossed his face. "We used to joke that one of them looked like a guard dog, like he was *watching over* the cathedral. Do you think that could be what he meant?"

"If we're right and these clues are old, it wasn't *him* leaving the clue, so I don't know . . ." I trailed off. "But who knows—he could have been priming you for this for a long time, for all we know. He might have said the guard dog thing just in case. One way to find out."

Jack offered to go up alone since he'd seen how much I disliked heights, but if we weren't being chased and there was a solid guard-rail, I'd be fine. We passed the gift shop after one flight of stairs, then continued the long trek—444 steps, Jack told me, in a dizzyingly tight spiral—to the top. I was breathing hard by the time we stepped out of the stairwell onto the narrow balcony. A rush of wind cooled the sweat on my face, and all of Paris spread out below us.

A few other tourists leaned out to peer through the wire mesh surrounding the deck like a safety net, and I followed Jack along the balcony. The Seine wound sinuously through the city, and the morning sun glinted off splashes of gold in the distance—the top of a dome here, a rooftop there—and made them stand out from all the cream and gray. Farther away, the Eiffel Tower pierced the haze of the morning.

"There," Jack said. He pointed down the balcony at one of the gargoyles. A couple about our age cuddled and kissed in front of it while the guy held his phone at arm's length, snapping pictures.

We both looked at them, then glanced at each other. I hoped he didn't know how many things were suddenly making me think about almost-kissing him. About what it would be like to really kiss him.

He glanced at my lips.

I turned around before my flaming cheeks were too obvious.

Jack cleared his throat. "Right. We'll just wait a minute, then—"

"Sure," I said quickly. "Yeah."

When they left, we edged our way toward the gargoyle, passing above the steepled roof of the main part of the cathedral. Jack searched the gargoyle and the area around it.

His shoulders tensed, and I leaned in close. "The symbol."

It was drawn onto one of the gargoyle's clawed feet in what looked like black marker, hidden well enough to escape the immediate attention of a cleaning crew. I squeezed Jack's arm excitedly, but just as quickly let go.

"He can't be telling us to steal the whole gargoyle," I whispered. "Is there something hidden on it?"

For the next few minutes, we combed the area until a guard noticed and moved to stand just a few feet away, eyeing us suspiciously. I gave him a tense smile, like we were just another couple of interested tourists. "The clue said 'watch over.' What about his eyes?" I whispered.

When the guard turned his back, Jack picked up a pebble and heaved it all the way toward the other end of the tower, where it hit and rolled down a drainpipe. The guard perked up, and hurried away to investigate. The only other tourists nearby were three Japanese teenagers making peace signs at their camera phones. Jack climbed onto the ledge and stuck his arm as far as he could through the stiff metal mesh, reaching into the gargoyle's eyes. He shook his head, and I deflated. Nothing. Not another clue, not another symbol, nothing at all.

"'He watches over our lady above the coronation site. Where he looks, it will be found,'" I said under my breath once he'd hopped nimbly back down beside me. "'Where he looks.'" The realization dropped into place with a jolt. "Jack. Where he looks, it will be found. Where is he looking?"

We stared out in the direction of the gargoyle's gaze.

"Oh God," I said. "The whole city looks exactly the same." The matching cream-and-gray buildings weren't quite as charming when they made it impossible to pick out anything. From the other side of the tower, the guard once again rounded the corner to watch us, a disapproving look on his face.

I got right behind the gargoyle and followed his line of sight as closely as I could. Jack came behind me and peered over my shoulder.

At that moment, the bells of the cathedral pealed out again, the chimes round and clanging and *directly* behind us. I gasped and jumped—straight back into Jack. He steadied me, and for a second, all I was aware of was the warmth of his body against the chill of the breeze, his hands secure on my shoulders. It was like I could ignore how much I wanted to touch him until it happened, and then I couldn't think of anything else. I leaned back into his chest involuntarily. He didn't stop me. In fact, unless I was imagining it, he drew me closer. It was dangerous how safe it made me feel. It was dangerous, period—we were in public, and someone could see us. I shook his hands off and stepped away, to the other side of the gargoyle.

And then I looked back up and saw it immediately.

"That white Ferris wheel." I pointed. "That's where he's looking. Is there anything in that direction that could be significant?"

Jack grasped the railing and stared out over Paris. "Yes, in fact," he said, a smile in his voice. "That's the Louvre."

CHAPTER 27

Luckily, the Louvre was a few short blocks away. Vendors were setting up their stalls of shiny Eiffel Tower postcards and dusty used books and vintage absinthe posters along the Seine, and the rush of traffic scented the air with diesel fumes.

We waited for a light to change, then crossed a busy street into the Louvre courtyard. The glass pyramid in its center gleamed blindingly in the morning sun, a modern contrast to the museum's classic facade.

"Let me guess," I said, my flip-flops slapping against the sunbleached concrete. "The pyramid was put in by another family to spite the Dauphins."

I laughed, but Jack frowned. "How did you know?"

I stopped, hands on my hips. "Seriously?"

Jack actually grinned. "Seriously," he said over his shoulder.

I shook my head and hurried to catch up. A quick glance at the Dauphins' wing of the complex showed that no one was watching, so Jack made a phone call. He'd gotten a new phone from the plane, and had grabbed me one, too, like there was a constant supply of extra equipment just lying around. While he talked to a security guard he knew, I called my mom again. Still no answer.

We sat on the edge of one of the courtyard's many reflecting pools, waiting for the guard to get us—and Jack's gun—past the metal detectors. I pulled up the Louvre website, hoping it would give us some kind of clue about what we were looking for. I stopped on a picture of the *Mona Lisa*. How ironic that we were this close to one of the most famous paintings in the world but wouldn't have time to see it.

"It's not that impressive in real life," Jack said, like he was reading my mind. "It's much smaller than you'd think. I have always wondered what she's smiling about, though."

I trailed my fingers through the reflecting pool, sending ripples across its surface. "She's pretending," I said. "That's not a real smile. It's what she wants people to see. It's how she gets by."

Jack looked at the phone for a long second. "Why?" he said. "Why does she have to pretend?"

"Because it's easier that way," I said. To me, it seemed obvious. "Then she doesn't have to get involved with people."

For once, Jack didn't study the face of every person who walked by, or scan the crowd for danger. He kept looking at the phone, then cut a glance to me. "I don't think so," he said. "I think she knows being independent doesn't always have to mean being alone."

I became very interested in the tangled ends of my hair. "So you and Mona were friends?" I teased, hoping it sounded light. "You knew her well enough to know her deepest secrets?"

He bit his lower lip. "I think I'm getting to know her better."

I was saved by a Louvre security guard in navy blue. He escorted us past the line and inside the pyramid.

I wasn't expecting it to look like this. The pyramid acted like a giant skylight, flooding the Louvre lobby with sun.

I glanced at the brochure we'd picked up. There were three massive main wings, all with some permanent and some rotating collections, plus a temporary exhibit.

"Since that bracelet said 'my twin,' I wonder if we're looking for jewelry," I said. "That would have to mean it's something that's been here since *Napoleon's* time. But if Fitz had this clue and *then* planted something for us, it could be anything."

Jack's eyes darted over the list of collections. "We'll just have to search as quickly as we can for anything that seems like a possibility."

As we started down the wide spiral staircase, something caught my eye, and my heart clawed into my throat.

Scarface, the redhead, and the rest of the Order crew marched past the pyramid outside.

I grabbed Jack. He stiffened.

"How did they find us?" I said. "We ditched our phones. We're in a whole other *city*."

A school group pushed and giggled and scrambled around us down the stairs. Jack pulled me to the side, something more like worry than surprise on his face.

"What?" I said, and then I thought of something. "Wait. Could one of the other families track your plane? What if they're not Order after all?"

"The other families can track our plane," he said under his breath, and then, "They're Order. But if they can track our plane . . . that wouldn't be good. I don't know. We don't have time to think about it now."

We hurried into the lobby, and Jack stopped short at the bottom of the stairs. "Or maybe them showing up here was a lucky guess." He pointed to a cheerful black, white, and red banner hanging down into the atrium.

NAPOLEON HALL

TEMPORARY EXHIBIT:

ALEXANDER THE GREAT AND THE ANCIENT GREEKS

"Think this might be where we're going?" Jack said.

"It does seem like an awfully big coincidence if it's not." I darted a glance back outside, where the Order was cutting the line.

"It has to be," Jack said. "In Paris. In *Napoleon* Hall. In an *Alexander* exhibit, for God's sakes. The Dauphins put this exhibit together searching for information about the mandate. What better way to find ancient Greek artifacts than encourage every small museum in the world to submit artifacts to the Louvre? And Fitz could hide it the same way he did at the Hagia Sophia."

I glanced around. We couldn't do anything about the banner, but a standing sign at the bottom of the stairs had an arrow pointing in the right direction. "This is officially the cheesiest, most cliché distraction ever, but hopefully it'll buy us a few more minutes." I spun the arrow so it pointed the opposite way. "Let's go."

We hurried down the stairs and merged with the crowds, darting glances behind us the whole time. When we got to the exhibit, Jack and I split up.

I found a bust of Alexander the Great, a slab of marble under a thick pane of glass, a head wreath made of golden vines. Next were various metal tools, and I got excited when I found a display of jewelry, but the pieces and their corresponding descriptive plaques didn't look out of the ordinary, and on the ring and the gargoyle, the symbol had been obvious.

I glanced across the room to see Jack, hands in his pockets, interested in some ancient coins, then part of a stone wall. When he turned, I raised my eyebrows at him, and he shook his head.

The next piece would take a minute to check, so I read its plaque first. *Ivory Sarcophagus, depicting scenes from the life of Alexander the Great. On loan from the Istanbul Archaeological Museum.*

Istanbul. And in the plaque's bottom right corner, the swirling symbol I knew so well.

"Jack," I whispered loudly. He strolled over like we were normal tourists, but his eyes danced with excitement.

I crouched in front of the sarcophagus, studying the mural, and Jack crouched beside me. "It's Alexander. And Aristotle, I think—he was Alexander's tutor."

I glanced over my shoulder, expecting to see Scarface at any second. I liked to think he wouldn't try to kill us in a public place, but that hadn't seemed to bother him in the Istanbul market.

Jack peered around the back of the sarcophagus until a guard across the room barked a warning and he had to step away.

The crowd of little kids we'd seen earlier came into the room, their shrill voices echoing off the vaulted ceilings. No Scarface yet.

"It's got to be something more than the scenes carved on here." Jack stared at the plaque. "Wait. The Istanbul Archaeological Museum. Fitz volunteered there, too. Did you read all the info?"

"What info?"

Jack grabbed a laminated sheet from a stand that held details on the piece in six languages. We both scanned it.

"There," I said. The middle of the second paragraph read: *"This is an especially interesting sarcophagus,"* says Emerson Fitzpatrick, *volunteer docent. "The false bottom was unique for the time, likely used to smuggle goods under the guise of a funeral procession."*

"False bottom," I whispered.

The sarcophagus was raised on four squat, round legs, so there was about a foot and a half of space underneath. If the Louvre had been as deserted as the Hagia Sophia had been, it would have been easy to get under it.

It wouldn't be easy here.

My eyes darted around, searching for an answer. The group of kids was making their way to the golden crown.

"Trust me?" I asked Jack. Without hesitation, he nodded.

I wondered what it would be like to be able to put your trust in somebody that easily. I couldn't deny that from this side, it felt pretty good. And it made me really not want to mess up.

As the group of kids moved between me and the guard across the room, I dropped to the floor and slid under the sarcophagus.

It was lucky I wasn't claustrophobic. The tons of stone hovering over me was bad enough, plus it was too dark to see. The rough stone caught on my fingertips as I felt around. So far, the bottom was uniform aside from a sticky spiderweb in one corner.

But here. Near the center. A long crack that, when I followed it with my fingers, made a square. And on one edge, a shallow trough. It felt like an old jewelry box I had. Rather than being on hinges, the top had slid open, using the same kind of fingerhold.

I put all my fingers in the hold and pulled as hard as I could.

It didn't budge.

The shadows changed, and I glanced to the side to see dozens of little feet headed toward my hiding place. I pulled on the sliding door again.

Nothing.

Frantically, I ran my fingers around the edge. Was there a latch?

Yes. Here was something. I moved the bit of stone as far as it would go, then grabbed the little door again.

"*Regardez!*" a child's voice said. "*Que fait-elle?*"

Jack said something in French and crouched in front of me, his hand on my ankle.

I yanked on the slider. This time, it flew open with a screech.

"My girlfriend's hurt!" Jack said loudly, in English now, obviously trying to cover the noise. "She's fallen!"

Despite everything, I couldn't help but notice he'd said *girlfriend.* He could easily have said I was his friend, or his sister.

A couple of little faces peered under the sarcophagus.

I stuck my hand inside the opening. Nothing to my right but cold, rough stone. I felt to the left.

Footsteps pounded the floor.

My fingers found something. I yanked a leather pouch out of the hole, along with quite a bit of dust. I stuffed the pouch into my bag and tried not to sneeze.

An adult face appeared, silhouetted against the light. "*Mademoiselle!* Miss. Are you okay?"

I edged out from under the sarcophagus, heart racing double time. Jack crouched beside me, helping me sit up, and I clung to him like I'd just passed out. He leaned in close. "Did you find anything?" he whispered, tucking my dusty hair out of my face like the perfect concerned boyfriend.

I nodded, and his whole face lit up, so much that I barely noticed the whole class of children and their teacher, all staring and whispering. And then the guard loomed over us, barking something in French.

Jack put an arm around me and replied, and I grabbed my head and winced as convincingly as I could.

"Like I said, my girlfriend has a *heart condition,*" Jack said, and I dropped the hand hastily to my chest.

"She'll be fine, though," Jack said. "Thank you for your help."

The guard frowned, gesturing to the sarcophagus and looking me up and down. Even though I had a jacket wrapped around me, I was still in the tiny cocktail dress, with scratched-up legs and bloodied bandages.

"I don't know how she fell underneath it," Jack said in English. He helped me to my feet, a little roughly, considering I'd supposedly just fainted. "We're sorry to inconvenience you. We'll get her back to our hotel now. No! No, we don't need a doctor."

The guard frowned and raised his walkie-talkie—and a familiar accent came from the other side of the room.

Scarface, the redhead, and the others strolled into the Alexander exhibit, so raucous that the guard turned to look at them. Jack grabbed my hand, and we darted in the opposite direction.

"*Arrêtez!*" I didn't have to turn to know the guard had seen us run. "There they are!" So had the Order.

CHAPTER 28

Jack pulled me past a pair of tall, red-headed tourists in too-short shorts, and farther into the museum.

The shouts followed us.

I looked frantically for the green SORTIE sign that signaled an exit, but there were none this way. Only bathrooms.

"Too obvious," Jack said, and made a sharp left turn through an open door into an office. He slammed it and locked it behind us.

A few moments later, the doorknob jiggled, then fists pounded an angry beat. "Open the bloody door!" Scarface yelled. I backed away, searching for another exit.

"They've got to have it or they wouldn't've run," Scarface's muffled voice came from outside.

More pounding. A kick to the door that bowed the bottom inward. That was the only door, but there was a window.

More footsteps, running toward us. Mumbles, curses. "Security guards," said one of the Order, and I thought I heard something about "the Commander" again. Finally, Scarface raised his voice enough to be heard.

"If you change your mind about letting the old man die, you have one day," he said. "Call this phone number in the next twenty-four hours with the name of the One, or he's dead. We won't give you this chance again." He rattled off a number, and I scribbled it on a scrap of paper I found in my bag.

A rush of pounding footsteps retreated. I stared at the phone number in my hand, but another set of steps reached us and the door handle rattled, much less violently. "*Sécurité!*"

Jack shook his head and gestured to the window. I stuffed the paper into my bag. Luckily, we were on the first floor, near some kind of employee exit. Jack helped me out, and vaulted out after me. He grabbed my hand, and we sprinted up a ramp.

"What was in the sarcophagus?" Jack asked, breathless, as he pulled open the wrought-iron gate leading off the Louvre grounds.

"Some kind of leather pouch. It felt like it might have a book—"

Down the block, an emergency exit flew open. The Order piled out. We skidded to a stop.

"Watch for them, you arse!" Scarface yelled, pointing away from us. "One of you go to the front, the other to the side. Girl's in a white coat, that little git's in a black one. They can't be that hard to find."

I dug my fingers into Jack's arm. There was too much traffic to run across the road, and they'd see us anywhere else.

Scarface started to turn.

Jack propelled me back down the ramp we'd just run up. It curved back on itself, so we ended up just off the street but down one level, next to a bike rack. We shrank back into a recessed doorway. I jiggled the doorknob frantically, but it was locked.

Jack gestured for me to pull off my jacket, and tossed it under a helmet in one of the bike baskets. He put his own jacket around my shoulders, then plucked a straw fedora off the ground. It looked like a tourist had lost it over the fence. Jack made a face, but it wasn't dirty, and he popped it on his head and pulled it low over his eyes. "Take your hair down," he whispered. I pulled out my ponytail holder and let my hair fall over my shoulders so I'd look as little as possible like the girl they'd just seen.

Scarface and another man's voices moved closer. If they looked down when they walked by, we were finished. We weren't hidden very well. Jack backed me as far into the shadows as possible, trapping me between himself and the wall. "Don't move," he whispered. His eyes darted behind him. "They'll think we're . . ."

I nodded. I was dressed pretty strangely for this time of the day, but it made it look like we could be coming home from an especially late night, trying to find a place to make out.

Jack stood so close that his forearms brushed my shoulders, so close that his cologne, or his skin, or whatever that musky sweet smell in the crook of his neck was, would have overwhelmed me if I hadn't been so scared.

The footsteps drew nearer. I tensed. I wouldn't put it past them to actually kill us to get this stuff. My pulse pounded wildly, and I glanced up at the street.

Jack's lips were in the hair at my temple, his breath warm at my ear. "It's okay," he murmured. "We'll be okay. They're almost gone."

My shiver then was only partially from fear.

The voices got louder, came right alongside our hiding place and paused—then kept going. I let out a breath and stood on tiptoe to see over Jack's shoulder. Nothing. Gone. I collapsed back down, a bubble of relief expanding in my chest—and then I stumbled. I flew into Jack's arms, and the beer bottle I'd tripped over flew back against the door behind me with a loud clink.

The voices stopped. I clutched Jack's shirt in both my fists. For a second, they didn't move, we didn't move, the whole world held its breath. Then footsteps, hurrying back toward our hiding place. Jack turned to see. I had the better vantage point, and watched as a shadow fell across the gate at the top of the ramp. If Jack turned any farther, he'd be exposed.

He started to crane his neck, and I grabbed his face and yanked it back around. His skin felt hot, his light stubble scratchy under my fingers.

He opened his mouth, but I shook my head violently, nodding above us. Just two kids making out in a dark corner. They wouldn't care about us then.

The shadow stopped. The wrought-iron gate squeaked on its hinges, and the shadow leaned over the railing.

I did the only thing I could think of.

I kissed Jack.

I yanked his face down to mine, holding it between my hands, hoping his hat was blocking our faces.

Oh God, please don't let him come down the ramp. Oh God, please don't let Jack freak out and pull away.

Oh God. I was kissing Jack.

Kind of. Our lips were mushed together but frozen, our eyes wide open and staring at each other in terror. I was holding my breath. I was pretty sure he was holding his, too.

A second went by, or a minute, or a week, and his eyes went midnight black and shining.

Over the noise of the traffic, I heard a sniff. "Just a couple of kids snogging in some grotty old stairs," the retreating voice said. It sounded like the redhead. "Not them."

"Then go find them, you wanker," Scarface said, and the voices faded away.

My hands fell away from Jack's face, and our lips came apart. I collapsed against the wall, limp with relief.

Jack still hovered over me, glancing over his shoulder. When he seemed satisfied they were gone, he turned back, and instead of saying anything, instead of even looking at me, he closed his eyes with a long, shaky sigh.

He knew I had done that to save us, right? Not that I didn't *want* to, but I wasn't trying to get him in any more trouble, or make things any more complicated. My unsteady breath echoing off the walls was the only sound I could hear, and it was entirely too loud. "Jack—" I said, and he opened his eyes.

Where I thought I might see exasperation, I saw anything but. There was something wild in his eyes, something desperate in the way his lips parted. But he was not upset. Definitely not upset. My mouth snapped shut.

Our faces hovered inches apart, frozen but twanging, like magnets we suddenly had to pull on as hard as we could to keep from coming together.

He started to say something, but stopped. At the look in his eyes—fear, frustration, longing—my end of the magnet got a lot harder to keep in check.

Then one—or both—of us let go.

His lips crashed into mine.

It was nothing like the fake kiss a minute ago. His lips softened to mine immediately, and his hands, usually so cautious, pulled me to him so tight, I molded to his body.

He was kissing me. Jack Bishop was kissing me. And I was kissing him back like I was drowning and he was air. The brim of the
fedora butted up against my forehead, and he shoved it out of the
way and onto the ground.

"Avery, God," he murmured. He parted my lips, and I grabbed
his collar and pulled him closer, closer, closer, and every feeling from
the past few days—the pain and the danger and the wanting and
the confusion and the need—all tangled together in that kiss, in his
mouth on mine, and down my collarbone, and my fingers sliding
under the untucked hem of his shirt.

I tipped my head back and let his lips find their way down my
neck, and his neck tasted like salt and spices, and his hands, my
hands, all over everywhere, and I was falling, falling, falling, with just
his arms holding me up.

Voices sounded from the street. I didn't think it was the Order,
but over the traffic and our breath echoing off the walls, it was hard
to tell. The only thing I knew for sure was that I didn't care. I didn't
care about anything. I just didn't want him to stop kissing me.

And he didn't.

It wasn't my first kiss, but it felt like it. It felt like how kisses
in movies looked, which I'd assumed was just fiction. But this was
real. For an irrational moment, I thought we could kiss away the
mandate, and the Order, and the rest of the world. A kiss like this
could do that.

Finally we pulled away. Aftershocks of the kiss vibrated through
me.

Jack's shaky breath mingled with mine, his fingers wrapped
around my hips like they were all that was holding him upright. I
leaned up to him, my lips, of their own accord, blindly trying to find
their way back to his.

He bent toward me once more and brushed his mouth across mine. That kiss, that last whispered breath of his lips, gave me goose bumps over my whole body.

Jack suddenly dropped his hands and took a deep, shuddering breath. Without thinking, I reached out to stroke his sleeve. It felt wrong now to not be touching him. But instead of wrapping me up in his arms like I thought he would, he pulled away.

"I'm sorry," he said. His hands curled into fists. "God, I'm sorry. I wasn't supposed to do that. I've gone and made it worse."

My arm dropped to my side like dead weight. No. Kissing doesn't make things worse. Kissing makes things *better*, especially kissing like that. If everyone got kissed like that, there would be no problems in the world.

I wondered what it would have been like if Jack had been a normal transfer student and there was no Circle, and no Order, and no Saxons, and no fate dictated by the mandate.

Is it possible to feel nostalgic for something that never actually happened? If it was, it was a shade of *toska*. A craving for something you couldn't possibly understand. A craving I was finally letting myself feel, only to wish I hadn't.

Jack turned his back to me. He straightened his shirt, put on the blazer I shoved back at him. He was so achingly beautiful with his hair mussed up from having my fingers tangled in it that I could barely breathe.

As if he'd read my mind, he smoothed his hair back into place.

I stared at him for a beat more, sure he could feel the longing pulsing out of me—and then I deflated. My heart slammed shut so hard, I shuddered.

"I'm sorry, too," I said, as blandly as I could muster. "That was obviously a mistake."

He turned around. His eyes didn't say it had been a mistake. "I'm just trying to do the right thing," he said. "You know that, right?"

Of course I did. Whatever else I felt, I knew he always tried to do the right thing. I turned away, pulling my hair back into a ponytail. "How do you know what the right thing is?" I whispered.

"That's the problem, then, isn't it? I don't anymore. The thing that feels right . . ." He shifted his eyes to me, and back away just as quickly. He paced to the bottom of the ramp. "The only thing that feels right is as wrong as it can get."

CHAPTER 29

We skirted the back side of the museum, past a sidewalk vendor slathering chocolate onto a sizzling circle of crepe batter. Jack led us down a set of stone steps to the bank of the Seine.

The only thing that feels right, he'd said. What felt right to him was *me*.

He wasn't allowed to say things like that.

The sun was straight overhead now as we walked under a bridge and down the river, past dozens of Sunday brunch picnickers. All around us was the hum of traffic and the laughter of kids chasing each other and the ding of bike bells, but the silence between us was starting to get too loud. "What's with all the padlocks?" I finally asked, pointing to a bridge with thousands of glimmering locks attached to its railings.

Jack shoved his hands into his pockets. "That's the love locks bridge. If a couple puts a lock on it and throws the key into the river, they'll be together forever. Supposedly."

"They've never heard of bolt cutters?" I said. Jack glanced at me out of the corner of his eye.

I saw a bench in the shade and headed toward it, brushing off a dusting of pale pink petals from the tree overhead before I sat down.

Jack sat about a foot away, which was too close. I shifted a few more inches.

Kissing *had* made things worse.

I pulled the leather pouch out of my bag like it was the only thing on my mind. At least I was good at lying.

Inside was a very old, leather-bound book. I felt Jack looking over my shoulder as I slid it out. The cover shed flakes of faded black onto my white dress. I set it gingerly on my knees and paused, feeling the weight of it in my hands, the weight of things far more important than boy drama.

Mr. Emerson was way more important. This—whatever history I held here in my hands—was way more important.

"If this says who the One is, and we tell the Order, we'll be handing that person a death sentence," I said. It could be somebody my age—somebody like Luc. Or even a little *kid*.

"If we don't, we'll be handing *Fitz* a death sentence." Jack shrugged out of his blazer and rolled the sleeves of his shirt. It had gotten a lot warmer since early this morning. "And the Order's killing people who they think might be the One anyway. Having it all end with one person dying will actually *save* lives."

I couldn't believe I was in a place where that was up to us to decide.

The sun glinted off the river as a line of baby ducks followed their mother in a neat row. Two little blond girls threw them pieces of a baguette.

"We'd also be stopping the mandate from being fulfilled," I said. "The Circle would never find the tomb, if it does turn out that the mandate is necessary for that."

Jack rubbed the bridge of his nose. That part had to be killing him.

"And Mr. Emerson said tell *no one*," I went on. "He could have texted you where he'd hidden this stuff, or just left it in his safe, but he really, really didn't want anyone but us to see it."

Jack rested his chin in his hand and looked at me. "Are you saying you don't think we should turn over the One to save Fitz?"

The breeze stirred the strands of dark hair that had already escaped my ponytail. "Do you think they'll actually kill him? They said they would at the Hagia Sophia and didn't. Wouldn't it be smarter to keep him alive for information until they get what they want?"

"Are we willing to risk it?"

I deflated. "No, I guess not." At the end of the day, I'd do whatever I had to for Mr. Emerson, even if the thought of deciding someone's fate made me sick. "I just really don't like it."

"I don't either." Jack sat with his elbows on his knees, his shoulders hunched. "But being part of the Circle, you learn that what's right isn't usually what's pleasant."

I looked down at the sun-dappled book and opened the front cover. A diary, it looked like. In French.

Jack reached out a hand. "May I?"

I watched as he scanned pages. "A lot of it's about battles." He turned to a later spot. "And then it seems like the writer got sick."

Nothing that sounded useful to us. I watched the stream of people go by on the ornate bridge overhead and hoped the Order wouldn't think to look down here.

Jack squinted at a page. "A lot of these battles are Napoleon's." He flipped another page, and another, running his index finger down each one. "At first I thought this was one of his soldiers writing, but the way he's talking . . . this might actually be *Napoleon's* diary."

I suppose that made sense after the "coronation site" clue.

Jack turned a few more pages and drew a sharp breath. I sat up straight, and he pointed.

The Celtic knot symbol from my locket was penciled onto the back endpaper.

Jack held the book close to his face, inspecting it.

"Let me check something." I took the book and my fingers brushed his, zinging sparks through me. I jerked my hand away and leaned over the diary. Close up, I could see a tiny edging of bees interspersed with the Dauphin sun symbol. Definitely Napoleon's. But just as I was hoping, the leather on the outside of the book wasn't attached. It was just a sleeve.

I slid the back cover out, and one corner of the endpaper was loose.

I worked it open further. After a second, my fingers found the edge of something hidden inside. I pulled it out and unfolded a single sheet of paper, one of its edges ragged.

"*Le trésor . . .*" I tried to translate, and then handed it to Jack. "What does it say?" There were two sets of words on the page. One looked like a normal diary entry, and below it, a message was scrawled more shakily, like the writer was having trouble holding the pen.

We both got quiet while an older couple with a striped picnic blanket tossed an empty wine bottle in the trash can behind our bench.

I held my breath until Jack started talking again. "It says,

"*The treasure is not what they think. They are wrong about the union.*"

My heart stuttered. Jack glanced up at me, then kept reading.

"*The One's true identity will shatter the Circle.*

"*The One, the true ruler, the new Achilles. Superior to the false twelve.*

"*For everyone's sake, I must pretend I never found any of it.*"

"That kind of sounds like it could be more of the mandate," I said slowly.

"Yeah. It does." Jack pointed to the shakier writing, and I leaned closer, looking over his shoulder. "This part says,

I cannot take this to my grave. I've left clues to the tomb, and if one of my descendants chooses to follow a path that will renegotiate our fates, it is a braver man than I."

"Is he talking about *the* tomb?" I breathed.

"It's always been rumored—even outside the Circle, in regular world history—that Napoleon found Alexander's tomb." There was awe in Jack's voice. "But he denied it, and anyway, there's never been a union between the One and the girl. How would he have found it?"

"It says they're *wrong* about the union," I reminded him. "And even if that doesn't mean anything, maybe he did it the old-fashioned way. By looking." The sun hit my feet, warming my toes. "Mr. Emerson did say 'wrong about the mandate,' and whoever wrote this—whether it's Napoleon or not—seems to think it's wrong, too." I held out my hand for the paper. "Do you think his clues to the tomb are the same as the three things Mr. Emerson wanted us to find? Or since this diary is one of Mr. Emerson's three things, maybe only the *bracelet* is Napoleon's clue?"

Jack rubbed his forehead. "It's something to think about eventually, but we can't get off track now. The One is our immediate concern. And if this riddle really is about the mandate, giving more detail on who the One is . . ."

It was our key to getting Mr. Emerson back. "It does say that stuff about the One, but it doesn't give us enough information to tell who it is." As I shifted on the bench, wrapping the blazer around me, I saw Jack pretending not to watch me out of the corner of his eye.

I pretended not to notice. "Was there anything in the other entries about the tomb or the mandate?"

"Not that I've seen. But I also don't see a ripped-out page." He held up the hidden paper. "This came from somewhere."

I sat up straighter. "Another diary?"

"If there were any other Napoleonic diaries, they'd be at the Dauphins'."

I looked over my shoulder toward the Louvre, right on the other side of this wall.

"I was thinking." Jack stood up. "Maybe we should go there anyway. Fitz did leave Stellan's photo, too."

I stiffened. "I'm not sure it's a good idea for me to go back there at all, and *definitely* not to talk to Stellan."

"I doubt he's as suspicious as you think—"

"He's been calling my phone all night." I crossed my arms. "Even at the prom—before either of *us* knew I was anything—he already thought I was something more. Prada made it worse. And then I ran off in Istanbul . . ."

"He might think it's odd," Jack said, grabbing his jacket, "but with the Dauphins hosting the ball tonight, he has other things to worry about. Everyone does."

I still didn't stand up. "Won't it be suspicious for us to be seen together?"

"There are loads of family members and Keepers staying there. It's probably the safest place for us to be together, actually."

I finally stood. I didn't like it, but there *was* another reason for me to go back to the Dauphins. My mom might be there.

"Okay," I said.

To help smooth things over, I dialed Luc while we climbed back up the steps from the river and crossed into the Louvre courtyard.

In the distance, the white Ferris wheel revolved lazily in front of a backdrop of gathering clouds.

Luc didn't answer, but I left a message with a quick apology for running off the previous night. Jack and I drifted silently through the throngs of tourists toward the Dauphins' wing, and only then did I realize the careful distance he was keeping. It wasn't just me feeling awkward and wrong. The realization didn't make me feel any better.

Jack was right—no one inside gave us a second look. There were people conferencing on settees in the sitting room, and Keepers talking into headsets, and attendants with dry-cleaning bags. We were told, to my relief, that Stellan was off preparing security for the ball.

We headed straight to the library, pausing only for Jack to ask whether an American woman had shown up looking for her daughter. She hadn't, and I tried not to worry. With plane connections and delays and her phone maybe not working abroad, it wasn't time to panic yet.

The Dauphins' library didn't actually smell like cigar smoke, but the warm dark wood and deep leather armchairs hinted that the smell would be appropriate. We scanned the lower level quickly, but it held mostly fiction and art. I climbed a set of rickety wooden stairs to a second story of books that stretched all around the room, and clicked on the dangling light overhead.

The must of old paper permeated the air, and I stopped at a history section. Jack climbed to the balcony, too, and touched my shoulder to squeeze past. When I glanced over, he was looking at me. We quickly turned back to our respective shelves.

"Here," he said after a few silent minutes. He was crouched on the other side of the balcony, a stack of books in front of him. He held one with a cracked black cover open to a title page, with *Napoléon*

Bonaparte scrawled unmistakably across it, in the same penmanship as the diary in my bag. "Looks like all these are his," Jack said.

He handed me the one he was holding and picked up the other three, and we made our way down to the first story and to a heavy oak table.

"You look for a ripped-out page, and I'll skim the entries for anything about the One," Jack said.

I nodded. As I opened the first book, the library door opened. Instinctively, I shoved the books behind us and stood shoulder to shoulder with Jack, forming a wall, but the woman—in all black, and with a duster in one hand—just muttered something in French and scurried back out the door.

I let out a breath. "Maybe we should go somewhere else. I have a room here."

Jack pursed his lips. "It's okay for us to be seen together in public, but me in your room? Not so good."

I tried to ignore any thoughts that his being in my room conjured up, and the pang that came with them. "A Keeper and a random distant cousin getting caught with a bunch of Napoleon's diaries and talking about who the One is? That wouldn't be great either," I said quickly.

"Right. Okay, then." Jack followed me down the hall.

I made sure there was no one around, then let him in and locked the door behind us. Without the hum of conversation from the hall, the room felt too quiet. "Give me one," I said.

I took the top diary and perched on the bed—realizing I still hadn't slept in it once—and Jack set the rest of them on the coffee table. As I flipped carefully through the gossamer-thin diary pages, I realized something that should have been obvious.

I jumped up. "Let me see the ripped-out page."

Jack took the leather pouch out of his jacket and handed it to me. I unfolded the paper. "Let's just check if any of the paper matches."

Jack's eyes lit up. We eliminated two of the four books immediately—the size was wrong. The last two were similar, but when I rubbed a corner of each between my fingers, the texture of what looked like the oldest of the diaries matched exactly.

While Jack leafed through it, I paced the room and caught a glimpse of myself in the mirror. My cocktail dress had smudges all over it and a bloodstain at the hem, the blazer had become wrinkled and dirty, and I swear the dark circles under my eyes got darker as I watched.

"Come look at this," Jack said. "He starts talking about the mandate here. About how there's no purple-eyed girl, and nobody knows who the One is. He decides someone as important as him shouldn't be forced to depend on the established route to the treasure, and he's going to take a more direct path." Jack flipped ahead, reading to himself. "There are a few pages about where he's sent troops to search, and then, all of a sudden, it stops cold. Back to battles and strategy. No more mention of the tomb, the mandate, *nothing*."

I perched next to Jack on the chaise. "Where's the last page he talks about the tomb?"

Jack turned back to it, and I pushed carefully on the binding. "There!" It was nearly hidden, but there were unmistakably the ragged edges of a ripped-out page.

"It's like he found it, decided immediately to hide the fact—maybe because he didn't like what he found—and never spoke of it again," Jack said, frowning.

"Until he hid this page in the diary he kept on his deathbed," I said. "Did we look closely at the rest of *that* diary?"

Jack shook his head. "Not yet."

While he did, I made a list of things we knew about the One on the little notepad on the vanity. "The One is a member of one of the families," I said out loud, "meant to marry the girl. 'Walk through fire and does not burn,' it said in the mandate."

I wrote that down, and wrote *(Means: good in a crisis?)* beside it. *"New Achilles"—from Napoleon's diary. (Invincible? Near invincible besides one flaw? Line of mandate mentions something about the One "becoming invincible.")*

Jack stood and paced, diary open in one hand, flipping pages with the other. "Oh," he finally said. "I don't know if this is anything *new*, but it's something."

We both sat on the edge of the bed, and he let the book rest open at a page filled with nearly illegible scribbles and sketches. He pointed to one scrawl, in French. "*Walk through fire unharmed. Not burned. He lives.*" Under it were hastily sketched flames, licking at the words.

He pointed to another scrawl. "*Heir of Achilles.*"

"Heir?"

Jack shrugged. "Like 'the new Achilles' in that line? But what it means, I don't know. It sounds like another metaphor."

It did.

"It's like he's trying to figure out who the One is, too. Why would he care if he'd already found the tomb?"

"We have to keep in mind that these are the ramblings of somebody who's about to die," Jack said. "But it seems undeniable that he did find something."

I added *Heir of Achilles* to my list. Jack closed the diary and my stomach churned.

"If this is it," I said, tearing the page off the notepad, "we're not much closer to knowing who the One is than we were before."

Jack scraped a hand through his hair. "If the Order touches him, I'll kill them myself," he said quietly, then out loud, he said, "We have to talk to Stellan. We have to go to the ball and find him."

"To the *ball*?" I *had* considered earlier that my father would be there, but it was starting to feel like tempting fate too much. "What do you think he's going to be able to figure out that we haven't?"

Jack stacked the diaries in a neat pile. "I honestly don't know. But don't we have to try? I promise, no one will even notice you there. It'll be fine."

A fleeting image darted through my mind of the tiny photo that used to be in my locket. Dark hair, dark brows, like mine. The reason I'd wanted to come back to France in the first place.

"It'd be better to show him—"

We both froze when a knock came on the door.

"Just a second," I called as Jack bolted for the window.

"I'll get to the service door outside," he whispered. "Hide the books. I'll see you at the ball. Please."

"Just go!" He was out the window before I could finish the words.

I glanced frantically around and finally shoved the stack of books under the bed. I opened the door, heart knocking against my ribs.

Luc stood on the other side, garment bag in hand. "Hello, *cherie*." He bent to kiss both my cheeks. "I got your message and brought your dress for the ball."

He handed it to me, and I unzipped the top of the bag to find the Prada dress, with a winged, glittering silver mask resting over its hanger. I'd forgotten they'd said the ball was a masquerade. "They saved the dress for me, after all that?"

Luc smiled vaguely, and only then did I notice he was still in the same clothes as last night, hair flattened, eyes dark. I set the garment bag on the bed. "Everything okay?"

He shook his head. "There was another attack last night. Colette LeGrand and Liam Blackstone's limousine was caught in a collision on the way here from the airport."

I gasped out loud.

"Colette made it." Luc's voice hitched. "Liam didn't."

"What?" I sat down hard on the bed. The Order had killed Liam Blackstone? I pictured his easy laugh, him patting Luc on the back as they talked about soccer, and Luc's shy smile. The last movie I'd seen him in, where he'd played a vampire, with comically bad white makeup.

"Luc," I choked. "I am so sorry."

Luc nodded curtly, but his chin wobbled. I got up and wrapped my arms around him. He hesitated, then hugged me back hard, burying his face in my neck.

After a minute, I felt him take a deep breath, and he pulled away. "I'm headed to the hospital to see Colette. I'll be back to escort you to the ball."

I looked up sharply. "The ball's still happening, when there was an attack *last night?*"

Luc pursed his lips. "We can't give in to their scare tactics. That's what terrorists want. The show must go on, *cherie*, just with extra security. And though Colette is part of our family, we're hosting the ball, so I will have to be there, too." He squeezed my shoulder. "I'll see you this evening."

I nodded and shut the door behind him, then sat back on the bed. I unzipped the garment bag and touched the dress with one finger, transported back to when I thought the glamour of this world was the most extraordinary part about it.

I couldn't believe Liam Blackstone was dead.

I couldn't believe Jack and I were considering giving the people who killed him license to kill someone else.

I couldn't believe that we were at the end of Mr. Emerson's clues and still had no idea what they meant, and that we were running out of time to save his life. Would my going to the ball really do anything?

I rubbed my eyes. On top of everything, my contacts were killing me after wearing them for this long; I just wanted to take them out and sleep. But I couldn't. It wasn't worth the risk of someone seeing my eye color. This one tiny thing sent me over the edge, and frustrated tears built up in the back of my throat.

I swallowed them down. Crying wouldn't help my itching eyes, and it definitely wouldn't help Mr. Emerson. I took a deep breath, put contact drops in each eye, and curled up on the bed next to the Prada dress, where I fell into a restless sleep.

CHAPTER 30

Even though Luc was a Dauphin, we'd waited in a security line and gone through a metal detector to get inside. Now our packed elevator shuddered to a stop, and the doors slid open.

"*Alors,* time for a ball," Luc said, but he sounded even less excited about it than I was. His eyes were still haunted, dark smudges standing out against his pale skin.

When I'd woken up, my head a little clearer after a couple hours of sleep, I'd realized Jack was right. The two of us had done all we could, and it wasn't enough. We had to tell Stellan everything, just in case. Mr. Emerson's life depended on it.

Plus, it would distract me from the fact that there was still no sign of my mom.

I adjusted the silver mask over my face, happy for the anonymity.

"Have I told you how breathtaking you look, *cherie?*" Luc spun me out to arm's length, and my dress swished around my feet. "This silk drapes fabulously on you."

Despite everything, the dress had taken my breath away when I changed into it, just like it had at Prada. I remembered what I'd been thinking then, too. How different I looked. Like maybe the person wearing this dress could find what she was missing.

I reached for my locket and found the pretty silver teardrop necklace the store had sent instead. My locket was broken, tucked into my bag, in my room. I wished I'd put it back on. I didn't feel free anymore without it. I felt naked.

"Thanks," I said tightly. "It's—"

We stepped out of the elevator and into the ballroom, and the view stole the words from my mouth. Chandeliers and dancing candlelight gave the space a darkly romantic glow, and streamers hung from the ceiling like it was raining gold. Adding to the illusion, the crisscrossing metal beams outside were lit as well, like we were floating hundreds of feet in the air in a luminescent web. I supposed that was almost true. The ball was on the third level of the Eiffel Tower.

"It's a gorgeous dress," I finished. That much was true. The dress was beautiful. The ball was beautiful. I was in Paris, inside the Eiffel Tower, wearing Prada. I still couldn't believe that.

A group of people stopped Luc, and for the next ten minutes, he chatted and introduced me as the distant cousin I was supposed to be, and it all felt incredibly inappropriate when someone had died last night. There *was* a damper over the festivities—laughs weren't as loud as they could be, and everyone offered Luc their condolences—but they certainly weren't acting like their family and friends were recent casualties of an ongoing war. Maybe the Circle has been through so much that a little spilled blood no longer meant much to them. Or maybe, like Luc said, they just had to keep up appearances.

If I thought about that too much, I'd go crazy. So instead, I searched faces. I quickly found a downside to the anonymity of the masks. Even if I knew exactly what he looked like, there was no way

I could find my father. And dark hair and purple eyes by themselves weren't enough to tell anything at all.

I slipped my arm through Luc's again. "Are your parents here?" I hoped at least to see Monsieur Dauphin without a mask on.

"It's too dangerous for my mother to come." Luc looked around the party distractedly. "The rest of us can take a risk, but a pregnant woman carrying the girl from the mandate? This party is technically for her, but she's staying home. And I don't believe Father's here yet."

I twisted a lock of hair around my finger. Maybe everyone would take off their masks at some point and I could think about my father then. Right now, I needed to find Jack, and the two of us needed to locate Stellan.

"Can I find you later?" I said to Luc.

He nodded. "Are you looking for Jack? You've been hanging out with him a lot."

I stiffened. If Luc had noticed, other people had definitely noticed. I muttered something about talking to the Saxons.

"Fine," Luc said with an exaggerated sigh, stroking the ends of my curls, then taking my face in his hands. "Leave me *all* alone." He kissed me on both cheeks with a smile that didn't reach his eyes. "Just be sure to save me a dance."

I promised, and left him talking to some diplomats as I made my way through the mingling crowds. Around the central dance floor, dozens of small tables flickered with candlelight, and at the end of the room opposite the entrance, a small orchestra played a lively waltz, the sound of violins and cellos mingling with the perfume of hundreds of pink peonies.

I was making my way past the dance floor toward a less-crowded corner where I might have a better vantage point when I saw

Stellan. He stood alone against a wall of windows, talking on his phone, nearly blending into the dark.

I could have approached him then, but I wanted to find Jack first and go over our plan. I'd keep an eye on where Stellan went from here, and we could find him in a few minutes. I turned to go, but then I heard him. I stopped. If I hadn't known better, I'd have said Stellan was speaking almost *sweetly*.

Curious, I inched closer—and only then did I notice Madame Dauphin approaching his quiet corner from the opposite direction, her hand on her full belly.

Stellan hung up the phone and snapped to attention, which looked vaguely comical, considering the gold mask perched on his forehead.

Unfortunately, I was right in his line of vision now. I pressed my back to the wall of windows, partially hidden by a jutting pillar.

"Madame," Stellan said. He wore a slim black tuxedo that made his shoulders look especially sharp. "I thought you weren't coming tonight."

"Hugo and the security staff decided I wasn't coming," Madame Dauphin said. "You know that *I* prefer to do things my own way." She wore a draping black dress, and with her severe blond hair and red lips, she looked both frightening and beautiful, like the evil queen in a Disney movie.

"So?" she said impatiently. "What have you found? I was expecting a report on her earlier in the day."

Her?

Stellan darted a glance toward the center of the room, like he wished he was anywhere else. It was odd to see him look uncomfortable. "I've found nothing of concern," he said.

Madame Dauphin stepped closer, and Stellan stepped back. "You and I both know there's *something* going on. The Order only attacks people who matter. And then you let her run off, after I told you specifically to keep an eye on her. Lucky for you, she came back today with that Saxon Keeper."

Stellan flinched, and so did I. I'd been right. Not only was Stellan watching me, *Madame Dauphin* was, too. And she'd noticed Jack and me. I pressed farther back into the shadows.

"I told you I'd report any findings immediately," Stellan said.

"I hope so. You know what it means if you keep anything from me."

Stellan bowed his head. "Yes, Madame. I am quite aware."

"In fact," Madame Dauphin said, looking around and lowering her voice even more, so I had to strain to hear her, "I wonder if we shouldn't capture the girl, to be sure. We can hold her until we're able to investigate more thoroughly."

I went cold all over.

Stellan looked behind him, almost at me, and I held my breath. "She belongs to another family. I don't think that would be looked upon kindly."

Madame Dauphin waved a slim hand. "The Saxons have hardly acknowledged her existence. I want you to take her and hold her, just for now. Make sure there's nothing inappropriate going on."

Stellan opened his mouth, but Madame Dauphin cut him off.

"Senator. Hello." Madame Dauphin's voice rose an octave. "So glad you could celebrate with us."

A man in a suit took Madame Dauphin's arm, and the two of them walked away. Stellan watched them go before disappearing into the crowd.

I waited until I couldn't see him anymore, then crept out of my hiding place. I needed to find Jack before Stellan could find me, we had to be careful what we told him, then I had to get out of here.

I stuck to the shadows around the edge of the dance floor. Not having any peripheral vision was starting to drive me crazy, but now I had even less interest in taking my mask off. Madame Dauphin could have spies everywhere. So I looked for Jack as well as I could from my limited perspective.

The CEO of one of the biggest software companies in the world ate a canapé and frowned at the crowd. A Victoria's Secret model tossed her long blond hair and leaned on the shoulder of a short, round man in a turban. A tiny white-haired woman smiled up at a basketball player even I recognized, and I didn't watch basketball at all. When the woman turned to set down her champagne glass, I did a double take. It was the queen of England.

Still no Jack.

The plume of an elaborate peacock mask skimmed my shoulder. I jumped, and the woman wearing it laughed drunkenly.

I let out a breath through pursed lips. Calm down. Think. If Jack was here, he'd be looking for me, too. I found an empty space by a pillar and, when I was sure no one was looking at me, pushed my mask onto my forehead. There were Keepers and security posted around the room, all in matching black tuxedos, but despite the black masks, I could tell none of them was him.

My eyes flitted all the way around the room—and then, no more than thirty feet away, I saw him. He was standing against a pillar next to the musicians, feet apart, hands in his pockets, searching just like I was.

My gaze lingered on the cut of the tuxedo jacket hugging his shoulders and tapering to his waist. How was it possible that he got better looking every time I saw him, and that, as much as I tried not to, I *still* noticed? And still couldn't stop remembering the feel of his hands cupping my face, me running my fingers through his hair.

The only thing that feels right is as wrong as it can get, he'd said.

It drove me crazy that I wasn't angry. That half of me wanted to slip my hand into his and face everything together, as a *we* again. But the other half wanted to forget anything could ever possibly happen between us. The wanting—and not having—hurt too much, and that was exactly why I'd always tried to avoid it.

I made my way toward Jack, the music getting louder as I came up beside him.

He whipped around, and his eyes, behind his mask, went from high alert to relief—and what I could swear was something more as he took in my dress.

It stabbed into my gut. "Hi," I said.

"Hi." His voice was nearly drowned out by the swell of the violins.

I waited for the music to sink back to a normal volume and glanced back at the dance floor. Jack had chosen this spot well—nobody seemed to be watching us at the moment. "Madame Dauphin wants Stellan to hide me away and interrogate me."

"What?" Jack pushed his mask to the top of his head and led me to a small bar table in a dark corner.

I took my own mask off, carefully detangling the strap from my hair. "I don't know exactly *what* she suspects, but she knows something's going on."

Jack tapped his mask against the table and frowned. "Well, now that you've told me, they won't be able to get away with it, but I'd rather they not even try. Do you want me to talk to Stellan about Fitz by myself? I'll get one of our security staff to watch out for you until I get back."

The orchestra struck up a waltz. I tucked a curl behind my ear, looking behind me again. "No," I said. "I want to hear what he says. I think we talk to him, you stay with me so he can't do anything, and then I get out of here."

"You don't want to try to find your father?" The candles in the center of the table cast flickering shadows on Jack's face.

I frowned. I didn't realize he knew that was my plan. Besides, that was looking like a dead end, too, unless everyone took their masks off. "I don't think it's going to happen tonight."

Jack took a breath. "Avery, I should tell you—"

"Jack Bishop," a girl's voice said teasingly. Jack whipped around.

A girl about my age sashayed toward us in a red dress with a cascade of ruffles that ended in a mermaid hem. She pushed sideswept dark bangs off a feathered red mask. Jack locked his hands behind his back.

"What are you doing back here?" she asked, in a pretty, proper British accent.

Jack glanced back at me. "Lydia," he said. "I was . . . Lydia, this is Avery West. Avery, meet Lydia Saxon."

My fingers tightened on the mask in my hand. Lydia Saxon. Alistair Saxon's daughter, I assumed.

"Avery West? As in, the cousin we've heard about but not yet seen? Where have you been hiding her?" She gave Jack a playful shove and turned to me. "Pleased to finally meet you."

"Nice to meet you, too." There was something disconcerting about this girl. I couldn't put my finger on it, but I could swear she was looking at me funny, too.

"Jack," Lydia said. She looked me up and down so quickly, I would have missed it if I hadn't been watching her. "My father wants to speak with you. I'm sure he and Cole will want to meet Avery, too."

"Thanks, Lydia." Jack gave her a tight smile. Unlike Stellan and

Elodie with Luc, Jack seemed to actually treat Lydia as his employer. "We'll be just one second."

Lydia waved her fingers and headed back onto the dance floor. When she was far enough away that I shouldn't have been watching her anymore, she shot one last glance over her shoulder and frowned.

"Let's find Stellan quickly, then," Jack said. He was all efficiency, but I could sense the tension in his face. "It sounds like the Saxons are looking for me. Cole is Lydia's twin brother. They're Alistair Saxon's children."

Jack seemed to only ramble like this when he was nervous. I watched Lydia go. "You didn't tell her anything about me, did you?"

Jack looked around the dance floor distractedly. "What?"

"Did you see the way she looked at me?"

"Avery." Jack slipped his mask inside his jacket and turned to me. "No. I did not tell her anything."

I let out a breath through my teeth as the orchestra started a fast song. I pointed to where I'd seen Stellan disappear and slipped my own mask back on. "Last time I saw him, he was over there. If we're going to do this, let's do it."

Jack left a few seconds ahead of me so we wouldn't be seen together again. I followed his back toward the other side of the dance floor when a man stepped in front of me. He was middle-aged, with a red face, a blue mask, and a shock of blond curls, and he grabbed my hand with a grin and pulled me toward the dance floor.

"Oh," I said, resisting. "No, I—"

"What?" the man yelled, yanking us into place at the end of a line of couples. Three couples down, an older lady with snow-white hair and a bird mask held both of Jack's hands. I met his eyes, but then everyone around me clapped twice, and the blond man spun me and I lost Jack in the crowd.

I gave a silent thanks to my mom for forcing me to take ballroom-dance classes years ago, and foxtrotted across the floor. All the couples ended up in a circle, and then the whole crowd clapped again and my partner released me down the line. I tried to find Jack, but all the twirling tuxedos looked the same. The next guy in the circle, with smiling eyes behind a sky-blue mask, was already holding out his hand, and I took it reluctantly, searching the crowd over his shoulder as the dance continued.

And then another new partner, and another, one in dark robes rather than a suit, squeezing my hand so hard, I was afraid he'd break my fingers, the next younger than me, and stepping on the hem of my dress as we ran through an arch made of everyone's hands. I tried to escape every time we changed partners, but kept getting swept back up. How much longer could this dance go on?

On the next partner switch, I fell into a set of arms that held me exactly how they were supposed to, if a little closer than normal. The man's palm wasn't even sweaty.

"Looking lovely as usual, *kuklachka*," he said in my ear.

My eyes snapped up to Stellan's, staring down at me through a gold mask. I fought the instinct to pull away, reminding myself I *wanted* to find him. If I could pull him off the dance floor, I could signal to Jack and we could get this over with.

"How are you enjoying the ball?" he said. The dancing and the nerves had riled up my blood too much. My skin prickled when he moved his hand from my waist to the open back of my dress.

"It's beautiful," I said tightly. The crowd formed two lines, and Stellan directed me to the end of one, holding both my hands between us.

When we came together again, hands above our heads, he said, "One more question." He leaned close to my ear. "What did you hear earlier?"

So he *had* seen me while he was with Madame Dauphin. He pulled me back into a waltz position. "I don't know what you're talking about," I said.

A lock of blond hair fell over his forehead as he stared down at me. "Who are you?"

My heart spiked. He didn't actually know. Just keep playing dumb and I'd be fine. "What do you mean?"

He tucked a finger under my chin. "I'm going to find out one way or another," he said. "You may as well tell me now."

"I'm not—" He stroked my jaw with his thumb. "Nothing." I gritted my teeth. "I'm no one. I'm not anything. *Stop* it." I twisted my face away, suddenly very aware of the music pounding through my feet like a heartbeat.

With a grating scrape of metal, Stellan drew his dagger at waist level.

"I asked you," he said, in a low, measured voice, "who are you?"

CHAPTER 31

What are you doing?" I couldn't scream. That would draw more attention I didn't want. "Is pulling a knife on me your answer to everything?"

He tucked the arm not holding the knife even closer around me and twirled us deftly away from the crowd, making no move to let go when everyone clapped for a partner switch. "*Qui êtes-vous, kuklachka?*"

"What?" I looked behind me frantically. We were nearly off the dance floor now. Where was Jack?

"*Quien es? Ni shi shui? Kto ty?* Or do you need it in another language?" The dagger shone in the dim light, scrollwork running down the blade like rivulets of blood.

I pulled away as far as I could. The fabric of my dress strained against his arm, still locked around my waist. "I don't know what you're talking about."

"If you won't tell me, I'll guess. I guess that you're a spy."

"What?" My eyes snapped back to him. "No!"

The blade touched my skin. I drew in a sharp breath. He wouldn't hurt me. He couldn't.

"At first I thought you were a spy for the Order, or even one of their assassins, coming after Luc, but Prada proved me wrong. So, a spy for the Saxons?"

"No!" He thought I was a *spy*? No wonder he'd been suspicious from the beginning. "I'm just a . . . relative." It wasn't exactly a lie.

He pressed the dagger hard enough to make a dent in my skin. It rose and fell with my feverish breaths. "You realize someone sent a *professional* to kill you?" Stellan drew out the word.

"That was just—"

"I know Prada wasn't a mistake, and so do you." He spun me to an abrupt stop, still holding me close. "And then you run out of the club like an insane person after taking advantage of Luc's inebriation to get him to tell you who knows what."

"I did not take advantage of Luc," I snapped. Now I knew why he hadn't told Madame Dauphin anything. He had no idea who I was, and couldn't afford to be wrong.

"What would the Circle do if they knew you were threatening a member of another family?" I said, glaring up at him, my fingers digging into the shoulder of his tuxedo jacket. "Let go of me. Now."

He stared back, eyes flashing, and, after a few more seconds, dropped the knife from my chest.

I peeled his arm from my waist, turned, and nearly ran into Jack, who was hurrying toward us as the music faded to a less rowdy number and the dancers dissipated. He gestured with his head and we made our way into the shadows off the dance floor. "What's going on?" he said. "Did you tell him?"

I wiped the tiny bead of blood from my chest with shaking fingers. I had entirely forgotten about asking Stellan about Mr. Emerson. "No. He threatened me," I whispered, and Jack tensed. "It's okay, I'm fine. I just got sidetracked."

I let go of Jack and turned to where Stellan was walking away. "Wait," I called.

We caught up with him at a tall cocktail table. "Changed your mind about telling me the truth?" he said to me. "Or have you two come to show me a slide show of the must-see tourist attractions of Istanbul?"

I stiffened. Jack wasn't kidding when he said they could track me anywhere. "If you'd given me time to explain before, I would have told you I had a panic attack at the club. I needed some air, but I got lost, and Jack was in Istanbul, so he picked me up."

I was proud of the lack of waver in my voice.

"Istanbul is what we need to talk to you about," Jack said. I watched for anyone watching us. We were alone. "It's Fitz. I was on my way to see him when I caught up with Avery, so I brought her with me. But he wasn't there—it looks like the Order's taken him."

Stellan's brows inched up.

"He left pictures of the thr—" Jack paused. "Of you and me, saying that we needed to help him." I gritted my teeth at the near-slip, but Jack went on. "Do you know why he might have said that?"

"Of course not." Stellan pulled his mask off and tossed it onto a table. "Are you seriously telling me Fitz has been kidnapped? Why in the world would the Order take a *tutor*?"

"We're not sure. We were hoping you might have some insight."

"Well, I don't." He looked between Jack and me, and his eyes narrowed. "What does *she* have to do with this?"

My heart rate spiked again. This was exactly what I didn't want. "I don't have anything to—"

I trailed off as a million tiny lights suddenly danced in front of my eyes. Maybe I actually *was* having a panic attack now.

But no, people were pointing out of the tower. Of course—the Eiffel Tower light show. It twinkled out over Paris every hour. If I had been a tourist, I definitely would have wanted to come see it, and now we were watching it from the inside.

"What are you not telling me?" Stellan said.

"We have some things to show—" Jack started to pull the diary out of his jacket, but Stellan looked over my shoulder. His face hardened, and I put a hand on Jack's arm. A tall man in a tuxedo was storming across the dance floor toward us. Jack hid the book again.

"You and the security staff were supposed to keep her home tonight," the man barked at Stellan, his face and light brown hair blurring with the twinkling lights. "And now she's off doing God knows what."

"Yes, Monsieur Dauphin," Stellan said, and I looked up sharply. The lights burned into my brain. "Madame was not meant to come tonight. But—"

"But she does as she wants." Monsieur Dauphin hit the table with a fist, and I flinched.

He looked just like Luc, only twice as wide. And ten times as mean. He didn't look like *me*. Not even a little bit.

I touched Jack's arm, motioning him away. We couldn't do this now. Monsieur Dauphin's eyes flicked to me and narrowed. I could see the wheels turning in his head—Madame must have told him her suspicions, too. He said something in French to Stellan, who glanced at me, too.

I turned, pulling on Jack's sleeve, and was surprised to see Lydia Saxon headed our way, with a frowning dark-haired boy who must have been her brother, Cole, in tow. And behind them, a man in a masquerade mask. Now Jack was the one who snapped to attention. My hand fell from his arm.

The lights kept going. Flash, flash, flash. They seemed to get brighter by the second.

Flash. I turned to Jack, to find his brows a tangle of unreadable emotions. He nodded to the man, who stepped forward, pulling off his mask.

Flash. The lights flickered faster, or maybe now it really *was* in my head.

Flash. I stared, unblinking, unable to move. The man's face was illuminated by a million tiny bulbs, dark-bright, dark-bright.

Flash. I couldn't tear my gaze away, and the man didn't move either as the edges of my world fell away.

As I stared into a mirror version of my own eyes.

CHAPTER 32

My eyes.

And not just the same color, like Luc's. The same *everything*. Intense, dark violet eyes, set a little too far apart. Rimmed with thick black lashes, bordered by dark brows. The rest of his face was entirely different—the square jawline, the pronounced cheekbones—and if I hadn't been looking for it, I wouldn't have noticed any more resemblance than distant family would be expected to have. But I *knew*. They were my eyes.

Lydia stepped up next to him, her hand on his arm. She'd taken off her mask, too. She didn't have the eye color, but I could see now that her wide-set eyes—and her twin brother's—were an echo of mine. *That* was what had bothered me about her. Even behind the mask, I'd seen shades of my own face. Lydia and Cole Saxon. That meant—

Something drew my gaze down, to Alistair Saxon's jacket, to the embroidered insignia on a handkerchief sticking out of the breast pocket. A compass. Just like Jack's tattoo, which I had always thought looked familiar. Then I realized when I'd seen it before.

I was five years old, searching the drawers in my mom's bedroom for something to play with. In one of them, my locket had rested on top of a sheaf of papers. Letters. Love letters, from what I could read of them. On top of each one, like personalized stationery, a compass had been embossed into the paper.

My head swiveled between the three of them, and the certainty of it all knocked the breath out of me.

This man was my father, and he was also Jack's boss, Alistair Saxon.

Jack shoved his hands into his pockets. He didn't look at all surprised. Obviously he hadn't found out just now. Finally, he flicked his eyes to mine, then back to his feet. "I'm sorry," he mouthed.

Jack had lied. He knew exactly who my father was.

My *father*.

Jack broke the silence that probably only lasted a few seconds but felt like a lifetime. "Sir, this is Avery West. She's the *cousin* we found in the States." He looked pointedly at Stellan and Monsieur Dauphin, who were talking just a few feet away, still shooting glances in our direction.

Saxon, my father, took a step closer to me. He knew I wasn't a cousin. I could tell. I could see him confirm it as he recognized me bit by bit. My mom's button nose and rounded cheeks. His own eyes. His daughter.

I wondered just how much Jack had lied to me—how much he'd told Saxon. If he knew I was the purple-eyed girl they'd all been waiting for.

"Yes," my father said with a bland smile. "Very good. Nice to meet you, young lady."

And then he turned away, like he was already bored.

I staggered like I'd been slapped, and had to grab the back of a chair. The lights outside stopped blinking. My father didn't bother to look in my direction again.

So Jack hadn't told him about my eyes. He didn't know how powerful I could make him, so he didn't care that I was his kid. After all that, he was just any old deadbeat dad. Maybe he had a dozen illegitimate children running around, and finding a new one wasn't a big deal.

"It's been a long night, Hugo," my father said to Monsieur Dauphin. "I know our guest has been staying with you, but I think we'll take her to our hotel, as we haven't had a chance to talk—"

I looked up, a flicker of hope running through me.

"Nonsense," Monsieur Dauphin cut him off. "It's nearly midnight. Isn't most of your family staying with us anyway? Sort it out in the morning. Speaking of, have you seen my wife? The headstrong . . ." He broke off, muttering under his breath.

My father glanced at me, then at Jack, and the hope coiled inside me like a spring. Then he gave a noncommittal shrug. "Yes. Fine. Lovely."

The spring snapped. My hand fluttered up to my chest, like I was trying to hold in the bits of shattered heart leaking out. My father knew I existed, and he didn't care a bit.

I really, really didn't want to cry in front of him. "I'm ready to go now," I said quietly. My voice didn't even hitch.

Jack stepped forward. "I'll take you—"

"No." I jerked away. My breath rattled in my chest. "Somebody else is probably going back anyway."

"I am."

I closed my eyes as Stellan stepped up beside me. Which was the lesser of the two evils?

Jack had lied to me. I'd asked him over and over about my father.

He knew exactly how much this meant to me. I'd told him embarrassingly personal things. And he knew his own employer was my father, and he didn't tell me. The betrayal burned through my blood like acid.

And yes, Stellan was supposed to interrogate me, but now that I'd met the Saxons and Jack knew Madame Dauphin's plan, he couldn't lock me up and throw away the key. Plus, it looked like there was no way I was ending up anywhere but the Dauphins' tonight.

I didn't look at Jack or my father as I followed Stellan out of the ball and rode silently in the elevator to the ground floor.

Thank you, world, for reminding me again exactly why I never let myself care.

We made our way to a line of waiting long black cars, and I stared up at the glowing tower, stretching nearly a thousand brilliant feet into the gray-and-purple night.

Stellan watched me. "What is your story, *kuklachka*?" he finally said.

I blinked, and the orange glow of the Eiffel Tower blurred into watercolor.

Stellan stopped in front of my room.

"So," he said. "You tell me you're no one, then almost get killed at a boutique, run away from a club in Istanbul, and now you're crying in a ball gown. You're sure there's nothing you want to tell me?"

"There's nothing *to* tell." My voice came out in a rasp. "You really don't believe me?"

Stellan unlocked the door to my room. "I learned long ago that I'm the only person I can trust, so no. I don't believe you. I just can't figure out what you're trying to cover up."

I pushed past him. "And I can't figure out why you're so temperamental. You were threatening to kill me a couple of hours ago, and now you're pretending to be friendly."

Stellan followed me into the room. "If I was actually threatening to kill you, you'd be dead."

"I'm going to sleep. Please leave." I stalked to the bathroom.

In the mirror, Stellan came into view and leaned against the doorframe. I turned on the sink and washed my hands.

"You know, spies are usually good liars. So are pretty girls," he said.

I tossed the lavender soap into the soap dish so hard, it bounced out and slithered to the bottom of the sink. I whirled on him.

"Really?" The water dripped down my forearms, and I grabbed a towel. "Sometimes I can't tell whether you're trying to interrogate me, or kill me, or sleep with me." I snapped my mouth shut and felt my whole body flush.

The corner of his mouth crooked up. "To be honest, I can't quite decide either."

"Get out."

Slowly, he pushed off the doorframe, blocking my way out. "You know, if you *were* a spy, I'd be impressed. Nothing hotter than a talented girl. I mean, I'd have to kill you. But before I did—"

"Go. Away." The tears were building behind my eyes again, frustration and exhaustion and bone-deep sadness. I threw the towel on the sink and swiped at my face with the back of my hand. "Seriously, go away."

Stellan studied me. "What *is* it that's upsetting you so much? Prada?"

I suddenly thought of that first morning, before Prada, when I was wearing nothing but a robe and my biggest problem was trying to forget how attractive Stellan was. It seemed like another lifetime.

"It's nothing. I'm fine. I just want you to leave so I can sleep." I had to brush against him to get through the doorway, and he blocked my way with one hand.

"You're rubbing your eyes a lot for someone who's fine," he said, not entirely unkindly. His hand was warm on my hip.

The tears swam even closer to the surface. I forced them back by sheer will and pushed the rest of the way past. "I'm *fine*. My contacts itch, that's all."

There was a pause. "You wear contact lenses?"

I felt the scowl drop off my face. Oh God. I forced myself to turn and glare at him again, but I couldn't cover the beat of hesitation. "I have really bad vision."

He pursed his lips, and there was a knock on the door. Elodie stuck her head in and said something to Stellan in French without even a glance at me.

Stellan sighed. "It appears I'm needed. Sleep well, little doll. There will be guards outside to make sure nothing *happens* to you overnight."

I covered my sigh of relief with a yawn. I could only hope that another purple-eyed girl was so far out of the realm of possibility that he wouldn't connect my contacts to his suspicions.

He made no show of hurrying, and I shoved him the rest of the way out with the door. I closed it behind him, locked it, and rested my forehead against the cool wood while I listened to the two sets of footsteps retreat down the hall.

I collapsed onto the blue velvet comforter, the fabric of my dress crinkling under me.

I lay there for a second before I pulled out my phone and called my mom again. Nothing.

I put the phone back in my bag and dug around for my locket. I set the Prada necklace on the bedside table and tied the two ends of my locket's broken clasp around my neck, then buried my face in the comforter. I felt about a hundred years older than I had a few days ago. I knew so many things I'd never wanted to know. And at the same time, I felt like a little kid. So much less sure of the world, of myself, of everything.

My father didn't care about me. Pretty soon I was going to have to accept that my mom was actually *missing*. And Jack had lied. I trusted him—I *finally* trusted him—and he lied. After everything we'd been through. I didn't even know what that meant. When had he told Saxon? Did they have some kind of plan that involved keeping me in the dark? It didn't seem like my father cared enough to have a plan like that.

I rolled over to my back and stared up at the canopy above the bed.

It felt so trivial to be sad about a boy right now. Jack lying to me shouldn't hurt so much, especially compared with everything else. Like Mr. Emerson. I reached into my bag again and found the piece of paper with the Order's phone number on it. Ironically, I'd written it on the back of the sketch of Jack's tattoo I'd done in Ancient Civ that day. I traced the drawing with one finger. I almost wished I had a compass tattooed on me right now. I could use some direction.

With a start, I realized I could get one on my seventeenth birthday if I wanted. I was a Saxon.

I shook my head. We only had about twelve hours until the Order's deadline. I flipped the paper back over and stared at the phone number until my eyes crossed. We were at a dead end with the clues. Maybe my father could help us find the Order and take Mr. Emerson back by force, if I could get him to care enough about me to go to the trouble.

I rolled off the bed and crossed the room to the window. Should

I suck it up and call Jack and have him get Saxon to start a search? I really, really didn't want to talk to him right now.

I slid the window open, letting the smell of the storm that had been threatening all afternoon wash over me. A low rumble of thunder sounded in the distance, and I leaned on the window frame and looked out over the Louvre courtyard.

"There you are," said a deep voice next to me.

I whipped around. There on the balcony, leaning against the wall outside my window, was Jack.

CHAPTER 33

What are you doing here?" I demanded. It came out part angry, part relieved, a lot worried.

He scrambled to his feet. "Please let me explain."

"Coming to my *room* in the middle of the *night*? Are you crazy?" I whispered, pointing at the bedroom door and putting my finger to my lips. I kicked off my shoes and climbed out the window onto the thin balcony. I refused Jack's hand when he held it out to help, and I eased the window closed behind me.

I stared him down. "Why did you lie to me?" The breeze flapped my dress.

"Avery, I'm so sorry." And he looked it. He looked as broken as I felt, from his pleading eyes to the loose bow tie around his neck, obviously forgotten. "I was wrong. I was going to tell you, so many times."

"How long have you known?"

I could tell he wanted to avert his eyes, but he didn't. "Since Prada. It's not exactly that you look like him, but I could see it, once I realized your father had to be one of the twelve."

I swallowed. "So you and the Saxons were just stringing me along that whole time? Why?"

"He didn't know until tonight."

"What?" I looked up, my eyes swimming.

"He found out at the ball, and it wasn't me who told him," Jack went on. "Lydia figured it out. She recognized you somehow."

Just like I'd recognized her. She looked like my *sister*. I still hadn't processed that.

I crossed to the railing. Even though the museum was long closed, people still milled around the square below, taking photos of the pyramid gleaming against the softer lights on the Louvre's stone facade.

"It was never my intention to hurt you," Jack said quietly. "Trust me on that."

"I *can't*!" I whirled around. "That's the point. I can't trust you. You knew how much this meant to me, and you lied over and over about having no idea who he was."

He paced a few steps down the balcony. "I didn't tell you because I wanted to know what Fitz meant before I let you walk into something dangerous. Or because you might run. Or . . . I don't know. I should have told you." His dark hair flopped onto his forehead, like even it felt defeated. "I thought it would be better for everyone if I told you when you were in the same place and let you approach him yourself. We were so busy, the ball was the first opportunity."

That was what he'd been about to say before Lydia interrupted us, I realized. "And what if I hadn't wanted to talk to him?"

"I was going to let you leave."

"You would have let me get away again? They'd kill you for that. Especially if they found out you knew who I really was," I said, half jokingly, looking at the spot on his arm where I knew his tattoo was. Beautiful. Deadly.

"I know," he said, not jokingly at all.

I leaned on the railing, not sure whether he was making me feel better or worse. "You can't say things like this, then do something completely different and expect me to believe you. To *trust* you."

If I shattered one more time, I might not be able to put the pieces back together.

"I know. I'm sorry," Jack said again, quietly. "That's what I came here to say." He reached into the breast pocket of his coat and pulled out an envelope with my name on it. "Saxon wrote you this. It was my excuse for coming to see you."

Avery,

I understand this is a shock. It is one for me, too, but a welcome one. I wish I could speak with you tonight, but I think it's best not to arouse unnecessary suspicion. I'll come get you in the morning. Security at the Dauphins' is tight—you'll be safe.

Best, Alistair Saxon

I read the note again. "So does he want to marry me off to somebody in the morning?"

Jack shook his head. "He doesn't know about the purple eyes. I should have told him, but I wanted you to at least be able to do *that* yourself."

I held the note so hard, it crumpled between my fingers. I turned back to Jack, who was rubbing the back of his neck uneasily.

"Why couldn't you have told me?" I said again. My voice cracked.

The confusion, the uncertainty, the relief still flowing through me at seeing Jack. The euphoric jump in my heart knowing that my father *did* care. The sound of the killer's head hitting the floor at Prada. The last thing I said to my mom—a lie about how I'd stay home from prom and pack.

I was falling. Falling, falling, falling. I clapped my hand over my mouth to stifle a sob that escaped anyway.

Jack's jaw clenched, and he crossed the balcony in one stride.

He folded me into his arms.

I pushed him away, but he didn't let me. He tucked me under his chin and wrapped his arms around me tight. And then I crumbled. I clung to him with everything I had, handfuls of his shirt balled up in my fists, sobbing the huge, choking sobs I'd been holding back for days.

It felt like the tears would never stop.

Jack held me close, and I felt his heart beat and his chest rise and fall under my cheek, and breathed in the inexplicable, musky sweetness of his skin—apples, I decided through the haze of tears. He smelled like fall, like autumn sun and ripe apples. Finally, I felt my shoulders relax and the sobs taper off.

I nuzzled my head into his chest and he tangled his fingers in my hair. "Sorry," I whispered, but that wasn't the right thing to say. "Thanks," I said, but that wasn't quite right either. I pulled away an inch and stared at his chest, where my tears had left a wet, mascara-smeared blotch.

"I can't betray the Saxons and the Circle," he murmured into the top of my head. "But I can't—I won't—betray you, either. I promise."

Hearing him say it felt like standing on the edge of a threshold we'd been dancing around since we met.

"Are those two things mutually exclusive?" I whispered.

"I hope not," he said. "I don't think so."

I didn't want to want him. I didn't want to wish I could run my fingers through his hair again, to touch a new cut on his cheek. I didn't want to forgive him, but I did want to, so badly.

"You didn't leave me," I said. I ran a fingertip around a button on his shirt, not meeting his eyes. "You didn't leave me and save yourself on Mr. Emerson's balcony. You didn't turn me in to make things easier. You didn't leave me alone tonight, even though you knew I'd be mad at you." I swallowed back a lump in my throat.

His fingers paused in stroking my hair. "Of course I didn't."

However misguided it was, Jack had done what he'd done to protect me. How was it possible that in a tug-of-war for his loyalty between the Saxons—his only family for years—and me, I was winning?

I finally disentangled myself from his arms. My hands lingered under his tuxedo jacket, palms grazing down his sides, his starched white shirt crinkling under my fingertips.

He drew in a sharp breath that sent a flutter through me. His gaze skimmed the curves of my silver Prada dress. It really was the color of his eyes. Moonlight and storms.

I pulled my hands away and sat cross-legged, my dress spread out around me on the balcony. I wiped my cheeks with the heels of my hands, and the quickening breeze dried them the rest of the way. The storm really seemed to be moving in now. Jack slipped out of his tuxedo jacket and draped it around my shoulders before he sat down, too.

"Did you tell my—Saxon about anything else? Mr. Emerson or the clues or anything?"

"I told him about Fitz being gone, but that's all for now. He's agreed to get someone in intelligence asking around right away. We can get him looking for your mom, too, if you're still not able to reach her."

A weight lifted off my chest. In the distance, the Eiffel Tower's hourly golden light show twinkled again against the clouds.

"Am I like him?" The words came out before I realized I was thinking them.

Jack kicked a pebble with the toe of his boot. "If anything, it's like two sides of the same coin," he said. "You both have this sparkle in your eyes. But his is . . . I don't know. Darker? Yours is light."

I swallowed back the lump in my throat. "Cheesy lines aren't going to make me forget I was mad at you."

"I'm not trying—"

"It's okay," I said.

I wondered if Jack meant it when he said kissing had made things worse. Or whether he *had* meant it, but what he'd said and done tonight meant he didn't care. Or whether he was here to be a good friend and that was all. I wondered if he was thinking about my hands on him as much as I was thinking about his hands on me.

Jack cleared his throat. "My second day in Lakehaven," he said. "It was a Monday."

Lightning lit the whole sky to daylight. I looked up at him expectantly, but he kept his eyes on the skyline.

"That was when I stopped watching you just because it was my job," he said.

I dug my nails into my palms. I guess I had my answer.

"The Saxons don't always pick me to go on recon missions like this, but they needed someone who would fit in at a school. I had this picture of you, and I thought it might be hard to find you, but the whole school was walking in one direction, and there you were, walking the other way, all by yourself, to sit outside and read. You fascinated me."

I stared at him. "Because I didn't have friends to sit with at lunch?"

His mouth crooked up. "Everyone with the Circle . . . they do what they're told. *I* do what I'm told. I know it probably sounds mad to you, but I'd never thought of doing anything else. And there you were, doing what you wanted."

I pulled my knees to my chest and tucked the dress around me, repositioning everything that had happened at school in my head in light of what he was saying.

Jack pulled the tie from around his neck and rolled it into a tight spiral. "I was supposed to find out whether you were a family member after all, then bring you in immediately, but I didn't. I liked it, going to classes, getting to know you. I knew it would stop the second we got back to the Saxons, back to real life, but it was worth it for the short amount of time I was there." He ran a hand through his hair. "It was completely irresponsible of me, but I was already planning to ask you to the prom, even before Stellan showed up."

I couldn't stop the smile that came over my face.

"And then through all of this, you've made me question everything I knew. You've been putting yourself in danger at every turn, not because you were told, but for somebody you loved, because you believed it was right." He paused, flicking the end of the tie with his thumb. "You know how the tattoos are an oath to be loyal to the family?"

I nodded. "To the death," I said. How could I forget?

Jack gave a small nod and touched his forearm. "I've never even considered breaking that oath before. Ever. But I did, for you. To keep you safe. Everything—from letting you go at prom, to tonight, at the ball—it's all been for you. As much as I tried to tell myself it was for the Saxons, it wasn't true. As much as I said I was going to Istanbul just for Fitz, it wasn't true. Every second I wasn't with you, I was thinking about you. Worrying about you. It wasn't for them." He cut his eyes to me, lowered his voice. "It was all for you."

All of a sudden, even with the breeze, it felt too hot out here. I pressed my palms to the cool tiles.

"Why didn't you tell me any of this before?" I whispered. The whole world had faded away to nothing but the two of us, and the storm, and everything I thought I knew, smashing into pieces again. "I'm sure it was obvious how I felt. How I feel."

My face got even hotter, and I was glad it was dark.

A ghost of a smile crossed his face. "No, I . . . I mean, after I kissed you, and you let me, I thought, maybe . . . I wasn't sure."

A laugh bubbled up, like champagne bubbles pushing past the ache in my chest.

"I told myself you couldn't possibly feel the same way. I'm only a Keeper. Even if you were just a *cousin*, it would've been impossible, and once we realized what you really are . . ."

He trailed off. I thought about the Emirs' Keeper, terminated when he was caught having a relationship with a family member.

I leaned my head back against the wall. My own father wouldn't be so harsh, would he? And anyway, we could keep a secret. So maybe if we started something now, we'd have to stop it later to not get found out. I could deal with that when and if it happened. The stakes were bigger for Jack, and I didn't want to put him in danger, but I was pretty sure he felt the same way I did. Some things were just worth the risk.

And suddenly, at least for the moment, I knew what I was longing for. I'd understand if he refused, but I had to say it.

"I want you to stay," I blurted out.

At the exact time, he said, "Is it okay if I stay?"

"I don't want to be alone, and we could be really careful and no one would know—"

"I don't want to leave you alone. Anything could happen—"

"Right," I said, butterflies fluttering in my stomach. I couldn't believe I'd said that. I couldn't believe it had worked. I stood up. "Yeah. Um. Come in."

Jack's face fell. "I . . ." He shook his head. "I can't risk getting caught in your room."

"Oh." I tried not to look as horribly disappointed as I felt. Of course he just meant staying here to guard me. Nothing more. Of course it was too dangerous. My judgment was clouded.

And then the crackling air burst open. Lightning tore apart the sky, and the clouds that had been threatening all day ripped apart.

I scrambled back through the window, dashing rain out of my eyes. Jack leapt to standing.

"You can come in," I whispered. "It's only us in here."

He hesitated, but climbed in and huddled inches inside. He glanced back out like maybe he should leave after all. Then back at me like he didn't want to.

I stood across from him awkwardly. I'd spent the past forty-eight hours running across Europe, being shot at, stealing antiquities, but I still couldn't deal with one boy. I knew it was wrong, and I knew it was dangerous, but I didn't want him to leave.

I crossed the room to the hallway door, made sure it was locked, and put the vanity chair under the doorknob. The rain hammered the roof, punctuated with pings off the metal railing. I thought I saw a smile on Jack's face in the dark.

"Come in," I whispered.

Water made my dress heavy and bulky, and in the bit of light from outside, I could see Jack's shirt dripping, clinging to the lines of his body, and now I really couldn't think.

"Clothes!" The word flew out of my mouth. No one would overhear. The rain was so loud now, I could barely hear myself. "Dry clothes! I can get you some."

"Yeah, that'd be brilliant. Thanks." I heard a smile in his voice. I hoped he couldn't hear how flustered I was in mine.

I felt his eyes on me while I flipped on the lamp in the closet and searched for anything that would fit him. I finally found a pair of flannel pants. I couldn't find a shirt that was big enough, so he'd have to decide what to do about that.

I tossed him the pants and gestured to the bathroom, then turned back to the pajama drawer. Nightgowns, a lavender silk shorts and tank top set, lacy black lingerie . . .

My face got hot just looking at the lingerie. I pulled out the shorts and tank top and slammed the drawer.

When I'd changed into them and hung the wet dress on a hanger, I looked in the mirror. In the pale lamplight, I looked soft, romantic. My damp hair fell in waves, dark against my skin, and my eyes looked wider, darker than usual. My heart was too empty and too full at the same time.

I came out of the walk-in at the same time Jack opened the bathroom door. He wore only the pants I had given him, his bare upper body silhouetted against the bathroom light. A cool, rain-scented breeze blew through the open balcony window, and goose bumps rose on my skin.

We could just sleep next to each other. Just so I wouldn't be alone.

Jack reached behind him to the bathroom light switch.

"You can sleep in the bed with me. If you want." The words rushed out of my mouth before I could stop them. "I mean, I know it's dangerous. And it's up to you. But no one knows you're here. And the bed's really . . . big."

As he flipped the switch, a flash of lightning made the room as bright as day, illuminating him, his lips parted, eyes wide.

Thunder crashed right on top of the lightning, so loud that it shook the floor. My heart, which had already been beating double-time, hammered so hard my hands shook.

Jack stepped out from the bathroom door. "I think that means yes," he said.

CHAPTER 34

I slipped under the covers and shivered at the crisp cool of the sheets. I shivered again when I felt Jack climb in on the other side. I was in bed with Jack. I'd asked him to get into my bed. And he'd done it, despite the fact that being caught here would be very, very bad. I would never have imagined a boy spending the night in my bed to be a life-or-death situation.

Neither of us had closed the window, and the rain pounded down wildly. A gust of wind stirred the chandelier, and the crystals tinkled.

"Good night?" I whispered. I hadn't meant for it to sound like a question.

"G'night," he said after a second. He didn't sound disappointed, which made me feel a little disappointed.

Whenever I slept over at Lara's, I barely knew there was another person in the bed. Now, though, I could sense the heat radiating off Jack's body, feel every shift of the covers.

Jack moved closer. If not for the rain, my full-body buzz might be audible by now. I shifted, too, a minuscule movement toward the middle of the bed. And then my pinky finger touched a body part that wasn't my own, and my buzz short-circuited. Jack's fingers twined around mine until I could feel his pulse where they inter-laced.

I tried to calm my racing heart. Holding his hand—even in my bed—was nothing. But it didn't feel like nothing. The warmth of his bare arm against mine edged out the cool of the sheets, and the band of tension around my chest started to relax. It was like even though I'd said all the wrong things outside, Jack had heard exactly what I meant.

And then the sheets rustled, shifted, and a lightning strike lit everything to neon. I could see the outline of Jack's shoulders as he rolled onto his side. After a second, his fingers wrapped around my hip, and he pulled me gently onto my side, too, facing him. He brought the sheet up and over our heads. My unsteady breath echoed off the covers and our bodies, louder now than the rain pounding outside.

Not only was I in bed with Jack, I was in bed, under the sheets, so close my knees pressed into his. I felt his face tilt down to mine, and I let my lips inch closer to his.

But he didn't kiss me. Instead, he pulled our interlaced hands up between us. He straightened my fingers with his, and ran his finger-tips down my palm.

I never thought I'd forget about kissing, but just then, I did. I wanted him to do nothing but touch my hand like this for the rest of my life. And then his fingers trailed over my wrist, down the inside of my arm.

I pressed my lips together hard. Air. I needed air. But I didn't pull back the sheets. If I moved, it might stop. Breathing wasn't worth it.

Jack took his fingers off my arm. Before I could wonder why he'd stopped, he grasped my hand, all its nerve endings wide awake now, and pressed it to his own chest.

There was something delirious about not being able to see, about just feeling the warmth radiating from his body, hearing the soft in-and-out of his breathing, smelling the rain through the open window and on his skin. It mixed with his own scent, warm, earthy, cozy, like a fall storm, making me want to bury my face in his neck. My fingers settled into the curve over his heart, and he swept my hair off my shoulder, the strands tickling my skin. His touch was slow, cautious.

Oh. I hadn't considered that he might not know how I'd react. When he brushed the soft patch of skin behind my ear, I let my neck arch into him, showing him just how okay this was.

I'd almost forgotten where my own hand was until I felt his heartbeat speed up. And then it hit me. After all we'd talked about outside, he thought he had to prove to me that I could trust him. That how he felt about me was real. He didn't know how to do it with words, so he was showing me instead. He couldn't fake the pounding pulse under my palm.

And at the same time, he was making me open up. And I was letting him. Here, in the dark, I had let down my guard without even realizing it.

All I wanted was to do the same for him.

I let my fingertips move, tentatively. I'd never touched a guy's bare chest before. It was hard and soft at the same time, smooth skin over firm muscle.

My fingers grew more confident as I traced down his side, where a few small, round scars marred his skin. I stopped at one and he tensed, like me noticing this imperfection made him feel too exposed. Maybe I should have moved on, but I liked knowing there were imperfect parts of him. I stroked the scar with one fingertip. It took a minute, but I finally felt the tension melt out of him.

This tiny moment felt more intimate than all the kissing in the world.

Everyone kissed. I'd kissed other guys. He'd probably done a lot more than kiss with other girls. But this was different. More. I'd seen cracks in his armor. Now I felt him taking it off.

I ran my hand over his forearm, over where my memory told me his tattoo was even if my eyes didn't. To his neck, where blood pulsed life through the surprisingly delicate skin at his throat, pushed aside a lock of still-damp hair clinging to his forehead. It had gotten warmer under the sheets, but every new bit of his skin still felt cool.

All the time, I fell closer into the kind of trance I didn't ever want to wake up from, half asleep and wide awake all at once.

Jack traced a path down my nose, across the bow in my upper lip. Then catching on the chain of my locket. To my shoulder. Our lips still weren't touching, but I was breathing his air and he was breathing mine.

Something in the far back of my mind told me it would be too easy, in this trance of our breath and our fingers and the rain pounding outside, to sleepwalk ourselves into something I wasn't sure I was ready for. Jack traced my forearm.

Yes, too easy.

One fingertip stroked the inside of my palm. My body felt unfamiliar, unsteady.

His hand settled on the curve of my hip.

With considerable effort, I made myself take hold of his wrist. He froze. My eyes fluttered open, blinking in the dark. I hoped he didn't think anything was wrong. It wasn't that at all.

After just a second, he exhaled softly. He straightened my fingers once more and pressed a kiss to my palm, then to each of my fingertips in turn. I felt a smile tug at my lips.

Finally he pulled the sheet off our heads, and cool air rushed in. I shivered, and Jack pulled me close, until I snuggled into the crook of his arm. His lips brushed my forehead and settled in my hair, and when I pressed my palm to his chest again, his breathing fell into a steady in-and-out within minutes.

I breathed a small, contented sigh into his chest. After everything that had happened, how was it possible for me to feel this happy right now?

I didn't know if I'd be able to sleep at all, and a part of me didn't want to. I wasn't ready to lose tonight to unconsciousness yet, wasn't ready to face the real world again in the morning. But with the steady beat of Jack's heart under my hand, and his warm skin against my cheek, I finally drifted off into dreams.

CHAPTER 35

I thought I knew what it felt like to wake up, but I'd never woken up like this. I opened my eyes to the unfamiliar and incredibly pleasant sensation of my head rising and falling to the rhythm of someone else's breath.

For a second, I didn't remember where I was.

My head was still nuzzled into Jack's chest. One of his arms held me close to his side, and his other hand rested on top of mine over his heart. Only our legs had moved, tangling themselves together.

Last night had seemed like a dream, but he was here, his skin cool under my fingers, his soft breath stirring my hair.

As I watched, his brows knitted together and his eyes flicked back and forth under his lids like he was having a bad dream. I stroked his chest with one fingertip. He stirred, and his eyes fluttered open.

His heart sped up under my palm and we stared at each other silently. We were both still dressed; we hadn't done anything, really. So why did it feel like we'd done everything?

The morning light flooding the room suddenly felt wrong. Like it was forcing us back to the real world, the world where something other than the two of us existed. Where we had to do something now besides stare at each other—where we had to either acknowledge what had happened the previous night or pretend nothing had happened at all. We already had too much to deal with. Maybe not complicating things more would be for the best.

Still, neither of us had moved so much as a toe. Why was this so hard?

Finally, my fingers rebelled against the silence, tightening on Jack's chest.

The corners of his lips turned up. "Hi," he mouthed.

A grin spread across my face. "Hi," I mouthed back.

Jack's smile grew and I let mine take over. For the first time, maybe ever, my chest wasn't empty and aching and cold at all. In fact, it felt so full, it could have burst. This was worth the possibility of getting hurt a million times.

Had I never understood because I never let myself, or because I never had anyone to understand with? It turns out falling for someone doesn't feel like falling at all.

Jack glanced at the chair still under the doorknob, then settled back and tucked a strand of hair behind my ear.

"How did you sleep?" he whispered.

"Really well." Despite everything, it was the best I'd slept in a long time. "You?" I wondered if he'd slept at all, or if he'd been as alert all night as I should have been.

He threaded his fingers through mine. "Best I've slept in ages," he murmured. The hint of self-consciousness looked out of place on his face. "I should probably go, though."

I wanted to protest. I didn't want him to leave, ever. But I knew he was right.

He pulled back the sheet and sat up, and the sun no longer

seemed wrong. Now it was fine, bathing the beautiful, half-clothed boy in my bed in light.

He took his clothes into the bathroom, and I grabbed my phone out of my bag. First I called my mom again—no answer. But I'd thought of something else in that fuzzy place between asleep and awake.

As I dialed the number to retrieve my mom's phone messages, I hugged the pillow that smelled intoxicatingly like Jack and stared out the window at a clearer morning, like the edges of the world had been sharpened overnight. The sun shone on the top of the pyramid, the music of the traffic below came softly through the window, and I was almost able to forget that Jack and I—that apparently Jack and I were now a *we*—had made things even more complicated. And infinitely more dangerous. Even so, I couldn't stop grinning.

I typed in my mom's code and skipped through message after increasingly panicked message from myself—and then my insides went cold.

Jack came out of the bathroom, buttoning his still-damp shirt. "I'll be back with the Saxons and our guards within the hour—"

I held up a finger, listening, more confused by the second. Finally, the message ended.

"What is it?" Jack said. He perched on the edge of the bed next to me.

"I thought I'd check my mom's messages, just in case there was anything from the airlines about a delay or something, but . . . I think this one's from Mr. Emerson."

I pressed the button to replay it and put it on speaker:

"It's me. People have been watching me. They're here. If I don't make it, I need you to find what I've left." Mr. Emerson was breathing raggedly, rushing through the words. "The tomb. I've been searching for years. Napoleon found it, and hid it again. I have three clues he left, but there are more. I've hidden them, and you've got to get them before the Circle does. Start at my—the office I sometimes call you from. Follow from there. I'm sorry I've never told you.

"It's the union—Napoleon discovered some disturbing things. And there's more. I was searching for information about the One, and . . . you won't believe it, Carol. I can't say any more, but I believe I've found one of them, and brought—I've been trying to protect— never mind. Both of them are in great danger. You have to find—"

The message cut off abruptly.

My mouth was hanging open. "What—"

Jack replayed the message again. "Some of it's what he told us in the note. But he told her a lot more. Your *mom*. Which means what?"

I shook my head. "I don't know." I stared at the phone, still ticking off seconds as the mechanical operator's voice asked whether I wanted to save or delete the message. I pressed save. "Maybe we can go through the diary again. See if this connects?"

"Definitely." Jack turned down his collar and stood up. "But first, I want to get you out of here. We can talk about it all when you're safely with the Saxons."

I got out of bed and looked down at our feet, his stuffed into shoes, mine bare and cold.

"I'll be back as soon as I can." He paused, then ran his fingers down my arm. "And, um. Thanks. Last night. Thanks for letting me get in out of the rain." He grabbed his jacket and stepped out the window and down the long balcony.

I watched him until he disappeared, then locked the window behind him. I collapsed on the bed, my mind spinning. What could Mr. Emerson possibly think my mom could do with the clues? How was *she* involved in all this?

There was a tapping at the window, and I jumped out of my skin. Through the panes, I saw Jack standing outside. I leapt off the bed and threw the window open.

"I forgot something," he said. He reached through the window, took my face in his hands, and kissed me.

I meant to only kiss him back for a second, but then my hands were around his neck, my fingers in his hair, my body pressed into the windowsill between us. He still smelled the tiniest bit like last night's rain. And then he was climbing over the sill, back into the room, tossing his jacket onto the bed, his lips not leaving mine the whole time.

"Why didn't you do this last night?" I murmured against his mouth.

He let his fingers slide over my shoulders, down to my hips. He broke away far enough to let his eyes follow their path, tracing lines of fire over my skin. "Avery, if I'd let myself do this last night . . ." His thumbs slipped under the hem of my shirt. "I might have lost what hint of self-control I had left."

"Oh," I whispered, and all of my own self-control flew out the window.

I waited for him to tell me that we couldn't do this here, now, that he had to go—waited for myself to come to my senses and tell him this was dangerous. That we had more important things to do. That we just couldn't. He didn't. I didn't.

We stumbled backward onto the chaise. And then I was on his lap and he was kissing my cheeks, my eyelids, the tip of my nose, always back to my lips.

Finally, he pulled away. "We shouldn't be doing this," he murmured. I knew he'd be responsible. I started to pull away with a resigned sigh. "But I don't care," he finished with a grin.

I forgot where we were, all the danger we could be in or not or why it ever even mattered. It all faded away as my body melted into his, and the daylight streamed through the window and wrapped around us.

A buzzing sound made me jump. It took me a second to realize it was Jack's phone.

"I don't have to answer it," he said, but I saw his eyes dart to his pocket.

"No, you should." I shifted on his lap enough that he was able to pull the phone out.

He frowned down at the text, and his grip tightened on my waist. "It says there's an emergency. And—" He cursed. "There are more, from early this morning. We must have slept through them. It doesn't say what it's about. I have to go."

I stayed on his lap for as long as I could, fingers tracing over his shirt. Even through the worry, a smile lit his eyes and he leaned in for one last lingering kiss.

A noise in the hallway stopped us both still, his arms tight around me. Jack put a finger to his lips. We both held our breath, and I leaned toward the noise.

And then, I heard the most frightening thing I'd ever heard.

A key, turning the lock on my bedroom door.

CHAPTER 36

We both jumped up. The door opened a few inches, then got stuck on the chair I'd wedged under the knob. Jack bolted for the window, grabbing the incriminating tuxedo jacket on the way. Someone kicked the door open, shattering the little gold chair into pieces.

Monsieur Dauphin strolled in. He nodded at Jack, halfway out the window, and a dozen guards streamed into the room, their guns trained on him. Jack stopped still and raised his hands above his head, jacket dangling from his fingers. The guards surrounded him and wrenched him back inside.

Behind Monsieur Dauphin, Stellan slipped into the room.

How did they know? They cuffed Jack's hands behind his back. I was going to throw up. But he wasn't the Dauphins' to punish. They'd have to give him back to the Saxons. I could reason with my father. Couldn't I?

A guard pressed a gun to Jack's side. "This isn't what it looks like," I pleaded, even though it was obviously exactly what it looked like. "He was helping me, um . . ."

"I couldn't care less what he was doing with you." Monsieur

Dauphin's cold, low voice sent a shiver down my spine. "He won't live long enough to do it again."

"No!" I lunged toward Jack, but another guard grabbed me and turned me to face Monsieur Dauphin. Between him and Stellan, Luc peered out. His eyes were rimmed with red, and he looked shaken.

"What I care about," Monsieur Dauphin said in that same eerily calm voice, "is what you've been hiding from us."

My stomach dropped to my toes. Monsieur Dauphin crossed the room toward me. "I don't know what you're talking about." I struggled against the guard's iron grip.

"Don't touch her," Jack snarled from behind me, but he cut off abruptly, and I turned to see a knife at his throat.

Monsieur Dauphin, towering over me, grabbed my face in one massive hand. He leaned down, peering into my eyes, so close I recoiled from his hot breath on my face.

I squeezed my eyes shut, and then a hand from behind me was forcing them open, holding my eyelids apart.

"Stop!" I tried to yell, but Monsieur Dauphin gripped my face so hard, the word came out as a whimper. His other hand came up to my eye, and I knew what he was doing.

His thick fingers swiped at my eyeball, and I could feel my contact lens, dry and sticky from having been slept in overnight, ripped from my eye. Half my vision went blurry, made the world look unreal.

Monsieur Dauphin let go of my face. I blinked involuntarily, and a gasp went up from the room.

"It's true," Luc breathed. "Why didn't you tell me?"

Beside him, Stellan watched impassively, but I could see his jaw twitch. It was him. He'd figured it out and turned me in.

"She didn't tell you because Saxon had some kind of plan with her." Monsieur Dauphin continued to peer at me curiously. "But now, she'll help us instead."

"No." I shook my head desperately. "There's no plan. Saxon doesn't even know about my eyes," I said, then had a flash of inspiration. "Don't you need his permission to do anything to me? He'll be here any minute. He'll stop this."

"Ah, but he's been told you've run away. He's off looking for you right now. Unfortunately, he won't find you until you're already ours. He won't be happy about it, but it'll be done." Monsieur Dauphin wiped his hands on a handkerchief.

"But you're not even sure who the One is," I choked out. "You don't know it'll work."

He handed the handkerchief to a guard. "And we're not going to know, so it's time to take matters into our own hands."

The room looked fuzzy, wrong. "You don't need me," I said desperately. "You have the baby."

I saw nothing more than a flash of movement before the back of Monsieur Dauphin's hand hit my cheek with a deafening *thwap*. I fell to my knees, choking on a cry.

Luc stepped out from behind his father to help me up. I wiped the tears out of my eyes and could see, up close, that Luc had been crying, too. I looked at the others again. At the unfamiliar dark circles under Stellan's eyes. At the rage in Monsieur Dauphin's.

"Luc?" I whispered.

"The Order attacked my mother on the way home from the ball last night," he said. His Adam's apple bobbed as he swallowed. "She'll pull through. And the baby boy is fine."

He didn't say anything else, and it hit me. The baby girl was not fine. "Oh, Luc—" I whispered.

With a flick of Monsieur Dauphin's hand, the guards holding Jack bundled him out the door. My eyes swam.

Monsieur Dauphin turned to Luc. "The tailor is waiting for you, son," he said. "I got you a new suit for your wedding."

The hard wooden cot was a far cry from the plush mattress on the bed upstairs. I shifted my weight, trying to find a position where it didn't jab into my shoulders or hip bones as I stared up at the ceiling. I'd already been in this cell for a couple hours, and I had no idea how much longer I'd be here.

We'd passed a whole hall of these sparse rooms—probably some kind of servants' quarters—and as soon as they'd left, I'd yelled for Jack, but got no answer. I could only hope my father found us before anything happened.

I stared at the dress hanging on the wall. It was ivory, with a V-neck and a delicate lace overlay. It was beautiful. It made me want to throw up.

Out in the regular world, some girls might see this place, think of the clothes and the balls and the fact that they would be literally in charge of what went on in the world, and sign on the dotted line.

I glanced up at the ironwork across the windows. The Circle might be a beautiful, gilded cage, but it was still a cage. Even before I knew about them, my whole life had been about running from them. They'd taken my past, and now they wanted my future.

On top of it all, if the mandate was fulfilled, if the union happened, I had no idea what would happen to Mr. Emerson. What good were hostages when the ransom didn't matter anymore? And it was unlikely my father was out looking for him if Jack and I were missing.

There was a knock at the door and I bolted upright.

Stellan poked his head in.

"Stellan, please. Let me go." I jumped up. "I'm not trying to hurt the Dauphins. I promise."

He scowled. "Here."

He held out a box. I'd insisted they bring me clear contacts if they were going to make me take mine out. I ripped open the box and popped a contact first in one eye and then the other. I blinked, and the world fell into place again.

Stellan couldn't keep the hint of wonder out of his expression as he watched me. But then he hardened again. "You should have told me. All those times I asked you what you were, and you lied."

"You would have just turned me in even sooner." I crossed my arms over my chest, shivering in the pajamas they hadn't given me time to change out of.

"But if I'd known . . . if I hadn't been watching you last night, and I'd stayed with Madame—" Anguish twisted his face, and for one charged second, his hands curled into fists at his sides and I winced away. I realized just as quickly that the anger wasn't directed at me.

"I'm so sorry about what happened to Madame Dauphin, but it is not my fault. And it's not yours either," I said. He started to protest and I went on. "Madame Dauphin told you to follow me. I heard her, remember? In fact, if I heard correctly, she seemed to be blackmailing you or something."

"That is none of your business," he said under his breath. He turned to go.

"Wait," I said. "Is Jack . . ."

Stellan stopped, his hand on the doorframe. "He's in a cell. Someone will deal with him later."

Relief filled my chest. I stood up. "How did you know?"

He turned halfway. He was wearing a simple white T-shirt and gray jeans, like the first time I'd seen him in Lakehaven. "Does it matter?"

"Then why *not* tell me?" He must be feeling especially dejected. Normally, he'd jump on the chance to brag about how he caught me.

He sighed. "I saw you talking to the Saxons. I noticed you looked alike, but since you were supposedly a Saxon yourself, I didn't think much of it. Then you mentioned the contact lenses. And I remembered how you were looking at Alistair Saxon, and the pieces just fell into place."

He spread his hands and turned to go again. "Wait," I said. There was nothing more Stellan could do to me. If I had any chance of helping Mr. Emerson, I had to tell him the *whole* truth. I stood up from the edge of the cot. "Fitz knows something about the mandate, and the tomb." Stellan stopped short, and I barged ahead. "That's why the Order took him. He left us clues, including a diary of Napoleon's that talks about everything. The tomb, the mandate, the One. The Order wants to know who the One is, or they're going to kill him."

Stellan turned, one hand still on the doorknob. "You just said a lot of things that make no sense. The Order's *ransoming* Fitz? Are you talking about *the* tomb?"

"Yes. We'll tell you everything. Let's just go talk to Jack."

Stellan stepped the rest of the way back inside. "Why would Fitz know anything about the tomb and the One?"

"I have no idea, but he did. And he wanted us to find clues. He left us a note, with photos. Of Jack, you . . . and me."

Stellan raised his eyebrows, but I plunged ahead. "I knew Fitz, back home. Long story," I said before he could ask the obvious question.

Stellan's eyes narrowed. "And you expect me to believe this? You've lied to me over and over."

Footsteps went by outside, and voices speaking French echoed down the hall. I waited, then lowered my voice. "I lied because you would have turned me in to the Dauphins, which you *did.* I'm telling you the truth now." I realized with a jolt that this was the same thing Jack had told me outside the club in Istanbul, when I trusted him as little as Stellan trusted me right now. It was odd being on the other side.

Stellan shook his head. "I doubt Fitz would leave whatever this is for *me.* He . . . he always liked Jack better."

I felt a quick pang of sadness for him. At least Jack knew he had Fitz on his side. "Apparently he trusted you with this, too."

Stellan eased the door closed. "You say Jack has this diary right now?"

"Unless they took it. Just come see. Please. For Fitz. And if that's not enough, you'll want to see the rest of what we found. The stuff about the tomb might be interesting for the Dauphins."

He hesitated, and I took advantage of it, pushing between him and the door. "We only have until noon to contact the Order, and it's not like I can escape."

He ran a hand through his hair. "I'll go get it from Jack, then, and tell you if I find anything."

"No!" The diary mentioned something about the union, too. It was a long shot, and Mr. Emerson had said not to tell the Circle, but if we discovered something that could get me out of this wedding, I'd have to take it. For Mr. Emerson, for my mom, *and* for myself. "The three of us should talk through it together, like Fitz wanted. We have to be missing something." I looked up at him.

"You've already ruined my life by turning me in. You owe me this much."

Stellan pursed his lips. "Okay, but only for Fitz. It'll be hours until the wedding, but they'll be looking me to work soon. I'll give you"—he looked at his watch—"ten minutes. Let's go."

CHAPTER 37

Jack was unhurt, sitting on a metal cot, his tux jacket lying beside him. I was so relieved, I almost cried. He jumped up and stared from me to Stellan, eyes bulging when Stellan demanded to see the diary. Jack pulled it out of the jacket.

Stellan glanced through it. "Okay. I need to go make an excuse so no one bothers us. Don't try anything."

He left, and I fell into Jack's arms.

"Can we trust him?" Jack murmured into my hair. "He turned you in."

"What other choice do we have? We must be missing something. And if not, we can at least get him to call the Order. Ask for more time. *Something.*"

I felt Jack nod, his chin moving on top of my head.

"I'm assuming they took your phone?" I said. I was sure he would have called Saxon if not.

"Yeah."

It was colder down here. I shivered, and Jack rubbed my arms. "At least they didn't find the diary."

"They took my gun and my phone, but they barely looked at the book," he said. "It's actually lucky we got caught how we did. They didn't suspect there was anything more to it than me taking advantage of the pretty new family member."

I couldn't believe the corners of my mouth inched up at that, but they did. And then they fell again, just as quickly. "What will they do to you?"

There was a pause. "That's not our main concern right now."

Jack pulled away and looked into my eyes. A sweet, sad smile twitched at the corners of his mouth.

"Don't look at them," I said, twisting away. The violet felt like a betrayal. "They're ruining everything."

He took my face in his hands and turned it gently toward him. "But they're the real you," he said. "They're beautiful. *You're* beautiful, either way."

He brushed my cheek with his thumb and I leaned into his hand, wishing we could have stayed under the covers this morning and shut out the world.

A voice that wasn't Stellan's echoed in the hall, and I jerked away from Jack. He shielded me, and I grabbed the diary and searched frantically for my bag, forgetting they'd taken it away. The door started to open, and I did the only thing I could think of—I shoved the book up the back of my pajama shirt, tucking it into the built-in bra so it would stay.

The door opened the rest of the way and Stellan stepped in. "I told the guard outside I was ordered to interrogate you. You may have to scream occasionally."

I let out a breath and worked the book out from the bra's elastic, wincing when it got caught.

Stellan watched my hand under my shirt and quirked an eyebrow. "I may have been misinformed about the purpose of this meeting.

I'm not sure I'm into this kind of thing," he said, shooting a look at Jack.

Jack glared back.

I stood up between them, clutching the diary. "Quit it, both of you," I said. "Like you said, we only have ten minutes." I shoved the book into Stellan's chest.

We told him all we knew, from the bracelet, to the gargoyle, to the diary. How the lines in the diary—*The One, the true ruler, the new Achilles. Superior to the false twelve*—sounded like they could be about the mandate, but we didn't know how to interpret them. How also, in the diary, Napoleon seemed worried for the Circle, because of the union and the One. We repeated all we could remember of Mr. Emerson's message to my mom, and told him everything about the Order's ransom and the impending deadline.

Stellan leaned against the wall, turning pages of the diary. "So what you're saying is you dragged me away from my duties for puzzle-solving time?"

"It wasn't exactly our choice," I said.

To Stellan's credit, he didn't offer a snarky comeback. I could see him checking where we'd taken the note from the endpaper, looking closely at the words. Flipping back through the book.

While he looked, I paced the cell. Five steps across one way, my bare feet—they hadn't given me time to put on shoes, either—slapping the concrete. Five steps back.

I stared up at the low concrete ceiling. Superior to the twelve. The Circle of Twelve. Twelve. Dozen. A dozen eggs. Twelve months. I couldn't think of anything where one of the twelve was *superior*.

I fingered my locket. The symbol on it had to have something to do with the Circle. It had been with those letters from my father.

I was suddenly sure there was a twelve in there somewhere. Twelve loops in the knot design, maybe.

I counted them absently, and then stopped. Counted again. My fingers froze on the necklace. There weren't twelve spaces made by the design. There were *thirteen*.

I counted once more. The swirling Celtic knot pattern made twelve loops around a central loop. Altogether—"Thirteen," I said out loud. Jack looked up questioningly, and I had a sudden flash of inspiration.

I sat next to Jack on the cot. "Let me see your tattoo." I yanked up his sleeve. I'd counted the twelve compass points, but I hadn't thought about the circle that connected the points. A thirteenth thing.

I crossed the room to Stellan. "Take off your shirt." He looked at me strangely, but stripped off his top, tossing it onto the chair. I made him turn around.

I touched the twelve points on his sun tattoo, then the circle in the middle, connecting them all.

"The tattoos represent the twelve families, right?" I said to myself. "Did the families make their own symbols, or did someone else do it?"

"Aristotle assigned the symbols just after Alexander died," Stellan said.

I tried to picture the other symbols on the spines of the books upstairs. There was an olive branch with what must be twelve leaves—and the branch would be a thirteenth thing. And a wheel, with twelve spokes—and the outer rim.

My mind turned in a different direction. Twelve plus the one extra that *connected* them. My brain was so fried, I'd been looking at it wrong. It didn't say "the best of" the twelve. *Superior* meant *separate.*

A superior thirteenth thing, the one extra holding the twelve together.

"What?" Jack said, watching me.

I tried to explain my line of thinking.

"So you're saying maybe 'superior to the twelve' means somebody who's not part of the twelve?" Jack leaned back against the wall, pulling down the sleeve of his tuxedo shirt.

"Twelve things plus one more thing connecting them," I said. "It's on all the tattoos."

"Twelve plus one more." Stellan looked up from the paper in his hand. "*The One* true ruler."

I sucked in a sharp breath.

Jack stood abruptly. "In all the lore about the mandate, I've never heard of the One being someone outside of the Circle. That can't be what he means. It wouldn't make any sense."

"It would mean *they're wrong about the mandate* is an understatement." I took his place on the cot and pulled my knees to my chest. "It's not impossible."

"It's not *impossible.*" Jack paced. "But the mandate is about the twelve Diadochi. Some random person wouldn't make sense."

He was right. It wouldn't.

Stellan had been leaning against the doorframe, but now he stood. "Unless it's not a random person. Like if the Diadochi's thirteenth was Alexander the Great himself."

My feet fell to the floor with a thud. Not a random thirteenth person. The *ruler* of the twelve. The one who held them together. Like the twelve knights of the round table, and King Arthur. The twelve apostles and Jesus.

But if Alexander was the thirteenth for the Diadochi, if his was a *thirteenth* family of the Circle, then Mr. Emerson must mean the One we were looking for now was . . . from Alexander's bloodline?

"But he didn't have an heir," Jack said, like he was following the exact same thought pattern. "Alexander's bloodline died out immediately."

"Are you sure?" I said, my head spinning with ideas. "Maybe that's the missing piece. That's why nothing's fit together yet."

If somebody from Alexander the Great's own bloodline was the One, how would anyone find him? Would the Circle even accept him?

Probably not. He'd be in *great danger* . . . just like Mr. Emerson had said.

"Mr. Emerson said in that message he'd found something about the One. Like he was maybe talking about a *person*?" I said slowly. My gaze flicked to Jack, who paled. "And that he's been protecting him."

Stellan snorted. "Not even you two could be that dumb."

Just as quickly, the shock fell off Jack's face. "I remember that part of the message. He said he *brought in* whoever it was," he said to me, ignoring Stellan. "I didn't meet Fitz until I'd been with the Saxons for years."

I nodded. "Yeah. Of course. Okay. Dumb idea anyway. If that's even what he meant, which it might not be, he probably has him hidden somewhere far away." Still, my heart hadn't slowed down yet. It felt like we were so close. I pressed the heels of my hands into my eyes.

. . . the One who walks through fire and does not burn . . . the new Achilles . . . the One true ruler . . .

I kept coming back to the *walk through fire* thing. If we knew what it meant, it might give us some ideas. Jack had said it probably meant a "trial by fire," like that they were good in a crisis. But what kind of crisis?

I sat back and closed my eyes. Fire. Trial by fire. *He lives,* Napoleon had said, with pictures of flames. *Make the One who walks through fire and doesn't burn* . . . Burn . . .

When I opened my eyes again, they flicked not to Jack, but to Stellan, who leaned against the wall, his back to us, studying the book again. He hadn't put his shirt back on yet. But now I wasn't looking at the lines of muscle down his arms. Instead, my eyes were drawn to his tattoo again, and the scars under it.

Scars from a fire.

I read a lot of fantasy when I was younger. In some of those stories, the term *trial by fire* wasn't metaphorical. To choose the next ruler, candidates would walk through a fire, and the one who didn't die was special.

He was the one who literally walked through fire and didn't get burned.

I snapped out of my trance to find Jack watching me stare at Stellan. "The new mandate line," I said. "Repeat it for me again."

"'The One, the true ruler, the new Achilles,'" he said.

Achilles.

Achilles was invincible, except for a spot on the back of his heel. When struck there, he could be injured, or even killed. That's where we got the term *Achilles heel,* because it was his only weak point.

And now, thinking in terms of Alexander's bloodline, I remembered hearing that one of the legends about Alexander the Great was that the night before he was born, his mother had a dream about her baby being consumed by fire and coming out unscathed. *Walks through fire and does not burn.* All his life, Alexander cheated death so many times that people started saying *he* was invincible, too. Even that he was descended from Achilles. In fact, some followers *called* him Achilles.

The new Achilles. Alexander's bloodline. *Does not burn.*

I looked at Stellan's scars again. Strange scars, unlike any burn I'd ever seen. That weren't really like burns at all.

All the shouting voices in my head coalesced into a perfectly in-tune chorus, singing a song that didn't make any sense.

I had to check anyway, to prove my absurd hypothesis wrong.

"Take off your shoes real quick," I said to Stellan. "And your socks."

Now both of them looked at me like I had lost my mind, and maybe I had.

"If you're trying to get me naked, there are easier ways to do it," Stellan quipped, and then with a sideways glance at Jack, "and more appropriate times . . ."

"Will you shut up and take your shoes off?" I must have sounded serious, because he sat down on the cot and did it. I motioned for him to prop his feet up.

Holy mother-freakin' hell oh wow oh no.

"Oh my God," I said aloud.

Stellan had a burn. Not a quasi-scar like the translucent ones on his back, but angry, puckered skin, scarred like every old burn I'd ever seen. And it was on his right heel.

CHAPTER 38

I don't believe it for a second." Jack paced the room.

At any other time I might have appreciated the irony. I'd spent the last few days learning about a world-controlling secret society, and *he* didn't believe *me*?

Stellan stared at his foot. "After the fire, the doctors called it a miracle I'd lived," he said slowly. "My sister, too. They'd never seen anything like our scars."

I thought of something. "Your parents. If it's a bloodline thing, one of your parents would have it. One of them wouldn't have died."

"My mother died in the fire. My father had died earlier. Car accident," he said quietly.

"You both seem to be forgetting the laws of reality." Jack paced back and forth. "How would people from a certain bloodline physically not burn?"

I glanced at Stellan. "I have no idea. Maybe we'll find an explanation in the tomb, if we get a chance to look for it. It seems like that's where Napoleon got his information."

"Fitz was the one who found me after the fire. He brought me to the Circle," Stellan said quietly. He touched the scars snaking over his shoulder.

Jack shook his head.

"If it *is* true, and Mr. Emerson knew, why wouldn't he have told you?" I said.

"Sounds like he was looking for more information first. About whether the *rest* of it was true, maybe." Stellan gave a nod in my direction.

The tension in Jack's shoulders spread through his arms, and he eyed Stellan with an even greater animosity than usual, and all of a sudden, I realized the really important thing I'd overlooked.

"Oh," I said under my breath.

The girl and the One. The One was supposed to unite with a girl of the bloodline.

Or, in other words, me.

"Napoleon mentioned the union being wrong. It doesn't necessarily mean—" I couldn't say it.

Stellan leaned back against the door and crossed his arms over his chest. He looked from the book still in his hand, to Jack, to me. He frowned.

"Forget it. Let's assume for a second we're right, and there's a conspiracy within a conspiracy going on here. That the One is a thirteenth. Is possibly even Stellan," I said. "I know it's crazy, but for argument's sake, for *Mr. Emerson's* sake, we have to think about it. What would it mean?"

Stellan didn't say anything, but he closed the book, and his eyes narrowed.

"It would mean Luc's not the One," Jack said.

"The Dauphins would have to let me go, and then we could

contact the Order—" And tell them it was Stellan they were look-ing for. I met Jack's eyes. We couldn't do that.

I started over again. "It would at least mean they'd have to call off the wedding. We could get out of here in time to tell the Order *something*."

Stellan stood up abruptly. "Of course it would mean no wedding. Of course that's what it all comes back to."

"Well, it does—"

"How incredibly convenient," Stellan said with a sneer. "You even thought you'd get me on your side with this ridiculous thirteenth theory."

I looked from him to Jack, back again. "What?"

Stellan tugged back on his shoes and socks. "That's enough. I'm not stupid. How long have you two been planning this pathetic cha-rade for when she inevitably got caught?"

"No!" I said. "It's not—"

"I can't believe I let you talk me into playing along for this long. I'm taking you back to your cell." Stellan shrugged his T-shirt back on, grabbed my arm, and steered me out the door.

"Thank you," Stellan said, opening the door to my room. "The strug-gling and crying was a good touch, in case anyone thought I was getting sucked in to your schemes."

"Arrrrgh!" I threw myself on the hard wooden cot. "It's not a scheme. Yes, I want to get out of this, but we're not lying."

Stellan stood in the doorway. "Even if this thirteenth thing were true—this whole conspiracy of . . . *us*—" He looked me over with a frown. "Do you think anyone would accept it?"

I sat back against the wall, my bare feet dangling from the edge of the cot. "They'd have to accept it if we had proof. If you don't believe me, maybe I'll tell someone else."

Stellan crossed his arms. "If Monsieur Dauphin hears about you telling anyone, he'll cut out your tongue so you can't do it again. He's not a nice man."

I flinched.

"If you tried to spread this story, the Dauphins would destroy your 'proof' immediately. Then they would kill Jack and me for knowing about it." He shook his head. "You think you're so smart, but you're completely naive in the ways of this world. These people are playing for a lot more than you can imagine."

"Then I can run." Fighting obviously wasn't going to work, so flight was all I had left. "At least let me run. Pretend I got away."

"No." He smacked a palm on the doorjamb. "Pay attention. You can't run. If Monsieur Dauphin can't have you, do you think he'll let anyone else have you?"

I swallowed hard.

"And it turns out I don't want to see you get killed, *kuklachka*. So don't do anything stupid."

My mouth went dry. Stellan turned to go.

"How old is your sister?" I said desperately. I didn't want to admit it, but Stellan was a lot like me. He'd heard us out because he cared about Mr. Emerson. The way to appeal to him was through the people he loved.

Stellan opened the door partway, but hesitated.

"What's her name?" I said.

He stayed at the door. "Anya. She's seven."

I bit my lip. "What's she like?"

His shoulders rose and fell with one deep breath, and he pushed the door closed again. He pulled a tattered photo out of his wallet. A tiny blond girl with huge blue eyes sat under a tree, laughing. Those same scars-that-weren't-scars covered the whole right side of her face. Seven years old. She must have been a tiny baby when they were in the fire.

"Why don't you leave and be nearer to her?" Hurt flared in his eyes, and I remembered this was why he was trying to transfer to Russia. I handed him the picture, and he gently put it back in his wallet.

"Even if I could get another job that would let me take care of her, you don't just leave the Circle. It's not a job you can quit, if you hadn't noticed."

I glanced at his neck, where I could see the top of his tattoo.

"Maybe I would have done things differently if I'd known what I was getting into, but I was a child. My parents were dead. It was this and have Anya well taken care of, or have both of us go into the foster system in Russia, which wasn't an option." He broke a splinter off the wooden doorframe and picked at it. "So I do my best so that I can try to move nearer to her someday. But it means I can't make mistakes. Like letting someone beat me to an American girl I have very specific orders about."

He gave me a meaningful look, but the sarcasm had already crept back into his voice, displacing any vulnerability. It didn't matter. Somehow, in the space of thirty seconds, he had managed to make me feel bad that I'd made my own kidnapping and interrogation so difficult.

He cleared his throat. "You'd better put on the dress and get ready. They'll be unhappy if you delay the ceremony."

My eyes were drawn to his neck again, to the tendrils of scar tissue. "There's a way to see," I said, suddenly realizing the obvious. "At least about the burns. It won't be fun, but if you have a lighter . . ."

He reached into his pocket and pulled out a lighter. Realization dawned on his face.

"You know it's not true," he said, staring at the lighter. "It won't prove anything."

He flicked the lighter, and an inch-tall blue-and-orange flame sparked from its tip. The second it did, he flinched, such a small movement I wouldn't have noticed if I hadn't been watching so closely.

He let the flame die, and his Adam's apple bobbed with a hard swallow. Then he scowled and flicked the lighter again, defiantly. We both stared at it for a second, watching the flame dance in the drafty room.

In one quick motion, he brought it to the inside of his forearm and hissed through his teeth. He grimaced, and looked away, but left the flame in place for five incredibly long seconds.

When he started to shake, I batted his hand away. "Stop. Enough."

Stellan dropped the lighter to the ground and clutched his arm to his chest.

I reached for it, and he rested his forearm in my hands. I looked for the burn.

There was nothing there.

I stared, then grabbed his other arm. He shook his head. "It's this one. Right there." He pointed to the spot and grimaced. "Hurts like hell."

I had burned myself with a curling iron a few months earlier. It went bright red immediately, and within a few minutes, it had blistered. I reached my fingers to the back of my neck. Even now, I could still feel the welt, and I'd only touched the iron to my skin for a fraction of a second.

On Stellan's arm, there was no mark at all. I touched the skin carefully with my thumb. It was warm, but no redness, nothing. "Not even like the ones on your back," I whispered.

"Those burns were much worse." He sounded as awestruck as I felt. "I got them saving Anya. A burning beam fell on us. It took me a minute to get out from under it, and—"

He looked up, and I could see the doubt shining in his eyes.

I latched on to his uncertainty. "Think about it. If we were right, and you were the One, and if we all got away before the Dauphins could catch us, *and* we have all those other clues to the tomb? We might be able to find the treasure ourselves. You wouldn't have to count on the Circle anymore. You could take Anya and go anywhere you wanted."

He still didn't look convinced. I caught his hands. "Please," I said, changing tactics one more time. "Just let me out of here so we have more time to investigate. If you sneak me out before Monsieur Dauphin notices—"

He took his hands back, letting mine fall limply to my sides. "I can't risk—no. I'm sorry, *kuklachka*, but no."

I closed my eyes, defeated. "Then at least call the Order," I said.

Stellan ran a hand through his hair. "Do you even have the phone number?"

"I memorized it last night." I rubbed my eyes. "Give me your phone."

He pulled his phone out of his pocket hesitantly. "If I got caught talking to the Order—"

"Fitz is going to *die* otherwise!" I grabbed the phone and punched the number in. "Tell them we're still trying to find the One. They can't blackmail us unless they keep him alive. I hope."

Stellan took back his phone. "I'm sorry," he said again. And he was gone.

CHAPTER 39

Without windows to judge the passing of the day, I wasn't sure how many hours had gone by, but it had to be evening by now, and no one else had come in to see me. Maybe they'd changed their minds and were putting it off. Or maybe it just meant a wedding took more than a couple hours to plan, even for the Circle. I stared at myself in the small, utilitarian mirror. This bathroom was rustic compared with the marble and gold of the one upstairs, and the version of me staring back from the mirror was an entirely different Avery, too.

Even if Stellan had called the Order and gotten a reprieve for Mr. Emerson, it was starting to sink in that I was really about to get *married.* Could they do this without my permission? Would it be legally binding? I'd refuse to sign the papers. I'd run away later.

But if they could track me as a random girl in Istanbul, there was no way I'd be able to escape as a wife.

Wife. The word sent a violent shiver through me.

As if on cue, the door opened and I jumped, flattening myself against the bathroom wall. Elodie came in, along with four other maids who chattered at me in rapid French. So much for putting it off.

"Sit," Elodie said, brushing her bangs out of her eyes. She dragged the single chair in the room across to the mirror and pushed me into it, then pulled at a limp strand of my hair. "This is disgusting. Have you even showered today?"

I glared at her. "Silly me. I must have missed the spa in this cell."

She rolled her eyes and studied me in the mirror, pulling my hair back from my face. This was eerily reminiscent of the plane to Istanbul, when she'd put me in the Herve Leger dress.

"Up," Elodie said. "We don't have time to wash your hair, so dress first, then I'll see what I can do with . . ." She waved a hand at my head.

I didn't say anything while one of the older maids pulled the wedding dress over my head and adjusted the fitted waist so it flowed in a graceful A-line over my hips. The cap sleeves settled onto my shoulders, and she laced up the corset back so tight, I gasped. She gave it one more pull for good measure, and then Elodie gestured to the chair again. I sat gingerly, my back rod-straight in the corset.

Elodie went to work on my hair.

"Does Luc actually want this?" I remembered him smiling at that boy at the club. For that and plenty of other reasons, I was pretty sure he had no interest in a relationship with me, but the political implications of it were something different entirely. In the mirror, I could see the older women whispering behind me while one pulled a pair of blush-pink heels out of a box.

"I can assure you Luc is just as excited about the nuptials as you are." Elodie tugged a little harder than necessary on a piece of hair before securing it with a bobby pin.

"Can't we put it off until we can talk about it?"

"No."

"Because it's *fate*?" I said sarcastically. "Our fates are mapped together, as the mandate says."

"Do you know what a fate map is in biology?" Elodie twisted half of my hair up and set to curling the other half. "It's a map of which cells in an embryo should develop into which specific adult tissues. But what they *should* develop into isn't necessarily what they actually *do* develop into. They can be manipulated, or change on their own, and end up as something completely different from what they were fated for."

I turned to stare at her. That was a strange thing to say.

She wrenched my head forward again, her honey-dark eyes still trained on my hair. "I've always loved science," she said sweetly.

So she was just torturing me. I sat in silence while she finished. Another maid handed her a cascade of white lace, and Elodie draped it over her arm.

"Amazing that you managed to keep your eye color a secret," she said, smoothing the lace with her fingers. "And now, only the Dauphins and a few of their staff members know. Good thing you have this to cover your eyes." She affixed the white fabric in my dark hair with a comb. "Your father wouldn't be the only one who was angry if the Dauphins' plan was *unveiled*. If anyone else at the wedding saw your eyes before the union was official . . . it would be a riot."

I glanced up sharply. That was it.

I watched Elodie, who kept her eyes trained on my hair. Maybe she *wanted* me to make a scene so Monsieur Dauphin would have an excuse to kill me.

Elodie stood me up from my chair. There, staring back at me from the mirror, was a bride.

"Doesn't it seem wrong to you that a girl has this much power but has no say in what happens to her?" I said, still staring at my reflection. This couldn't be where the past few days—really, my whole life—had led. "This is so Middle Ages."

"Oh, *cherie*, it's much older than that." Elodie worked her fingers under the veil and to the back of my dress. "Now let's make sure this is tight enough."

She undid the corset strings and I started to protest, but rather than pulling them tighter, she let them out enough for me to breathe. I looked at her in the mirror again, and she continued to avoid my eyes.

Could she actually be *helping* me? Why?

"There," she said. "Now don't do anything to muss yourself up before the guards arrive to take you to the church. And take this." She pressed a large black umbrella into my hand. "It's raining, but don't be sad. Rain on your wedding day's said to be good luck."

CHAPTER 40

No one told me where the wedding was being held, but I should have guessed. The drive to Notre-Dame felt like the longest few minutes of my life. I barely even noticed the lights reflecting off the Seine or the golden glow of the ornate bridges arching over it, radiant against the dusk. When we got out of the car, the Dauphins' guards stayed far enough away to accommodate my umbrella as I sloshed through puddles. The bottom of my dress would be ruined, but it wasn't like I cared.

From across the square, a rowdy group of tourists laughed and catcalled at us. I thought for a second about yelling for help, but I knew it'd be a bad idea.

I hugged the handle of Elodie's umbrella to my chest, trying to let the rush of raindrops on its canopy drown out the rushing in my head. And then, I felt a click. Where the handle had been smooth a second earlier, now it wasn't. A thin ribbon of shining metal protruded from it.

I worked at it with my fingers, drawing the thing the rest of the way out.

A knife.

A small, thin blade, about four inches long, its handle part of the umbrella handle.

Whether it was because Luc was Elodie's best friend and she didn't want him to have to do this, or because she'd rather see me gone from France altogether, I wasn't going to say no. I was so much smaller than the guards that my umbrella hid me, so I was able to work the little knife down the bodice of my dress, under my arm. Its tip dug into my side, but it should be okay if I stood very straight.

Now I had to figure out when to use it.

Maybe that little bit of subterfuge opened my eyes, because all of a sudden, I noticed a phone on the belt of the guard in front of me. I didn't know my father's phone number, but I might be able to call the Order, just in case Stellan hadn't. Plus, I could try my mom again.

I waited until we stepped up on a curb, then cried out and fell into the guard, careful to stay upright enough not to stab myself. As he whipped around, I pulled his phone out of its holder and stuffed it under my arm. "Sorry," I said, standing back up. "I tripped."

The guard scowled, but didn't say anything. I worked the phone down the other side of my bodice.

As we got to Notre-Dame, I remembered Jack telling me that the left-hand door, with the triangle over it, represented the Circle *watching over the common people.* I sniffed. Unlike yesterday, when tourists had flowed in and out of the main entrance, only that left door was open now. We stepped inside.

After the thundering rain on the umbrella, the inside of Notre-Dame was silent and as echoey as a cave. Tall candles lined the entrance, their flames casting elongated shadows, and dozens of chandeliers bathed the soaring archways along the nave in warm light. When my ears had adjusted, I heard the whispers of the crowd and saw the occasional head turn to sneak a glance at us. I let myself hope for one second that my father had heard about this surprise wedding and showed up to stop it, but no outraged Saxons ran toward us. How ironic. The fact that he actually did care enough about me to search for me meant he wouldn't be here when I needed him.

The guards deposited me in a small room near the entrance to wait. I locked the door and pulled out the phone, dialing the Order's number.

All I got was dead air. No signal. I cursed under my breath.

My gaze darted around the room. One small window, high up on the wall. A confessional booth. That was it.

I shoved back my veil and searched the room for something to climb on. There was a rickety stool in one corner, but it wasn't very tall. I pulled open the door of the confessional booth and found a chair. I dragged it across the room, climbed up, and tried to grab the windowsill.

I twisted too far and the knife in my bodice pierced my side. I bit back a whimper and dropped back to the chair, panting. It was too high. I'd never be able to reach, and probably wouldn't be able to get through the bars, anyway. What *else*?

Wait.

I jumped off the chair. Inside the confessional booth, behind where this chair had been, there was another tiny door.

Voices outside the room got louder. The guards were coming back.

I sprinted into the confessional and shoved against the little door. Nothing. I jiggled the handle, pulled. It stayed firmly shut. A loud knock came at the door. I lowered my shoulder, ran into the door, and it flew open. Inside was pitch black.

The outer doorknob rattled.

I stepped inside carefully—and my feet found stairs. I reached back out to pull shut first the door of the confessional, then the inner door, and fumbled my way up the steps.

I could feel cool, rain-scented air coming through tiny holes carved in the wall, but there was no way out of the dark, so I hurried up and up and up, as fast as I could, really glad now that Elodie had loosened my corset. I hoped beyond hope that this would somehow lead to an exit. Strangely, no one was following me yet.

Finally, an outline of a door. I held my breath and eased it open, not sure what I'd find. Empty.

I stepped out cautiously, and only then did I realize I wasn't in a room. I'd only made it to the balcony that surrounded the center of the nave, on level with the colorful stained-glass windows.

I stood behind a pillar, breathing hard, and peered down to see Monsieur Dauphin and Luc at the altar that had been closed off yesterday. After a few seconds, a guard approached. He whispered something to Monsieur Dauphin, who stiffened. He glanced up, almost at me, and around the rest of the balcony.

He said something to the guard, and the guard disappeared.

How was I going to get out of here?

I kicked out of my too-loud heels and tried not to trip on the heavy, soaked hem of my dress as I hurried down the balcony, sticking as close as I could to the wall, trying every door I came across. There had to be another stairway. I kept expecting to hear the clomp of guards' boots, but the balcony was eerily quiet.

The clearing of a throat directed my attention downstairs. Then, the sound of Monsieur Dauphin's voice.

"Thank you all for coming this evening. As you all know, our family's tragedy is just the latest in our adversaries' plan to take down the Circle, family by family." Murmurs went up in the crowd. "I know some of you suspect, as I do, that the Order's information about us is too detailed to be coincidence. I am happy to report that we have caught the traitor who has been passing information to the enemy for months."

What?

A roar went up from the crowd.

"Bring him," Monsieur Dauphin said, and I had to peek out from my hiding place.

Below me, a guard dragged a prisoner to the front of the cathedral. All eyes were on him as he passed, handcuffed and bound at the ankles, a dark hood obscuring his face.

When he got to the front, Monsieur Dauphin yanked off his hood.

The whole audience gasped.

I gasped with them.

The man the guards were holding was Jack.

CHAPTER 41

This boy has been using his status as a Keeper to betray us." As Monsieur Dauphin said it, he glanced up to the balcony surrounding the nave. "And now, all of you will watch as his crimes are punished."

A guard drew a huge knife. Monsieur Dauphin threw Jack to the ground, then looked up again.

He knew I was up here. He was using Jack to draw me out. Oh no. Oh no no no. If I showed myself now, we'd never get out of here.

But I thought of Jack, saying that the Saxons and Mr. Emerson were all he had in the world. The only people who cared about him.

It wasn't true, not anymore. They weren't all he had, and Monsieur Dauphin knew it.

He raised a hand to the guard.

"Stop!" I screamed.

The guard paused. The whole congregation whipped around to stare up at the balcony. I made my way to the railing.

"I'm here." My voice, so small, echoed through the now-silent cathedral.

Monsieur Dauphin waved his hand, and a group of guards ran off. I stayed exactly where I was, staring at Jack. He held my gaze, and it helped calm the desperate thoughts running through my head. We'd find another way. We'd have to find another way. No more than a minute later, the guards burst through a door on the other side of the balcony.

They bundled me back down the stairs. One of them pulled the veil over my face, and another tossed my abandoned shoes at my feet, and I slipped back into them. We emerged into the nave. My heels clicked loudly on the black-and-white marble floor. A small blood-stain from the knife was spreading on my side, staining the wedding dress. The congregation stared.

"I'm sorry," Jack mouthed as I got closer. I shook my head.

"Let him go," I murmured to Monsieur Dauphin. "That's the only way I'll do this."

Monsieur Dauphin glanced around at the dozens of guests—the president of France a few rows away, glowering at Jack. Padraig Harrington, the golfer, wearing an amused grin, like this was the most fun thing that could have happened today. "You have my word," he said.

He pulled Jack to his feet and propelled me toward Luc, who stood at the altar, looking nearly as lost as I felt. But to him, the mandate was fate. *Destinée.* Especially since they'd lost his baby sis-ter. I knew that, as much as he might want to, he wouldn't stop it.

Luc steadied me with a hand on my elbow, and I spun to watch Jack stumble away down the aisle, his ankles still restrained. Not twenty feet away, a pair of guards jumped up and caught him, and a man in a white turban gestured with a flick of his wrist for them to hold him to the side.

"Wait—" I cried.

Monsieur Dauphin leaned in close beside me. "I said *we* wouldn't catch him. I didn't promise no one would."

I choked back a whimper. I'd thought maybe he wouldn't kill me if I exposed what he was doing in front of all these people, but suddenly, I wasn't so sure. But even if it was ridiculous—me against the whole Circle—I was going to have to try, and not just for myself now. We were in a semi-open space. It was possible one of these doors led to the outside. If I caused enough of an uproar, I could try to free Jack and run.

Monsieur Dauphin stood in front of us. "I do apologize for the dramatics," he said. "We'll now move on to the purpose of the day. The marriage of my son, Lucien."

I shuddered, and felt Luc tense beside me. Down a side aisle, Jack stood suspended between two guards.

I blinked through the veil, itching to yank it off. I couldn't do it yet. If I was going to have any chance, I had to choose the right moment.

A priest stepped forward and took my hands and Luc's. He bound them with rope, then produced a knife. "Rule by blood," he said, and I remembered the saying from the books I'd seen that first day. He made a shallow slice across each of our palms. I hissed at the sharp sting but tried to stay still, not fight, lull the guards into backing off farther.

The priest pressed our two palms together and tied the rope tighter. Then he held up a candle. "Light in the dark," he said, and passed the flame under our hands, searing the knot shut. Luc laced his fingers through mine and squeezed, and I squeezed back. This wasn't his fault.

The priest leaned over our hands and began an incantation in a language I didn't know. As he did, another priest approached and, to my surprise, pulled my veil off my back so my shoulders were exposed. And then, there was a snipping sound, and I felt the priest touch my head. He held up one wide, dark ringlet.

My free hand flew to my head. They'd *cut* part of my hair?

"In the *gamos* ceremony, the blood ritual and the offering of a lock of hair symbolize purity and commitment to the marriage," the priest continued, switching to English when he'd finished his prayer. "And now, the marriage vows."

The timing still wasn't right, but this was the last chance I'd have.

With my free hand, I ripped the veil off my head and tossed it in a pile on the floor. "Do you realize what the Dauphins are trying to do?" I yelled. "Look at my eyes!"

A murmur rippled through the crowd; a few people in the back rows stood to get a better look. Monsieur Dauphin rose from his chair.

"I have purple eyes," I said. I yanked as hard as I could, and my hand came free from Luc's with a spatter of blood across my white dress and the bite of rope burn on my wrist. Luc's mouth fell open, but he didn't stop me. "I'm Alistair Saxon's daughter, and the Dauphins were going to marry me into their family without telling you."

The room burst into an uproar. Monsieur Dauphin lunged for me, but I leapt off the altar and ducked behind the huge gold cross. Out of the corner of my eye, I saw guards surge between Monsieur Dauphin and the crowd.

In the chaos, I managed to slip into an alcove, where I worked the knife out of my dress. I'd gotten as lucky as I could have hoped—the whole crowd seemed to be turning on Monsieur Dauphin. Only a few people, and fewer guards, were headed my way. I waited a few more seconds, then ducked out the side of the altar area and ran toward Jack. I steeled myself to fight off the guards, but as I approached from behind, they shoved him against a wall and joined in the fray.

Jack's eyes widened when he saw me. "No, Avery," he said. "You might be able to get away. Just leave me!"

"Are you insane?" I dropped to my knees and started cutting through the rope around his ankles, the knife slippery from the blood on my hand. "I'm not leaving you." I sawed harder, but I wasn't going fast enough.

Someone else fell to the ground beside me, and I whirled, knife in hand.

Luc had his own dagger ready. Instead of reaching toward me, he sliced through the ropes. "Hurry," he said.

I gave his arm a quick squeeze, and Jack hauled me to my feet.

We turned around, but stopped when we almost ran into a dark-skinned little girl. She must have been about eight, and stared up at me with huge, awestruck eyes. Her mom dashed up and grabbed her shoulder—and then she noticed me, too, and stopped short. She dropped to her knees.

"My lady," she said in a heavy accent, and raised her hands to her forehead, palms out. "Blood save you."

I glanced at Jack. He looked as surprised as I felt. I took a step back from the woman, but then a man dropped to his knees next to her, and made the same sign with his hands. "May I offer my son," he said reverently. "To raise up the Circle. To save us all."

"What the—" I breathed as another man in a nearby pew noticed us and hurried over.

He didn't fall into the same position. "Guards!" he yelled. "Seize her!"

I backed up another step. Blood dripped from my palm onto the marble floor.

I had forgotten Luc was there until he stepped in front of me. "Friends. Brothers," he said with a quick glance at me and a nod of his head toward the back of the church. "We know this is a miraculous time." He circled the people smoothly until they were all facing away from me. Behind his back, he made a subtle hand gesture. *Go.*

I pulled on Jack's hand, and we backed away, toward a wide column. "Look!" Luc said. I saw him gesture toward the altar. "There she goes."

I yanked Jack fully behind the pillar. With a flurry of exclamations, the people noticed I was no longer behind them, and jumped up to follow Luc.

"What was that?" I whispered. Jack just shook his head. We rushed toward where I remembered seeing a side exit yesterday.

Halfway there, Stellan stepped into our path.

I almost screamed in frustration. Jack tried to dodge him, but Stellan caught my arm and pulled me behind another pillar that hid us completely from the rest of the church.

"You promise me you were telling the truth?" Stellan murmured. I yanked Jack to a stop.

"What—"

"And you'll stand behind me as the thirteenth, if we're right. Whatever we end up having to do."

I gaped at him. Beside me, Jack did the same.

"She cries herself to sleep every night I'm not there." Stellan squeezed my arm. "Every single night."

I thought of the pretty little blond girl. Anya.

"And you can't say a thing about me to the Order. Make something up," Stellan said. "Promise me."

"Yes," I said. "Yes!"

A shout came from the other side of the pillar. Guards. They hadn't seen us yet, but they would soon.

Stellan cursed under his breath. "I'll stall them. Second door on your left. It leads up, but all the exits on this level are locked. I'll find you later."

"How—"

"Hurt me. Hurry. Make it look convincing or they'll know I let you go."

Jack didn't need to be told twice. He hit Stellan with a quick right hook.

Stellan staggered back one step. "More convincing than one little punch."

Before Jack could do any more, I held up the knife.

Stellan's eyes widened, more with appreciation than fear.

I gritted my teeth and poked the tip of the knife into Stellan's arm.

He cursed under his breath in French. "More," he murmured.

More? I hesitated too long. Stellan took my hand and plunged the knife into his shoulder.

I cried out louder than he did, but he let go of me, and Jack and I sprinted to the second door on the left, slamming it behind us and plunging ourselves into blackness.

"Give me your shoe," Jack said. I tore both of my heels off, shoving one blindly in his direction. In the bit of light from under the door, I saw him work it underneath like a makeshift doorstop, then gesture toward the stairs.

My eyes needed more time to adjust to the dark, but time was something we didn't have. I dashed blindly after him up the narrow, steep spiral, holding my wedding dress as high as I could. A couple of flights up I tripped anyway, and felt the wound on my thigh from the fire escape rip open. I didn't even have time to cry out before Jack was helping me up, urging me forward.

We hadn't gone more than three flights when we heard the door open with a screech and a bang. The silence exploded with echoing voices, pounding footsteps. I gasped for breath, concentrating on the lighter spot in the dark that was Jack's gray shirt ahead of me.

We finally emerged into an open space a tiny bit brighter than the stairwell, and I put my hands on my knees, panting. It smelled like wood and damp. Flower-shaped windows let in what little moonlight made its way between the clouds, and illuminated what had to be rafters.

"We're in the bell tower," Jack said. Sure enough, there was the vague silhouette of a massive bell.

The guards' footsteps, and their shouts, came closer.

"If we're in the bell tower, that's the front of the cathedral," Jack said, ducking us under the crisscrossing wooden beams and dragging me toward the wall of windows. "I think there's a door."

We both felt frantically along the wall.

"Here!" Jack's exclamation was punctuated by a child-sized door thrown open to the night.

We jumped out of it into the rain and closed it as quietly as we could. I looked around in surprise. We were on the gargoyle balcony from yesterday.

"Where now?" I panted, dashing rain out of my eyes. We wouldn't have much time before they figured out where we'd gone.

He ran to the side and peered through the metal fencing. I gulped.

"There's construction scaffolding all down this side," he said. "They'd never expect us to escape from up here." He looked back at me. "I'll hold on to you. I'll help you. I know you're afraid of falling, but—"

I took the hand he offered. "It's okay," I said. "I'm not scared any-more." I realized it was true. Because I'd actually come to terms with the fear or because I'd found scarier things than heights, I wasn't sure, but I was no longer afraid of falling.

I hiked the dress up around my knees, and Jack helped me over the relative safety of the railing and onto the swaying, slippery scaf-folding. I clung to him for a second, then grabbed the railing and moved.

A slim ladder led down between each level. Luckily, my dress was easier to deal with going down than up, and we flew past the cathe-dral's stone facade, down down down. With our footsteps and the rain pinging off the scaffolding, I couldn't hear whether the guards had made it to the balcony. The cut on my thigh, and the new one along my torso, screamed. I could hardly breathe. Finally, when I was sure I couldn't go any farther, my feet hit solid ground. We'd ended up in a courtyard of what must have been some kind of caretaker's house next to the church. I gasped for air, and we ran for the cover of a small bunch of trees.

I collapsed against the fence. "Did they see us?" I panted.

Even though we'd been on the side of the bell tower and not the front, a girl in a wedding dress scrambling down the side of Notre-Dame wouldn't exactly blend in. Luckily, it looked like the rain had kept most tourists away tonight, and most of the Circle inside the cathedral.

I tried to stand and tripped over my dress again. I batted at it in frustration, and then I remembered the knife in my hand.

I plunged it through the lace and the satin and the layer of crin-oline underneath at thigh height, and ripped a hole in it. When Jack saw what I was doing, he helped me rip it the rest of the way around until most of the skirt was around my ankles and my legs were free again. I stepped out of the discarded fabric and Jack stuffed it into a nearby trash can.

"I have a phone," I said, pulling it out of my dress. "We have to call the Order."

"We have to get away from here first."

We did. The second they realized we'd gotten out of the church, it'd be a massive manhunt. But we couldn't just take off running.

Right as I thought it, one brave tour group hurried toward us under dozens of red umbrellas. On the street across the Seine, I could see their matching red double-decker bus waiting under a streetlamp.

"Time for a tour," Jack said. He took my hand, and when they passed our hiding place, we inched our way into the middle of their group. We left them at their bus on the other side of the river, then ducked down a side street and under the awning of a tiny *frites* shop.

A car drove by, splashing through a puddle on the cobblestone street. I pulled out the phone, and paused.

Jack read my mind. "Are we going to tell them about Stellan?"

"We promised him we wouldn't. And we're not even sure it's true." I stopped when the shop owner peered outside, but Jack waved him off. "Whether it's true or not, they'd kill him," I went on.

Jack ran his hands through his hair. The sloppy hoodie looked so out of place on him. "They'll kill Fitz if we don't."

The thought of handing someone over to the Order was bad enough when I didn't know them. I thought of Stellan taking the bobby pins out of my hair on the plane. Of him talking to his sister on the phone—his sister who had no one else in the world. "Maybe if we tell them we have clues but we're still working on it, they'll give us more time," I said. "Enough time for Saxon to go after them. We could even say we have leads on the tomb if we have to."

Jack frowned and looked back at the cathedral. The rain came down harder, beating on the plastic awning overhead. "Okay. Let's try it. You're right—if they've kept Fitz alive this long, he must be their only bargaining chip."

I dialed the number and put it on speaker.

Scarface picked up on the first ring. "You're late."

I clutched Jack's sweatshirt in my fist.

"We had a bit of a delay," Jack said over the rush of a car driving by.

"Well?" Scarface said. "Do you have it?"

"We need to know he's okay first."

I groped for Jack's hand, and he grabbed mine and squeezed. A rush of wind sprayed us with cold raindrops.

Scarface gave a derisive sniff. "All right," he said. And then, Mr. Emerson's voice came on the phone, and my eyes swam with relieved tears.

"Avery. Jack. Sweet kids. I love you both so much. Don't—"

The phone was snatched away, and Mr. Emerson's voice faded into the background. I hugged Jack's arm and felt a grin taking over my face. He was *alive*. He was still alive. We weren't too late.

"Happy?" Scarface said. "Your grandfather or whatever is alive and well. For now. We almost didn't give you that reprieve when your friend called and said you needed more time, but lucky for you, I was feeling generous."

Stellan. He had actually called them, and then he helped us escape. We really couldn't turn him in now.

"All right." Jack took the phone out of my hand. His voice was thick with emotion. "We do have some information, but we don't know who the One is yet."

"That wasn't our deal," Scarface interrupted.

"Wait," Jack said. "Listen. We don't know who it is, but we have clues. We just need more time. And this way you know we're not lying and making up a name."

"The deal was the name of the One for your grandpa's life."

"We know. We just need another few days." Jack looked at me, eyes wide. This wasn't going well. "The tomb," I mouthed. Jack nodded. "And we know more, too. We have information about the—"

Mr. Emerson's voice piped up again from the background. "No! Don't tell him anyth—"

An explosion cut off his words.

I grabbed at Jack with both hands. His face turned ghost-pale, and the hand holding the phone went slack. No. That wasn't what I thought it was. It couldn't be—

"Hope you're happy," Scarface said. "Your slipup just got the old man killed."

"No," I said. It was like I was talking underwater. Too slow. Too far away. "No. No!"

"If you'd like to try telling the truth again, we have someone else I hear you might be interested in."

A choked sob escaped my throat. "No!" I cried, not able to believe that had really happened. We'd gotten him killed. They had *killed* Mr. Emerson. They'd—

"Avery?" said a new voice.

I jerked away from Jack and stared at the phone, caught in the middle of a sob. "Mom?"

"Well," Scarface said cheerfully. "Lovely reunion. Now would you like to tell us what we want to know?"

My mom's plane wasn't delayed. Her cell phone wasn't dead.

My mom had been kidnapped by the Order.

I grabbed the phone out of Jack's hand. "We know who the One is," I said frantically. "We'll tell you. It's not somebody in the Circle. It's someone else—"

"Wrong!" Scarface said.

"No!" I screamed, but no gunshot came.

"Lie to me again and your mother dies," Scarface said. "If you want to keep her alive, you'll figure out who it really is. We'll know if you're lying. We'll be in touch."

"I'm not lying!" I screamed. "Don't touch her! Mom!" The phone clicked to dead air. I stared at it, helplessly, my hand shaking.

"No," I sobbed. "No."

Jack sat down heavily at the small cafe table. He reached blindly for me, and I collapsed into his lap, sobbing. And for that moment, it didn't matter that we were now fugitives from the most powerful people in the world.

CHAPTER 42

The sun came out the next day, which it had no right to do.

Jack pushed the last of his falafel around with a triangle of pita bread as we sat in the silence that was starting to become deafening.

"Are you sure he'll find us here?" I said. We couldn't call Stellan for fear the Circle would trace the call, but Jack said if we came here, to this little falafel place off a back alley in Montmartre at 6:00 p.m. today, the day after we'd escaped the wedding, he'd find us. We'd been here since 5:30. It was now 6:13.

"I'm sure," he said. "Are you sure we have to talk to him at all?"

I pulled off a corner of pita from our mostly untouched bread basket, just to give myself something to do. I barely tasted it. "If we're right, and he is the One, we're probably going to need him. And he helped us get away. He won't be happy if we leave."

I bit off the words as the waiter refilled my tiny cracked teacup. The restaurant was busy enough that they hadn't bothered us much, and we'd gotten the worst table in the place, squished in a nook by the bathrooms on the upper balcony, overlooking the restaurant.

Last night, we'd made our way to a tiny, seedy hotel we knew wouldn't check ID. Jack had gotten us two separate rooms, and

I hadn't protested. Anything else felt wrong after all that had happened.

We'd thought about calling my father, but decided against it. We didn't know what he'd do with me now that he knew about my eyes, and we weren't entirely sure Jack would be pardoned for knowing about it. After what had just happened, we weren't willing to take any risks.

And that wasn't even considering that Jack and I were now the two most wanted people in the Circle of Twelve, and therefore in the *world*. One person the Circle believed to be the worst type of traitor, and another they believed to be their salvation.

I twirled the short lock of hair at the back of my neck. I hadn't seemed to be able to stop touching it since they'd cut it at the wedding.

The door jingled below. Stellan. He strolled in between the plastic-covered tables. He looked so out of place in the dingy falafel shop that people stopped eating to stare. I wondered again what kind of connection he and Jack had to this place. To each other.

Stellan came up the stairs and pulled out the third chair at our table. "Either you kept your promise to not turn me in to the Order, or they're even more incompetent than I'd imagined." He plucked a pita triangle from the basket and dipped it into the hummus on my plate with a half smile.

Jack put a hand on my knee.

"We didn't turn you in," I said.

Jack's fingers tightened. I put a hand over his. "They killed him," he said through clenched teeth. "He's dead because we didn't turn you in."

Stellan stopped still, pita halfway to his mouth. His face went slack. "What?"

Jack pushed his chair back from the table. He'd been wound tightly all day, and it was like seeing Stellan was about to make him snap. I grabbed his arm.

"Don't," I said. "Stop."

Jack was shaking. "If we'd turned you in—"

I squeezed his arm, trying not to shake myself. "Will you check outside and make sure everything's okay?" I said quietly. "Please?"

With one last murderous look, Jack stomped down the stairs. I turned back to Stellan. He looked both dazed and furious. It gave a fierce edge to his almost too-pretty face.

"They killed Fitz." I picked off a flake of the peeling varnish on the table. "They have my mom. They'll kill her, too, if we don't give them a name. They're sure it's someone in one of the twelve families, so they wouldn't even believe us if we told them it was you, but they said they have a way of knowing if we're lying, so we can't just turn in someone random. I don't know what that means, and I don't know if it's true, but I'm not willing to risk my mom's life."

Stellan cleared his throat. "What are you going to do?"

"*We* are going to use the clues Napoleon left to try to find the tomb." I traced the edge of my plate. "We'll either tell the Order about it and let them have the treasure or whatever's there in exchange for my mom, or if there really is some kind of weapon, we'll use it against them. If Jack doesn't find them and kill them all first." When I said it that way, it sounded almost simple.

Stellan narrowed his eyes. "And you think it's going to work to use—what did you say you had, that diary and a bracelet?—to track down this tomb the Circle has been trying to find for centuries?"

I pushed away from the table. "Do you have a better idea?"

"For starters, I didn't let you get away purely out of the goodness of my heart."

I folded my arms. We were in this together now, and he probably wanted us to do something for his sister, too. That was fine. "What do you want?"

Stellan's own voice echoed in my head. *You wanted a change. A way away from the ache that is your existence,* he'd said. Toska. *Something is missing, and you ache for it, down to your bones.* I understood what that meant now. In so many ways.

He rested his elbows on the table. The last of the afternoon sun slanted through the front windows, casting a band of gold across his forearms. "I'm not sure you're entirely grasping the situation with the tomb. There's more to it than the Order and their—" He paused, pressing his lips together. "There are things at stake for you other than saving hostages. The Circle is in decline."

"I doubt that." I leaned on the table, too. "They're the richest, most—"

He held up a hand. "You might not see it from the outside, but haven't you wondered how they can maintain the kind of power they had centuries ago in modern times? The answer is they can't. It's been showing more and more the past few decades—the world is changing faster than ever, and they're not keeping up with it like they once were. It's scaring people. Soon they'll be nothing more than useless rich people whose ancestors were the kings of the world."

I swallowed.

"Did you see all those people bowing to you at the church?" Stellan went on.

I hadn't been able to forget. Them or the one who wanted to capture me.

"Yes, they want wealth. Yes, they want whatever magical power they hope to find in the tomb." He leaned forward until our faces were too close for comfort, but somehow I couldn't back away. "But they want more than that. The stress of the past decades has caused infighting like they haven't seen since the early days. They need something—someone—to rally behind. You represent this thing they've wanted for so long." He smiled wryly. "Don't you see? As much as whatever's in the tomb, *you're* their treasure."

A sick feeling settled in my stomach. The sound of Jack's boots came back up the stairs, and I flinched away from Stellan.

"If you want to find the tomb," Stellan continued, not even acknowledging Jack, "you're making it much harder than it needs to be."

My heart tripped irregularly. Jack sat down.

"Think about it. They all want to claim you as their *queen*. The Dauphins have demonstrated that at least some of them are no longer waiting for confirmation of the One's identity. If anyone else finds you," he went on, rolling a piece of napkin between his fingers, "they could snatch you and marry you off before you knew what was happening. Maybe knock you up for good measure so you wouldn't be able to get out of it."

I recoiled. Even Jack looked sick. "They wouldn't—"

"They would. Even before they actually find the tomb, whoever fulfills the union will gain a huge amount of power. Power that people can—and do—kill for."

I swallowed back the bile rising in my throat. "So?"

"So, we do the only thing that makes sense." Stellan sat back and propped one ankle on his knee. "You want to find the tomb. You have a great deal of power. You said you'd stand by me as the thirteenth."

I turned my chair to face him. So did Jack, his hand falling off my knee. "What are you saying?"

"I'm saying it's *us*, little doll. You might be the treasure, but *we're* the answer." Stellan motioned between us. Beside me, Jack tensed. "I know Napoleon mentioned something being odd about the union, but he doesn't say the Circle's interpretation is necessarily *wrong*. It could still mean you and me together are a veritable treasure map. And even if that's all made-up nonsense, it'd keep you safe from being taken by one of the others. And it'd give us a good deal of leverage over them, in case we needed it."

He trailed off and quirked one eyebrow.

I shook my head. He wasn't saying what it sounded like he was saying. "Stellan . . ."

A smile tugged at the corners of his lips. "That's right, *kuklachka*. Congratulations to us. It appears you and I are getting married."

ACKNOWLEDGMENTS

It may be my name on the front of the book, but a book isn't made by just one person. I'd like to thank all of you who have given me and this book your time and love and expertise along the way, especially:

My editor, Arianne Lewin. At times, I thought you might be trying to kill me, but your love of the book and your keen insight and your refusal to settle for anything less than just-right have (finally!) made it the book I'd always hoped it would be. It turns out you're pretty darn smart.

My agent, Claudia Ballard, who worked so hard to make the book the best it could be and find it a good home, and whose enthusiasm has never waned. Talking to you feels like giving my book a hug.

Katherine Perkins, who handles all the details with aplomb and has a sharp editorial eye on top of it. All the team at Putnam—design, copyediting, sales, marketing, everyone!—for your enthusiasm and support and tireless efforts to make this book a book.

Julie Chang, for all your enthusiasm. Eve Attermann, for being the first person in publishing to get excited about Avery's adventures. Laura Bonner and all the other rights agents and the rest of the WME team for getting the story out to the greater world.

Dahlia Adler, for when writing friends turn into real-life friends who watch *Sharknado* in our PJs and name our guest rooms after each other and have real-time conversations via e-mail. And for not disowning me over and over, when you probably should have.

Gina Ciocca for flailing or complaining with me, as need be, for the hilariously inappropriate jokes and for the novel-length e-mails when we should be writing actual novels instead.

Marieke Nijkamp for stroopwafels and "Bohemian Rhapsody" on the Seine and being an insanely fast, super-insightful reader and somehow never getting tired of my book.

Kim Liggett, sister-wife, who insists on loving my book even when I don't. By the time you see this, we will both have made it through.

Erica Chapman, for the marathon e-mails and the *squees*.

Leigh Ann Kopans and Chessie Zappia, for being two of my earliest pub friends and readers. The rest of the YA Misfits: Jamie Grey, Megan Whitmer, Jenny Kaczorowski, Naseoul Lee, Cait Greer—I'm so happy I met you ladies, and thank you for the beta reads and the friendship and the fun.

Seabrooke Leckie, for being with me through many of your manuscripts and many versions of mine, and for giving me friendship, enthusiasm and intelligent criticism in equal measure.

All the other writers who have beta read my book or taken this journey with me. Brenda Drake and Angi Black and Jenny B and all my Twitter friends and the new Fifteener friends I'm just starting to get to know and IRL friends who are confused by and/or excited about this whole publishing thing and if I listed all of you this would be another book.

Kristen Boers, for having lively YA discussions with me and being my first non-writer reader.

My earliest CPs, Sari and Jason, who read truly ridiculous versions of this book and lived to tell the tale.

Lisa and Laura Roecker, whose very early enthusiasm made me think this book could be worth pursuing.

My old IRL crit group, especially Antoine Ho, Sonja Dewing, and Jim Schnedar, for all the laughs and for reading my stuff before it was worthy of being read.

My parents, Jill and Dave. For getting me all the books I wanted when I was little and letting me spend all my free time reading them, and for being certain I'd make it when I decided to try to write one myself.

My brothers, Tom and John, who do a great job feigning excitement for a genre they know nothing about.

My in-laws, Chuck and Sara, for their unwavering support and mojitos when the publishing timeline seems interminable.

My husband, Andrew, for the back rubs and wine-pouring and dinner-making and putting up with my moods (see: wine). For filling plot holes and talking about Avery and Jack and Stellan like they're real people. For agreeing to set off on crazy adventures with me (including around-the-world travel and . . . life). Every writer (really, every woman!) wishes they had a husband like you.

All the tour guides and locals on our travels who answered crazy questions like how one might escape through the Notre-Dame bell towers, and who didn't turn me in to the authorities if they overheard me talking about what would happen if various monuments blew up.

Booksellers, and especially the crew at Bookworks. You showed me how fun this crazy book world can be.

Librarians and everyone behind libraries. I've practically lived in libraries my whole life, and can't wait to see my own book on the shelves.

To all the people I will meet between when I turn in these acks and publication, who will help with this book's journey into the world—I'm sorry I don't know you yet to mention you by name! Thank you!

To anyone I've forgotten, I'm sorry. I can assure you, I've probably remembered—too late— and I probably feel awful about it! I adore you anyway.

And thank you to *you*, for reading this book.